THE SHOE BOX WALTZ

KATHLEEN PATRICK

KATYDIDIT PUBLISHING

For anyone who has ever been on the boat
and those who love them.

So, I won't use my own name. I'll tell you this entire story, and you'll think I made it up. You'll have to; it's fiction. That's how fiction works. I'll write about the time when Cora Daneli was traveling around Europe with a friend she'd met in a youth hostel in Oxford. That was before the boat, but that's my story, so I'll start at the beginning...

CONTENTS

It doesn't matter if it happened… it's true.

CORA

When I first moved in with Ian, he was always trying to figure me out. Always staring at me. "Eyes are the windows to the soul," he'd say.

"I don't have a soul," I'd answer. "I outgrew mine. It shrunk in the wash." Back then I was working on a book. My first attempt at fiction. It took up a lot of time, and I never really put it away. Even when I wasn't writing, I was trying to figure it all out. When I finally let him read it, he quit asking all the psychiatrist questions, as if I had given him the answers in the chapters of that book, as if the character was me, and everything I wrote was absolutely true. He seemed to think he knew me then.

He stopped pushing to get married, stopped asking about children for a couple of years. For a while, I wondered which woman he was in love with. I invented the one on the page, gave her breath and allowed her to say whatever she wanted, whatever I wasn't able to say. I gave her eyes, windows to her soul. She had a soul. I know, I put it there. I wondered who he was in love with, because I didn't believe it could be me.

Maybe Caitlyn is wondering who loves her too. As the morning stretches into midday, I sit in my living room and wonder what I can do. I am the big sister. I used to hold her hand and make things better, but now we are both adults, and we have no mother, and the rules are all changed. Something is wrong, something under the skin.

I should invite her here. We can see the Black Hills from our window. We could talk and tell each other things.

CAITLYN

I'm not going to work. I'm not answering the phone. I'm not counting the snowflakes as they bash against the windowpane and pile up on the metal steps outside the door.

The trailer smells like after-shave. After-shave and stale beer. Greg drinks too much. Lately, the evenings are filled with empty beer bottles and blaring TV, and I could just as well be somewhere else, but I'm not. I'm here in my chair by the window watching winter come. My hands on my abdomen, trying to feel something growing. The silent hourglass has run out. The baby has grown too big to be ignored. I can't ignore it, but I'd like to. I'd like to ignore the telephone; it rings twice and then stops. Twice again in a minute, like my sister Cora used to do when we were still at home and she wanted me to get the phone. Maybe it's her. Maybe it's an alarm going off in my head, and there's no one on the phone at all. No answer if I pick up the receiver. No voice to match my own.

I. AT SEA

1

THE BEGINNING

So, I won't use my own name. I'll tell you this entire story, and you'll think I made it up. You'll have to; it's fiction. That's how fiction works. I'll write about that time when Cora Daneli was traveling around Europe with a friend she'd met in a youth hostel in Oxford. That was before the boat, but that's my story, so I'll start at the beginning.

Cora and Nancy first met while washing out socks and underwear in the huge communal bathroom at the Logan House hostel. Later, they strung a make-shift clothes line from the bedpost on Nancy's bed to the bedpost on Cora's. Nancy had majored in theater and just graduated from some college in Montana. Cora had finished up an English degree the winter before and had no idea what she was going to do with it. They spent the first night reading one-act plays out loud in their bunks.

Nancy had certain parts memorized, and Cora used the book. A young woman from Denmark wrote postcards on the next bed and laughed occasionally. They all went out for a beer later.

The thing that first struck Cora about Nancy was her beauty. She had long auburn hair. Cinnamon eyes. Around her neck she wore a flat gold chain that rested in the curved indentation above her collarbones. Small hoop earrings. Dainty things. And yet Nancy wasn't dainty. She had worked on a ranch while she was in Montana and had the biceps to prove it. "All you need to do to stay in shape is lug around a couple dozen bales of hay a day. Or move sets for the theater. Who needs exercise programs? They're a waste of money."

"I can agree there," Cora said. "I've been carrying a backpack around northern Europe for four months. Forty to fifty pounds on my back. Check these out." Cora flexed her biceps. "I've never been in such great shape before." She sat on her bed, folding dry T-shirts into small rolls and putting them back into her pack. "What have you seen so far?"

"Only London and here. I want to see the Pollack exhibit. He's amazing. Do you like Jackson Pollock?" Nancy combed through her wet hair with her fingers, shaking out the bangs.

"I don't know; I've never heard of him." It was getting easier for Cora to be honest. She found that traveling around alone, people would take her for what she was or leave her alone. It was so much easier than playing games and worrying about what others thought of her knowledge or lack of it.

"Tomorrow, I'll show you the Jackson Pollock world of color." Nancy smiled. "It's a little crazy; that's why I love it. Wild explosions of spattered paint."

The next day they saw the art exhibit and ate at The Bear, a tiny seven-hundred-year-old pub. Cora finished her cottage pie. "I'm going to hitchhike toward France Friday and head down to the Mediterranean. I want to get to the actual sun and sand."

"Want some company? I'm not in any hurry." Nancy took a big drink of beer. "I'd like to travel with you. You seem to know a lot about it. Is this your first trip to Europe?

"Yeah."

"Have you hitched much?"

Cora nodded. "A bit in Denmark. Lots around here. It's been fine. I'm pretty careful about who I ride with. I've got a tight budget. If I'm going to make it another month or two, I have to hitch some. I'd like to take a ship over to Greece for a few weeks. I definitely want to see Athens."

"I want to see Rome and Florence. You?"

"Sounds good, as long as the money holds out."

Cora had no preconceived plan other than her dream

of seeing the Acropolis. In the fourth grade, she made a model of the Parthenon in social studies class. Clay, milk cartons, and toilet paper rolls. Mrs. Sibley had told her she would see the real one someday; then she touched the spray-painted columns with reverence, as if they were the real thing. Cora believed her. In high school, she took Western Civilizations and studied all about Greece. She did extra credit projects on the history of the Acropolis and read mythology. She knew it was a matter of time.

After college, she took the money she had inherited from her grandmother out of the bank. She had given her twenty-seven hundred dollars, "to be used before it was too late." That was the kind of grandmother she had. "College is okay," she used to say, "but you also got to get an education. See the world. Don't get married right away. You hear me?" And Cora listened. She listened and planned her escape. Six days after graduation from college, she packed and headed for Kennedy airport on a Greyhound bus.

2

WRITING A NOVEL

I've never written a long story before. I'm not sure how long it should be. There is a lot to the story, and it is difficult to tell. I don't know what to leave out, what you need to know to understand. I mean, the flat tire outside Bristol isn't important, not even that it was raining, but that is when Nancy told Cora about her mother. The professor of mathematics changed the tire on his old rusted Volkswagen while the two women sat in the rain and talked.

When he picked them up, Cora sat in the back seat along with the backpacks, textbooks, and a cardboard box of tools. She explained where Grace, Iowa was located, what her parents did for a living, how she'd been traveling for four months throughout Scandinavia and Britain. She told about Iowa's last cold winter. Seventy-four inches of snow and below zero twenty days in a row. Cold, but not too bad.

Nancy talked about her uncle's ranch in Montana. The mountains. The huge horse barns, her mare and colt. She talked about the private school she attended. How she went home for the holidays.

The two women found out about each other as they told their stories. Cora found Nancy worldly and intelligent. She knew British history and European art; she asked the right questions. The driver beamed with national pride.

Nancy thought Cora was gutsy and self-assured. She admired her for traveling alone all those months, taking care of herself. She thought Cora fit the "still waters" cliche, layer upon layer of stories left untold.

It was not until the flat tire two hours later that Nancy and Cora sat in the rain and talked about Nancy's mother. It's important to understand about Nancy's mother, since it sheds so much light on the way Nancy behaves.

But we all have those stories, don't we? And sometimes we hear the histories of other's lives, and sometimes we are out of range. Nevertheless, we still go on interacting with folks and living our lives. Maybe some stories just go untold.

I guess it might get easier as it goes on: knowing what to tell and what to leave out. I'll let them do the talking. I'll write it down. I don't know if this is a short story or a novel. I know the ending, but I can't see across the gap yet, from the hostel in Oxford across the miles to that boat. I'm not a writer; I've never done this before. I can tell you about Hemingway and Fitzgerald and Shakespeare and Woolf. I have studied literature. I have learned about writers' lives and have written papers on them. I haven't lived a writer's life; I don't know what I'm doing.

3

DEVON

Cora stood on a thick castle wall, looking out to the sea. This was the place where the pilgrims departed for the New World. She tried to imagine the wooden ships stocked with smoked meat and kegs of water for the long voyage. "I found a fun place for some lunch." Nancy came up behind her, wearing sunglasses and holding her student guide book to Europe. "It's back near the post office."

"God, there sure are lots of tourists," Cora said.

"Yeah, despicable creatures." Nancy smiled. "Nothing I like less than a tourist. I'm hungry. You?"

"You bet."

After lunch, the two young women cinched up their backpacks and walked out of town. They followed the coast for about five miles, heading toward a small village. It was a warm, cloudless day. Cora had a pocket radio tucked into her backpack, and they listened to the BBC. Fleetwood Mac and Neil Young. The music reminded Cora of home. Dancing in college hangouts. Seeing her friends. Closing her eyes and letting the music take over. She thought about home most when she was listening to American music. She missed her parents and her younger sister. Missed her house. Especially the bathroom: piles of thick clean towels on the shelf, small perfumed soaps in the shower, hot showers. Long, hot showers, and privacy. Traveling the youth hostel circuit made privacy impossible. Most of the time, it didn't matter. Occasionally, when the showers were dirty or the water ice cold, she would have given anything to be back in Iowa. But today, the south coast of England was exactly where she wanted to be.

They rounded a curve in the narrow, paved road. Out ahead, a long-deserted beach stretched before them like a quarter moon. The cove was a long way down from the road at the bottom of a slow, grassy slope. A rocky cliff formed another wall of the embankment. The two looked at each other and smiled, knowing what the other was thinking. As they tumbled to the bottom, Cora thought of how good it would feel to get the pack off her back. She thought about the warm sand on her feet.

They went for a swim in their shorts and T-shirts and then sat down on the sand to dry off. Nancy braided her wet hair. "So, were you in love with anyone when you left home?"

Cora shrugged. "Probably. I've always used the term rather loosely." She paused. "Not as loosely as most men I've dated, though. You?"

"No. I thought I loved my senior advisor for a while. He was fifty, married and gorgeous. He helped me with my senior project. In theater we had to do a one person show as part of the graduation requirement. I was Lillian Hellman. I did a cutting from her book, Pentimento. Fascinating material."

"Was this a crush or what? I mean..."

"You mean, did we get involved?"

"That's what I mean." Cora raised her eyebrows.

"Sort of."

"Not good enough. Details, please."

Nancy shrugged. "We might have gotten more involved if I hadn't realized that I was his senior project too. I think he had one every year."

"Wonderful."

"Yup. He used to give me private coaching on some of my parts in the plays, like I wasn't getting it or something and could I work on it and meet him in his office after the last act. The first time he touched my shoulders and looked straight in my eyes... God, I was gone. I was supposed to be Antigone and devastated over my older brother's death. And there I was, looking at these gorgeous blue eyes. He kissed me. We started finding excuses to rehearse a lot more after that."

"I would have gone into shock if a professor of mine showed that kind of interest in me." Cora shook her head. "Weren't you scared?"

"Yes. No. He was in charge. He was my sexy teacher. I wasn't afraid of him, so where was the threat? His wife was a picture in a brass frame on his desk. He never brought her up, and I certainly didn't."

"So how did it end?"

"The night of my senior recital, I was backstage and glanced out from behind the curtain to see if people were showing up. He was standing by the door, running his fingers through his hair and talking to this junior who had volunteered to hand out programs. I knew right then. I asked her later if he'd made some comment to her about her show being only a year away. She looked shocked, like how did I know?"

"What a jerk."

"Exactly. It's getting late. We'd better get to Strete if we're going to find a bed-and-breakfast before the tourists in their motor coaches catch up with us." Nancy stood and brushed off her shorts. They were dry and warm again.

"I don't think this is a big stop on the tourist trail. No pilgrims or castles, from what I can tell in my book."

"Fantastic," Nancy said. "Let's go. I could use a lager and lime."

They spent the evening in a cozy pub, playing darts and talking to two young couples who had lived in the village all their lives. They explained where Montana and Iowa were located, gave the facts about the weather, how big their houses were, and what cars their fathers drove. Nancy lied and said her dad was a doctor and drove a Lincoln Continental. She said it was so big four adults could sit in the back seat. It was what the young man who had asked wanted to hear, since he knew Americans drove big cars and lived in outrageous houses. Someday he wanted to buy an old American Chevy. "Me too," Nancy said with a smile. "Me too."

4

WRITING EXERCISE

Backgrounds. College. Cora went to the University of Iowa. Nancy to Montana State. I would borrow experience from my own college days, but my four-and-a-half years at the university were uneventful. I was an excellent student. I made my share of mistakes. I didn't want to teach literature, so I pretended that studying literature was enough, and that I would find a job somewhere in the academic world. Employers would appreciate my vast knowledge of the classics and contemporary fiction. I could write a damn fine paper about the place of women in short fiction written by women in the early 1900s.

After a brief hiatus, I began working at a mortgage company writing letters to customers who were behind on their monthly mortgage payments on their mobile homes. I told them how far behind they were and what the consequences were going to be; eight or nine hours a day of typing letters to families who couldn't make their payments on a trailer house. I used to wonder what each home looked like inside, how the place was laid out. What the trailer park looked like. Carnation Acres. Melody Hills. East Lake Estates. It was an escape, a way to ignore the fact that my life was wilting.

My parents moved to Florida with my aunt and uncle for a trial semi-retirement. I left my hometown because I didn't have any reason to stay there and ended up in Rapid City, South Dakota. I had intended to go to the west coast, find a job, and see a different part of the country. My car broke down in Rapid City, so I stayed there. I was seeing a different part of the country. Folded into the pine-covered hills of South Dakota, I began again.

I rented a room from Geralyn Hendricks, a lifelong native of Rapid City. Her pale, yellow house sat in the hills just blocks from the main part of town. The room was small and musty, with faded red rose wallpaper. But she had a front porch and two wooden rocking chairs. She was seventy-three years old then and living alone. I figured one of the rocking chairs could be for me; I could sit out there evenings and read and forget about everything.

It turned out that Rapid City has a progressive, artistic pulse in the middle of a very conservative prairie. There's a new and used bookstore that sells more poetry and philosophy than self-help and cookbooks, a classical dance studio, and a health food restaurant. I got a job as a server at The Sunny Side. They serve mostly vegetarian food and have an open stage on Saturday night for local musicians and poets just getting their start.

I serve walnut, raisin, and cream cheese bagels and make enough money to live on. It makes as much sense as anything else. I never thought about what I wanted to be when I grew up. College was simply a stepping stone for getting on to the next chunk of my life. Sitting on the porch with Geralyn on a cool summer evening, drinking a lemonade and rereading *Moll Flanders*, sometimes I get that content feeling that I am right in the middle of my life, that I'm where I'm supposed to be. Sometimes that feeling is harder to get a hold of, and it takes so much work to feel comfortable in my own skin.

5

PARIS

The night ferry from Dover to Calais was full. Cora stood in the public restroom, brushing her teeth. It was her first time on a ship. She held the counter with one hand as the water in the sink slipped lazily back and forth, almost splashing over the steel rim onto the counter, moving with the graceful roll and tilt of the large vessel. A woman stood next to her with a baby cradled in one arm. She wet a cloth at the next small faucet and washed the child's face. The baby fussed and resisted. It was late, and the water was cold.

Nancy stood at the mirror braiding her long, thick hair. She smiled at the baby, at the woman. They smiled back.

Later, Cora and Nancy sat next to the woman and her family in the large open area for travelers without sleeping berths. Rows of uncomfortable chairs filled the room, every two rows facing each other. The woman, her baby, two other children, and the father sat across from them, pillows and small blankets spread out on the floor for the children. Their skin was a rich brown, and they all had deep black hair. Nancy thought they looked Indian or Pakistani. "Where are you going?" she asked politely.

"Home." The woman smiled a tired smile. Then, as if uneasy speaking English, she turned to her husband.

He nodded, opened his hands and looked at them, as if the story sat on his palms. "We travel home to Brussels from family funeral. Funeral of my young cousin." He looked at his wife, then at the two young Americans. "My cousin, he gave up living." The man said nothing more about it. He shrugged and furrowed his brow as the answer seemed puzzling even to him.

Later, the family shared their lunch with Cora and Nancy. The chairs were hard, and it wasn't easy to sleep, so they stayed awake and visited, the children nodding off for brief naps.

Nancy talked about her home in Montana, the mountains, and the wide sky. She said she wanted to be an actress and hoped one day to be in films. She did some pantomime for the children, but they lost interest quickly. The woman and man spoke softly and asked broken questions about politics in America. Nancy spoke highly of the American government, telling them why it worked so well, why it was such a wonderful system. She talked on and on, and Cora played with the children.

Cora wasn't so patriotic; she thought things were a mess back home, but she liked to listen to Nancy talk. She had a trained and smooth voice; she was on stage, performing her charming routine. Well read, well versed, well received. Cora played with the children, telling fairy tales and stories of snowbanks that reached the sky above Iowa.

Paris was more than they had expected. It was beautiful. It was terrible. The night crossing on the Channel and the long bus ride into Paris wore both women out. They arrived at 8:30 in the morning, hungry, tired, and stiff. The station was a muted gray. People spoke in soft voices, dragging luggage on wheels. Stretching their shoulders.

Nancy spoke some French, but not well enough to suit most of the people they talked to. She wanted to see the Louvre and the Champs-Élysées. Cora wanted to see the Eiffel Tower. They asked for directions. An older man who was walking his bike waved them off, got back on the bike muttering, and rode in the opposite direction. A woman with three loaves of fresh bread sticking out of her colorful bag smiled and said, "Take a taxi. You Americans are rich!"

"This is not starting out well," Cora said, looking at

her watch. It was 10:15. "Let's hunt down the youth hostel first and try to get a bed for tonight. We can get a city map and go from there, don't you think?"

"Sure." Nancy pulled out her guidebook and directed them down a maze of streets to the subway. After finding the public transit, the rest was easy.

The city was only a backdrop for the people. Dirty streets, gray, and black buildings. Cement. The air tasted of diesel and bus fumes. It was a city, like New York or L.A., but the people seemed different. Proud, inaccessible, busy people finding their way around on a hot summer day. Cora wasn't impressed. It was the first place she'd been where she felt like a foreigner who wasn't welcome.

"For five francs you could talk me into getting on the next train out of here and heading south. Paris doesn't impress me." Cora was setting up camp at the hostel. She put out her bedroll and was digging in her pack for dirty clothes. The bedroom had four sets of bunk beds lining the wall. A small sink and a bidet stood along the other wall. The toilet and shower were down the hall. Outside the window was a string clothesline attached to the brick building across a narrow courtyard. Cora planned to catch up on her washing.

"Give it a chance. I've always heard the people here were stand-offish. Maybe they're shy."

"Right."

"Give it two days, then you can pick the next place on the map we head. Deal?" Nancy smiled her gracious smile. All white perfect teeth.

"Two days. Okay, whatever. I'm in. I can handle anything for two days, right?"

6

CHARACTERS

I want you to understand some things about Cora. She isn't as interesting as Nancy, so it's hard to get her story out. She is not beautiful, so she seems less interesting. People don't look at her on the street the way they look at her friend. She is average. Like some census taker compiled data about young, college graduate females and made up a composite picture of the average one. Five-feet six-inches tall. Wavy, reddish-brown hair. Average body. A few freckles.

The thing about Cora is that she seems more attractive when she isn't around Nancy. Comparisons are human nature. She could go into a small disco in Copenhagen alone, and men would look at her. They would ask her to dance, and she would have a delightful time. She's pleasant and intelligent and if the men are decent, things are fine. But when Nancy showed up, Cora dissolved slowly out of the picture. She could see less and less of herself as the days went on.

Nancy is the center of the stage; she knows all the jokes and can make any ordinary event charming. She is social, and graceful, and well educated. Although Cora is friendly, she has never been one to dazzle people.

Everywhere they go, men look at Nancy. Women follow her with their eyes. Even children are not shy around her. Cora can sense this. She doesn't blame them, and she doesn't blame Nancy; she's mesmerized by her charm too. But, day by day, her strong will and confidence dwindle. She becomes dependent. Nancy knows more about art and French cuisine and culture. Nancy can speak the language. Without realizing it, Cora lets her make the decisions. Then she rationalizes it all. She doesn't care where they go, as long as she gets to Greece. By the middle of August, she wants to be standing on the Parthenon steps.

So, Nancy never even hears much about Cora's past. It was uneventful. Her mother wasn't a famous dancer whose life ended in tragedy. Her mother was a secretary. Her father worked his own small business and came home every evening. Her little sister was starting college in the fall.

How does one weave the daily workings of a person's life into their story? Cora Daneli lived for twenty-one years before she boarded a plane and headed for Copenhagen. She lived through adolescence, a house fire, a broken leg and four years of piano lessons, but for whatever reason, she didn't tell Nancy much about her life; she is left walking around Paris like some flat paper doll.

It might take an event to get her talking. Like the rainy night and the flat tire. Maybe the next time Nancy will listen, but Cora needs to have something to say. I expect she'll start talking one of these days. I'll wait around and take notes; I have nothing better to do.

7

CAFE

The two women were good at stretching their money. After a long day of sightseeing and a nap in the sculptured garden of Versailles, they stopped and bought baguettes, Brie, and a couple of pears for dinner. They ate in a park.

Nancy stretched out in a patch of fading sun and read a book. Cora got out her journal and recorded her impressions of the Chateau at Versailles, the elaborate decadence of it all, the beauty. A riddle, she decided. Was she supposed to like it or not? It was overwhelming and interesting. All the glimpses of European history were making her appreciate the literature of the period even more. It was helpful to see the buildings and jewels of the time.

As the evening cooled, they wandered the streets and watched the night city come to life. There was romance here. Paris was well-dressed at night. During the day her wrinkles showed, and she looked tired to Cora, but at night — at night the lights and glitter revealed a woman who loved to dance.

Nancy spotted a small cafe close to Notre-Dame. "How about a cup of coffee? We can afford that."

"Point the way." Cora smiled. "I could use some fabulous French caffeine." They found a table near the back. People were drinking wine, eating, laughing. Smoking cigarettes. A worn record played Edith Piaf in the background. "Classic." Nancy shook her head. "This looks like a set to a play. I want to star in this one."

"I'd give you the part." Cora had eye contact with a handsome man across the room. She figured he was watching Nancy. "Do you ever see your father?"

"What brought that up?" Nancy's voice carried an edge of anger and frustration.

"I was thinking about you starring in a show. You know, would he ever see you?"

"My father doesn't exist. He melted into thin air the day he decided my mother wasn't a fine enough dancer to have his name. His child either, for that matter, but it was a little too late for him to have much say in that." Nancy sipped the strong cappuccino. "No, I don't have a father. I imagine sometimes that he died of loneliness in a small flat in New York. After he was no longer in demand." She brightened. "But I have an uncle who would be there. Right in the front row. And he'd send roses to my dressing room. God, he'd probably videotape the whole thing for his archives."

"Is he your mother's brother?"

"Yes. Four years older. He took me on when he was only twenty-six. Can you imagine suddenly having an eighteen-month-old baby in your life? You can't imagine how grateful I am to him for being so brave. For loving me from the start. It's more than I can say for my mother."

"Is he married?"

"Yeah. I was four when they got married. He was already the center of my universe. It took a little time to allow another woman into the family, but she's great. I'm very lucky."

8

TRANSITION

I t's not easy to get people from one place to another even if they have train tickets and are headed for Florence on an almost cool evening, and they both have seats. Even if they are compatible and have been getting along well.

It's not easy, because they are looking out different windows. Nancy faces the night ahead of them; Cora sits straight across from her and watches stars.

Their knees almost touch. They try to avoid each other's feet. Not to be polite, but to feel alone. Even friends need solitude, and it's hard to find on a train in the heat of summer.

For almost two weeks they have traveled together, checking out each other's tastes for food, preferences for music and art, and patiently asking one another where she would like to go next. Sometimes it's awkward to disagree, because they want to be traveling. It seems inappropriate to complain about the rattle and sway of the train, the slight smell of sweat, when they are pushing south in Italy, headed for one of the most romantic cities in the world.

Cora thinks about her sister, Caitlyn. She concentrates on the room they shared as children. The bunk beds. The wallpaper with pale yellow daisies. They were friends then. Nine and fourteen. Clean after long baths, they painted their toenails.

In the night, when it's hot and she needs a shower, Cora remembers being clean, sitting on white, starched sheets in babydoll pajamas, wet hair dripping down her back and soaking into the cotton.

Nancy's in the barn. It's hot there too, but it smells of sweet alfalfa. Horses. Hay. Dust. She is talking, brushing Glory's thick, black mane, telling the horse all about her plans. They will pack a lunch and ride down to the creek. The grass grows thick there; Glory will love it. Nancy will go wading. She'll work on a suntan and do her algebra homework.

Both women jolt to the present when a man sits down next to Cora. He smells of wine and stares at Nancy.

Cora knows it. Nancy knows it. The story goes on, and they need to get to Florence. They are there by morning. An orange sun slips above the bridge. An egg yolk.

Something has happened. It is not because of the

man; he is as harmless as such men can be. He is only disgusting because he looks too long. He does not touch, but something has changed. A gap widens without Cora or Nancy knowing it. Underground, sand falls away and things pull apart. It is hard to sense this happening. The train is overpowering, the smell of wine, fingernail polish, and alfalfa hay fill the car.

Two young women are traveling. The train is at the station. They crawl down the steps and stretch stiff muscles. They think the tension is from a lack of sleep.

But I know better. It's my job to explain it; I will have to start again. Maybe I should have the man touch Nancy, move over near her, and fondle her knee. Have her do something. Make him responsible. Maybe he needs to touch Cora, so she can hate him for it.

I don't know; he's a faceless shadow. It's dark, and he's drunk, and everyone is sleepy. He just wants to get home. I just want to get to Florence. Nancy and Cora haven't slept all night.

9

DAVID

Cora stood in the cool marble hall, gazing up at Michelangelo's sculpture of David. For the first time, looking at a piece of art moved her beyond words. The walls dissolved into a spiritual mist. Nancy was non-existent in a crowd of tourists and flashcubes. David's hand was the center of the universe. Cora leaned in to look at the marble veins, expecting a pulse. The flow of life underneath the stone exterior. She blinked twice: the fine muscle definition, the eyes, the nails on the fingers. For the first time, she understood Nancy's love for art, for movement and dance, for the celebration of living.

Nancy leaned against a far wall and caught glimpses of David between waves of the crowd. She fought down a knot in her throat. This was something her mother would have loved. She hadn't thought of her mother in a long time, until she saw David in the natural, filtered light: his incredible honesty and beauty. The human body. Nancy was certain, if her mother would have lived, would have gotten away from New York and long-running shows and small apartments without enough heat, she would have come here. She would have wanted to see this. Maybe they would have come together. Saving for years. Discussing it at the dinner table. Nancy working after school. Or maybe there would have been a tour and Nancy could have tagged along. A seven-year-old kid playing in the curtains behind the stage.

Tour groups filtered past the statue. Cora and Nancy stayed and took in everything. They healed themselves from the days of travel piling up behind them. They reminded themselves that they were lucky to be here, that this was more than a stop on a guided tour, that somewhere inside they were recharging themselves with the genius of Michelangelo's vision. It was helpful.

LATER THEY WALKED the crooked streets and watched the world grow dark as the sun slipped away. They sat at a small restaurant near the Ponte Vecchio, the old bridge stretched over the Arno River, and ate veal and bread and drank wine.

Nancy licked her fingers and squinted down the street. "Do you believe suicide is wrong? That it's a sin?"

"I don't believe in sins. I'm not very religious."

"Do you believe in God?"

"Which one?" Cora smiled.

"Seriously. I mean it."

"I did my part in Sunday school. Made Popsicle-stick crosses and tissue paper church windows. But I don't remember it having anything to do with God. I think there have to be rules. Societies need guidance, but I don't know where the rules should come from, and I sure as hell don't think we've got all the best ones now."

"Then you don't believe in heaven?"

"I don't know." Cora shrugged. "I've never been there." She was flippant and felt the most comfortable discussing religion in such contexts, but looking over at Nancy, she realized it was inappropriate. "Are you wondering about your mother?"

"Yes." There was a long pause. "Just wondering."

Cora pulled her hair up and held it in a pile on top of her head, elbows out. "If there's a place like heaven, I'll bet your mom is there. Dancers belong in heaven. And I'll bet you two will get a chance to catch up someday. Maybe she's around now, like a part of your spirit. Maybe sometime you'll be thinking about her and close your eyes and she'll be right there, almost close enough to touch, you know? Some Eastern religions view death quite differently."

"Are you getting flaky on me? Like maybe my mom came back as a koala bear or something?" Nancy smirked and shook her head.

"Christ, no!" Cora paused. "A gazelle, maybe..."

10

SLEEP

I'm uncertain what to say about the nights. If it is necessary to describe the way two young women sleep in sacks made from cotton sheets. Youth Hostel guidelines for hygiene. Sleeping bags to slip under a wool blanket on cold evenings. A place for the pillow. Both women have followed the rules. It is necessary if one wants inexpensive accommodations. Travel on a budget. And the cots. There are several beds in a room: women are often in one room and men in another. It depends on the country. Some parts of Europe seem to care less about sorting it all out. The Pandolfini youth house is segregated. Nancy and Cora sleep, or do not sleep, under the window facing the street. The moon is bright and spills across the bedroom floor. Nancy's thin gold bracelet glistens on her tan arm. She is on her stomach, hugging her pillow. I don't know what she is dreaming. I don't know if she dreams at all, or even if she is asleep. Perhaps she only closes her eyes to think.

Cora lies flat on her back, arms at her sides. She is not wearing jewelry. Her eyes are closed too. The world slows down at night. It is the time to cocoon into the familiar sigh of memory. Cora walks down to a lake where her grandfather is fishing. He says "You're back."

"Yes," she says. "I flew in this morning."

"Sit down here; tell me all about it. The places they rebuilt after the war. Are they okay? Did you eat any of those warm bread things, those little twisted rolls? What do you call them?"

Cora smiles in her sleep. There is a fish on his line. There are people up at the old house she wants to see too, but the dream wrinkles and dissolves on the surface of the clear little lake.

Moonlight covers the floor of my room now. I write this by longhand, so as not to wake Geralyn with my typewriter. It is electric and shakes the desk when I hit the return key.

I am writing by candlelight; I find it romantic. It is four o'clock in the morning, and Cora will not let me sleep. More and more often, I find it difficult to get a full night's sleep. There are so many strings, like a bouquet of helium balloons. I feel a sense of desperation when I try to hold on to all of them, to keep track of this mess I've started, this thing I am trying to write down.

Outside the garbage truck begins its morning work. It grinds its way up the meandering roads around the neighborhood. I cannot see other houses from my window, only trees and telephone lines. But after the trucks begin, dogs bay, calling back and forth to each other. Empty cans hit the ground and ring with a hollow sound. The place settles back down about four-thirty. Then nothing more happens until six o'clock when the alarm goes off downstairs in Geralyn's room, and I smell coffee.

11

DIARY, 20 JULY

Dear Diary,

I am sitting at the fountain in Loggia dei Lanzi. The Neptune Fountain. Nancy slept in and I wanted time alone. The sun is hot, and I'm drinking cold sweet tea. Italy is already tiring me. I find it fascinating and beautiful. But each day the itinerary grows longer. We spend more time looking at art. The gardens by the Pitti Palace. Laurentian Medici Library, Medici Chapel, Uffizi Museum. I could say I wanted to go off on my own, but it is easier to go along with her. I don't know what I would do alone here. I'm growing bored. Maybe I've been traveling too long, like an overdose of beauty and history has caused me to grow numb. Still, part of me wants to see these places. What if there is another David and I miss it? I mean, what if there are other masterpieces with as much power? It is worth the walking and blinding repetition of gilded-frame shadows.

Besides, I don't know how to say no to her. I don't know if she has ever heard it before.

CD

12

HISTORY

S ex. Who slept with whom. When Cora lost her virginity. The lovers Nancy's had. Young men have sex for practice and enjoyment, but Cora and Nancy are women, and women's sexual histories are a part of their beings, their resumes of the body: past lovers and one-night stands, clues about their personalities, their morals, their resilience.

Cora and Nancy have their own histories. Alcohol was or was not involved. Birth control was an afterthought; birth control was always an issue. Love was mentioned, and it mattered, or it didn't. Sometimes they said words without thinking twice. Each woman had said yes out of a sense of complacency, because it was easier than saying no. Each woman had gone to a party, woke up in a strange bed, wanted to erase the night before, and then resigned herself to the feelings that would cling to her back like a monkey for days.

Sexual details. People seem interested in other people's sex lives — anything about it: sensual, or seedy, or second rate. Anything, except maybe that which deviates too far from the norm, but Cora and Nancy are right in the middle and have average sexual appetites. They watch young Italian men. They know how to flirt and play the game.

These two young women come to this place in Europe, this Italian city, with histories. Each has her own set of convictions, her own set of mistakes. They both have dreams. And all the imprints of the past play into the way they act this August. Fingerprints on a window. So what?

13

PONTE VECCHIO

"I'd like to leave for Rome in the morning." Nancy curled a long strand of hair around her finger as they walked along. They were on the Ponte Vecchio; merchant booths filled with gold jewelry and souvenirs lined the bridge. Most of the stalls were closing for the day.

"Sounds good. I was thinking I'd like to head for Greece soon. I want to have a full two weeks there, and I'm running low on cash. Have you decided if you want to go to Greece?"

"Not yet. It's that or spend some time in Switzerland. I guess it depends on my cash supply too. It would be a lot cheaper to travel in Greece."

"Well, whatever." Cora was hoping to see Greece alone, but she would travel with Nancy if she wanted to go. They could always take a day or two off by themselves. Whatever they needed. She had to start saying what she wanted, sticking up for her own wishes.

"I'll try to decide by tomorrow," Nancy said.

"No hurry. Next week I want to see the sunset from the top of the Acropolis. That's all I know."

The two women walked down a side street along the Arno River. Cora would remember the city of Florence as being orange. Everything turned a shade of orange at sunset. Every night had been clear as the sun dipped below the old buildings and fell into the river's arms.

It was dark when they walked back toward the hostel and stopped at a little sidewalk cafe and bar. Two white wrought-iron tables sat out in front. They were both empty until Cora and Nancy sat down and ordered a carafe of wine. Wine was cheap in Italy and very good. Nancy slid off her sandal, ran her foot against the smooth calf of her other leg. "I wonder if I'll ever be back here. I hope so."

"Of course. You'll start acting and get a part in some big show and vacation here in the offseason."

"I'll probably end up doing soap commercials or singing telegrams or something just to pay rent, if I end up in New York at all."

Cora leaned back in her chair, squinted across the table at Nancy. "You don't sound very sure. It isn't like you."

"Well, now we're talking about the real thing. I'm not as good at playing the leading role in the real thing."

"Would you do soap operas?" Cora asked.

"Yes. To pay the rent. Soaps pay very well, I hear." Nancy twirled the stem of her glass. "I'm afraid of New York. I'm afraid to live there."

"The crime's pretty bad. I don't think I'd ever be a good New Yorker."

"It's not the crime that worries me." Nancy took a long drink of wine and squinted down the darkened street.

"What then?"

"My father. I'm scared to death of running into my father someday. I'm worried I'd recognize him. See myself in the face of a stranger, or my eyes or my shoulders… "

Cora couldn't imagine not knowing her father. But the fear was easy to understand. "Wow. What a thought. Did your mother ever tell him about you?"

"He knew, and he wasn't interested. Made it for rehearsals, but missed my opening night, so to speak. He offered to help Mom get an abortion somewhere. He'd pay for it. When she refused, it was the end of that romance."

Two young men in jeans and pale cotton shirts sat down at the next table. They spoke Italian. "Then she couldn't stand the idea of not dancing. I guess a year and a half with a kid was all she could take. When I found out how she died, I used to worry about what I'd done wrong. I was in junior high. I thought maybe I'd cried too much, been a sick baby. If only I'd been a quiet kid. I spent a large part of my adolescence working on that one."

Cora refilled both glasses. "I'm sorry."

"For what?"

"For all that sadness. For how sad you look now."

Nancy smiled. "It's not your fault. I've got lots of folks I can blame for my blues, Cora, but you certainly aren't one of them. To a young evening." Nancy raised her glass, looked to the next table, and raised her eyebrows. Both women smiled.

14

IAN

Ian is not a South Dakota name. Chuck. Bill. Bob. People mispronounce it. When people come into the restaurant, they talk before they order, leaning over the counter, scratching under baseball caps. Most of the cowboys and farmers eat elsewhere. It's a young crowd. Some are curious and eat here once. Others are aware of the daily specials, while we keep track of Perdy's kittens and if they are all going to make it. It is comforting to share the details of other people's lives. I find it strangely helpful. I stand, picking at the paper pad I take orders on, smiling, inviting them to continue. People tip me well; everyone wants to be listened to.

Ian owns the Sunny Side. It used to be the Sunny Side Up, but he dropped the last word and started serving fewer omelets. Too much cholesterol talk was dangerous for business. Now it's mostly whole grains and organic fruits and vegetables. Some chicken and fish for the daring or accustomed.

Ian is a transplant from Boston. He said his childhood dream was to be a cowboy and live out West. Like me, he ended up land-locked in the middle of South Dakota near the soft personal hills. Sometimes Ian talks with a thick English accent and confuses the patrons. He is never the same person twice.

I began coming to the restaurant right after I moved to town, or after my car broke down. Either way you look at it, I was in search of healthy food and anonymity. I could be as unobtrusive as the artwork hanging in each booth. Framed covers from National Geographic magazines. Ian makes his own political statements in a quiet whisper, offending no one. You could look right past the words and just see bright lettering and a nice photograph. I knew right away I liked this place. It was the first place I had liked in a long time. I ate many meals there before even meeting Ian.

The details kept me occupied. I liked the bare wooden floors. I liked the maroon Formica on the tops of the booths. I liked the smell of chicory coffee and hot bread. I was in love with the light. I could go in at noon and read in a booth by the window. No one bothered me. I read thick novels at first, four or five a week. Chain reading Lawrence and Defoe and Elliot. It was when I started running out of money three months into my stay that I applied for a job. I'd sold the old beater car and had enough for next month's rent, but that was it. I couldn't afford to eat there if I didn't work there too.

Ian gave me the job right away and seemed interested in me soon after; I wavered between wanting desperately to be held by him and wanting nothing to do with him. Sometimes I'd run into him in the kitchen, and he would just be a tall man with a body and no distinguishing features. On those days, we did not flirt. We rarely even talked, and if we did, it was business or politics.

Ian understands moods. Sometimes I think he invented them. Sometimes I think I did. It is never important. Like cats in a cramped apartment, we avoid each other. When we cross paths, it is deliberate and almost always good.

15

PENSIONE TINA

Cora and Nancy sat in a dark movie theater waiting for the film to begin. The two handsome young men from the cafe sat on the outside, like bookends. White shirt and blue shirt. Cora was a little dizzy from the wine and carried on a hackneyed conversation with the guy to her left. "You like American films?" she asked.

"Very much. Sometime I go to America."

"Yes. It's a friendly country."

The movie was *Silkwood* about the nuclear power plant in Oklahoma. Cora didn't know what to expect. Maybe it would be dubbed, and she wouldn't understand a word. Maybe there would be subtitles. Neither Cora nor Nancy had been to a movie in Europe. They were at the late show, full from dinner and happy to be young and carefree. They flirted and felt at home, sitting next to each other in the soft seats. They were on an adventure.

The movie began and Cora felt the images and sounds wash over her and send a rush of emotion and sensation through her being. Banjo music. Prairie grasses. A farm. A white clapboard house with a rundown porch. A highway ran past with white lines skipping along. Traffic signs that she could read. Miles and miles of air. She was homesick; she was almost home. The show had Italian subtitles. All those characters stood up there on the big screen, handling plutonium pellets in glove boxes and speaking English. All those American jokes and recipes. It was a rare treat after being away from home for so many months.

Nancy smiled and leaned into the blue shoulder on her right. He smelled of clean cotton. Italian words danced across the bottom of the screen while the actors chewed bubble gum and talked like back home. Cowboy boots, pastures, crickets through the window at night. It took her a while to grasp the movie's plot and the lingo used in the nuclear power plant.

Before Nancy knew it, Thelma was cooked. The pressurized hoses showered her down. Then it was Karen Silkwood who set off the alarms and got scrubbed. She talked about her momma and wanted her to send some conditioner up for her hair. Her momma worried about her fingernails and asked if she was chewing them.

Nancy absorbed the details, thinking about what it was a mother worried about. Imagining the woman who gave birth to you fussing over you, even in adulthood.

Cora leaned into the story, getting lost in the dark. "Try not to cry, 'cause salt's gonna make it worse," Karen said. And the welts on Thelma's face filled the screen. When Karen Silkwood went to Washington, white shirt leaned over and whispered "Is that your town?"

"Yes," Cora said. "There are always parades."

Blue shirt commented on the big cowboy hats. Nancy told him he'd look good in one.

The movie raced along then; Cora gripped the arm of her chair. Nancy let her hand rest in blue shirt's hand. It meant nothing. Then hands were everywhere. Plastic covered hands, scrubbing, spraying the poison from Karen's skin. Internal contamination. "I'm contaminated." she said. "I'm dying."

AFTER THE MOVIE, white shirt leaned forward with a smug look on his face. "You Americans sometimes are not so smart," he said.

Cora looked at him. Looked at Nancy and blue shirt. Looked at white shirt looking at Nancy and blue shirt. "Right," she said. "Want to go for a walk?

~

When Cora walked into the breakfast room the next morning, Nancy was already eating. "Hi." Cora smiled and sat down.

"Where were you? Don't you think I was worried?"

"What are you talking about?" Cora poured herself some coffee.

"You could have at least walked me back here."

"You looked like you were in expert hands."

"You hardly knew him."

"I do now."

"Very funny."

"You're not my mother. Lay off." Cora took a drink and closed her eyes.

"Fine. You can get bitchy. I just don't think you handled that at all well last night."

"Whatever."

"I was worried."

"I heard."

"So, I'm angry."

"So, get over it." Cora looked straight at Nancy. "You got something else you want to say, or are you through?"

"I'm done." Nancy folded her arms and looked out the window.

"Good. Then I'm sorry."

"Me too. How about we get out of here? Head for Rome right now?"

"I can't," Cora said with a smile. "I got a heavy date." Both women laughed and went to pack their things.

THE DOOR to Pensione Tina was easy to miss. Nancy and Cora walked the streets of Rome looking for hostels that were not full. They weren't having any luck. A small, thin man, probably in his late seventies, peeked his head out from behind the huge black wooden door after they passed. "You look for room? This nice place. You come see."

Nancy turned around and then looked at Cora. "Is this for real?"

"I don't think he can accost us." Cora shrugged. "What the hell." She turned to the man. "Maybe. We look."

"Okay. Okay. Berry good place. Me speak English." He pushed the heavy door open and led them through a marble entryway and up what had once been a grand staircase. Several small bedrooms divided the upstairs. The man took Nancy's backpack off her back, reaching up, struggling. Nancy frowned and stooped down to accommodate him. He shuffled into the first open door and laid the pack on the bed. "This be berry good, si?"

"We will..." Nancy looked at Cora.

"Okay. Berry good. Here. Here." He motioned for

Cora to follow him down the narrow hall to the open door at the end. Again, he helped her with her pack and laid it on the bed. He opened the window to the courtyard and motioned out. "Berry good, si? Come. Come." He waved them into a small room with a long table in it. "Breakfast. Eat here. Si?" Next, he showed them the bathroom. It was clean.

"How much?" Cora asked after the tour.

"No so much. Berry good." He smiled a cartoonish grin. He weighed around a hundred pounds.

"Great." Cora said. "I love him. Let's stay."

"He tries to soak us, and I'm sneaking out at night," Nancy said.

"How much?" Cora said, pointing to her hand.

The old man shuffled off down the hall, motioning over his shoulder for the two to follow him. He stopped at a desk and wrote a figure on a piece of paper, handing it to Cora. "Okay, okay?"

Cora smiled. "Berry good." She shot a glance at Nancy. Single rooms with breakfast for 7,000 lire? "A genuine bargain," she said, half under her breath, but loud enough so that Nancy could hear.

16

ORIGINAL DETAIL

In the back room of the Pensione Tina, there is a single bed and a small table. The room looks out over a square gray courtyard. Someone strings laundry between two first-floor windows. This room is on the third floor. This is Cora's room. She stretches out on the bed, reading *Anna Karenina*. She just shaved her legs and wrote postcards home to her family. This is the first time she has had a room to herself in over a month. She likes the pale green walls, the bare light bulb. Sounds drift up from the garden below. Someone is laughing.

Cora's pack rests along the wall. Clean shirts hang on the posts of the bed, drying. Her small collection of books is setting on the chair near her bed. On top of them is the miniature brass donkey she carries around for good luck. She likes to unpack whenever she is staying in a room for more than one night; it makes her feel at home.

Nancy's room is about the same size. It does not have a window. A wooden crucifix is on the wall over the bed. There is a metal bedside table and a chair against the wall by the door. The walls are pale green, like hospital walls. A crack runs the length of the wall behind the bed, starting in the middle and heading up to the corner. Paint has chipped away in a few spots along the crack. The floor is wide wooden boards. The bed has clean, stiff white sheets. Nancy smells the clean pillowcase and closes her eyes. She moves the chair out into the hall, takes off her tennis shoes and socks and sits down on the floor to stretch. She closes her eyes and connects to each muscle as she gently leans toward the floor.

Cora and Nancy disagreed earlier. Nancy commented she was getting low on money. "What's the big deal? Call home and ask for more. From your trust fund or something." Cora shrugged.

"It isn't like that," Nancy said. "This trip was my idea. I'll only use the money they gave me. I can stretch it out."

"Well, isn't that what you told me? That you didn't have to pay for college and your uncle was well off?"

"You don't understand."

"Maybe not. But don't you think it'd be okay if..."

"Just drop it, all right?"

Nancy tells Cora to mind her own business, please. Cora reads to forget about it; Nancy stretches.

It isn't clear to Cora, who comes from a middle-class background, why Nancy won't ask for more money. It seems like a game. She is angry, or envious, or both. She sold the old Buick she bought her freshman year of college to buy the plane ticket to Europe. The rest of her money came from savings and the money from her grandma. Her parents told her to call if she ran into trouble. They'd get her money if she ended up in the hospital or something. They wanted her to go. It was something they had never done for themselves.

The two women spend time alone in their own rooms and meet later for a walk around the city when it is cooler. Neither of them holds a grudge. It's a given that traveling together creates tension. Friends should be able to speak their minds and get it over with.

17

GOOD GIRLS

Diary: If I had met Nancy in high school, would we have been friends? Me, with my jean jacket and hidden stash of cigarettes. I bet she was a cheerleader. Probably rode on the homecoming float. I don't know that our paths would have crossed, but then what has changed? Why are we friends now? I don't know.

I wasn't a bad girl; I only wanted to look like one. What was a "bad girl" anyway? One who smoked pot? One who slept around? One who flunked classes, lied to her parents, got laid in the back seat of a car once by a guy she'd been dating for three years, got an abortion, stayed in school, took Home-Economics, had a kid, quite school, what? I spent half of my time avoiding certain groups of people and trying to become a part of other groups, all in the name of a reputation and fitting in. Maybe it was the same with Nancy. Maybe we just did our best to be happy. Maybe we still were.

In college, I finally took a deep breath and started making up my own mind about things. That was when I decided what was fun and what wasn't, what was worth doing, and what I would risk to do it. I read everything I could get my hands on; I fell in love a dozen times; I downhill skied with my eyes closed. Only once; it was great. I was in control.

Nancy. Sometimes I think she is fascinating: open, fun, adventurous, sophisticated. Other times, I feel like she lives in a glass bubble, a princess bubble of beauty. Not even the most difficult things seem to stop her smile. Christ, when she talks about her father or her deepest fears, she has that little smile, like maybe someone is looking, like she is always on stage.

I don't get it. I don't get her. I like her. She looks at the world differently. I am learning from her. She's an excellent traveling companion, although sometimes she gets obsessive about art and history when I'd rather just be watching men, but we can't have everything in a friend, can we?

Maybe I'm a jerk. Maybe I'm jealous. Maybe she's the most charming person I've ever met. Maybe I don't think I'm interesting enough next to her. Put it this way.

We are both standing against a wall, apples on our heads. A circus knife thrower tosses a razor-sharp blade. I can bet which apple is the target.

18

FEAR

Cora is afraid of horses, and water, and firecrackers. She has a scar on her right hand from a lady finger that exploded before she could throw it. She was eleven. It was at her grandmother's farm near Sioux City. She remembers the smell of burning flesh. She tells Nancy none of this. There is no point.

Talking about it would make Cora feel weak and vulnerable. She does not want to feel more inferior over such a distant thing. Horses don't exist in the present. They stand in stables in Montana on Nancy's uncle's farm. They turn in tight circles at the county fair, all bridles and blinders. Worlds away from this place.

Cora's fear of water is absolute. She is not familiar with pushing through water with cupped palms, deep in subtle currents when the cold slips over your back. Cora can't swim. She grew up land-locked in Grace, Iowa. She spent a few summers vacationing at a cabin on the shore of Lake Superior, collecting driftwood and making sand-castles. She believed the monster was in the water and wouldn't come out, believed the monster was the water, the tug and pull of force taking her down and under. Sand scraping her face and arms. Water slamming down her throat. Bubbles and blue sky. Arms flailing. She was six or seven.

In junior high, when it was required for physical education, she wrote notes in careful script writing and signed her mother's name. "Cora has another ear infection. Please excuse her for the next two weeks. Sincerely, Maureen Daneli." She never got caught, and she never learned to swim. The days she was in the water, she concentrated on staying in the outside lane and staying invisible. Don't make trouble. Don't stand out. That is why it is odd that she agreed to go on the boat with the men. The only explanation is Nancy's persuasiveness and charm and Cora's fear of looking weak. It is odd and troubling. There is an element of adventure, of being young and free, but a trip on a yacht to Sicily with three strange men? I'll need to be cautious, to plan carefully, to show her motivation for such a dangerous decision.

Nancy is afraid she won't be talented enough to make it as an actor. Her fears are based on the future. She is afraid she will end up in New York and not be working, not be acting. She'll run into her father someday and recognize him. Not from pictures, she's never seen any, but she will see herself in his face, the way he gestures, and she'll know they're related.

She's afraid she'll never be lucky. She thinks she has had her luck already, finding a life with her aunt and uncle, being taken in and loved. Loving them back, loving them incredibly. Now she's an adult on her own. She knows she is attractive and therefore people rarely take her seriously. "It's lucky you're good looking," one student in the college theater group told her. "You'll be able to get better jobs."

It is not luck, she thinks. It is a father/choreographer who never wanted her and disappeared. It is a gorgeous, thin ballerina who couldn't stand to be a mother and killed herself. The beautiful daughter grows up feeling like she has done something wrong. She thinks she may understand one day if she goes on the stage and stands at the footlights as her mother did. Each time she hears applause, she closes her eyes and thinks, "Mother, are you watching? Mother, was I all right?"

19

FEEDING THE LIONS

The Colosseum was a ghostly place for Cora. While Nancy commented on the sunshine and the beautiful weather, rolling up her sleeves to get an even tan, Cora stepped over the patchy grass, as if she were walking on the dead bodies of Christian martyrs.

"I don't think you ever told me." Cora turned to Nancy. "Do you believe in God?"

"Today? Yes. Today I definitely believe in God." Nancy smiled. She had a way of making every conversation, every event, seem choreographed.

"And what about today makes you particularly religious?"

"I didn't say I was religious. I said I believe in God today. Look at that sky. Look at this place. How can you not believe?"

Cora knew it was no longer her curiosity that led the discussion, her agenda. Once again, Nancy held the cards. She shrugged.

"Why do you ask?"

"I was thinking about the Christians and the lions. I never had to test my faith. Never had to prove anything to anybody." Cora sat down in the grass. No one else was around; no tourists in sight. It was an unusual scene in the middle of Rome in the summer.

"Sheltered life," Nancy smiled and joined her on the grass. "I used to pray a lot, in junior high and even high school. I thought maybe somebody out there was listening and could get a message to my mom. Like a person-to-person long distance call. Every time I was at a slumber party and we'd try a seance, when that was a big thing, I'd be shaking like a leaf, worried or hopeful that I'd come face to face with my mother."

Cora shook her head. "I don't know about God, but this conversation is too weird for me; it seems like there are ears all around us. Let's get out of here."

It was late afternoon when the two women got back to the hostel. They stopped at a market and bought some fresh fruit and cheese for dinner. Nancy wanted a shower and a nap before they planned the evening's itinerary. Cora sat in the piazza and wrote.

Diary: Tuesday, 4:15. I dreamed last night that Nancy was driving me around Rome in a sports car, an expensive little thing. And she was driving too fast, circling the old buildings in the city center, screeching around fountains and almost hitting pedestrians at every turn. I was screaming for her to slow down, but she just laughed. Finally, I grabbed her arm, and it came right off like a chameleon or one of those lizards that just let go and grow another one. She kept driving and laughing, her head back, her hair blowing in the wind. I sat there, with this arm in my lap, in shock, going in circles and getting dizzy. When I woke up, I couldn't get back to sleep.

We went to the Colosseum today. It dates back to about 72 A.D. and is the best preserved structure from ancient times in Rome. It held some 50,000 people who watched the gladiators and the hunts and the lion feeding shows. It gave me the creeps. I am growing tired of Rome. It is polluted, and hot, and the traffic never stops. Men look at you and hiss and whistle and touch your arms when you pass them in the market. Maybe it is only the city. I am tired of the city. I want tree-shaded beaches and a good book and iced coffee. I want to go to Greece. I wonder if I will go alone. It doesn't seem like it's up to me anymore. Maybe it never was.

CD

20

LOVE

Ian wishes I were more naïve, more in need of him. He asked me once if I had ever been in love before, assuming I was in love now. "No," I said sarcastically, "but I've been married six times." He hasn't mentioned love again. He is growing more comfortable with my ambivalence. He is making do.

21

POSTCARDS

Dear Tam,

Greetings from Italy!

I'm still alive and getting cultured and poorer every day. I spend half my time in train stations, the other half in museums. I'm getting tired and need a few days of standing still.

I have met a few handsome men. One in the train station in Rome said he was in love with me, but it wasn't as romantic as it sounds. Men seem to believe all American women are easy. I have a traveling partner. (Woman). It's safer to travel in twos. I am going to Greece next. Then home. Hope your summer is going well. Miss you lady.

Cora

~

DEAR VICTORIA,

As you can tell, we've reached Rome. The country is beautiful here. I could spend weeks in each museum. I saw this sculpture of Daphne and Apollo. Zeus turns Daphne into a tree to "save" her from being raped by Apollo. The postcard doesn't do it justice. It's a gorgeous piece, her toes are turning to roots, her fingers to leaves... it's amazing. Maybe I was a sculptor in a different life. I will write next week, maybe from Greece. Tell Todd hello.

Nancy

DEAR MOM AND DAD,

Well, I'm nearing the last leg of my trip. I plan to head to Greece in the next few days. Italy is fascinating, but I long to see the Acropolis. Nothing seems as exciting as that. I will take a boat (sigh... a BIG boat...) over and stay as long as my money holds out. I'll call when I know return travel plans.

Love you.

Cora

DEAR DEAN AND JUDY,

I am in love with Italy. I am learning all about its art and architecture. I think I will become a famous actor and buy a villa on the Mediterranean coast for vacations. You may visit as often as you like. How are things? I expect to be home in August. I am thinking of going to Greece, but haven't decided. I'll keep you posted.

Love,

Nancy

~

DEAR CAITLYN,

Are you getting excited about college? I'll have to visit some weekend after I get back. You'll love it. This trip has been great. I'm finding out how much I can do on my own, how much there is to learn out here in the "big world." Isn't that called growing up? Sigh. Anyway, it's beautiful and it ain't nothing like Iowa. Miss you! We'll have lots to talk about when I get back!

C

~

ROGER,

How's the Big Apple? Have you landed any acting jobs yet? You will, I'm sure. You'd love the food here:

pasta and wine. I am traveling with a woman I met in England. A great traveling partner and friend. She's from the Midwest too. I will be back in Montana in late August. I'll give you a call.

Nancy

~

JUICE,

Hello from the other side of the world. I am getting cultured, growing fat from the delicious food and getting tan. Great, huh? I doubt Iowa will ever quite measure up now; I may have to move to Greenwich Village or San Francisco or Las Vegas. You know, the cutting edge. So, our friendship will have to remain long distance. You aren't a handsome, sexy guy, and I don't miss you.

Cora

~

TIM,

I don't know why I chose to be halfway around the world to write to you. Maybe the miles make me miss the familiar. The past. And that is what we are, isn't it? Past. Oh well, no hard feelings. I just wanted to send you a postcard of the gorgeous Italian sights and make you jealous. Ha ha. I am happy and learning Italian from my pocket dictionary. Enjoy your summer. Maybe we'll get together for coffee sometime. Wouldn't that be adult of us?

Nan

DEAR BECKA,

I am writing to you from this small guesthouse called Pensione Tina. A little man, about eighty, runs it and looks after us "girls." He wakes us to little songs in Italian and strong coffee. It is a romantic place. You'd like it, especially all the handsome men.

I never promised a postcard every week, did I? Apologies. I can hardly afford postage; it is getting desperate, but I am sending my sincere greetings here. Considering my cash flow problems, this may be your only memento from my trip!

I'll call you as soon as I return from the sandy beaches of Greece. And no, I don't intend to SWIM in the sea, just bask in the sun next to it. No one needs to know I am afraid of the water. It's my little secret so far. Out of room.

Arrivederci

C

DEAR JC,

This may be my last postcard, as I intend to be heading toward home within the next couple of weeks. Rome is wonderful. Tomorrow we're taking a day trip to an ancient city that is still well preserved because it was buried until they started excavating it in the early 1900s. It should be fun. I've taken lots of pictures to bore you with upon my return. See you soon.

Nancy

22

FAUNA

I don't pay attention to trees. I don't know the names of the shrubs or flowers along the roadside where Cora and Nancy are walking outside of Rome. Halfheartedly hitchhiking. I do remember the gnarled trees — indecisive branches curling and turning toward a stark sky, but naming them is another matter. Of course, there must be olive trees. Cora is thinking about going to Greece.

I remember the smell of Crete and the morning sounds of goat bells on the hills near the sea. Here in the Black Hills, it smells of pine and spruce and white birch. I don't know. Naming plants isn't important to me. I suppose I could do my research. Go down to the public library and look it up. Talk to someone in the park service. Get some answers. A genuine writer probably would. I am not a writer. All I have are questions and faint memories of smells in Mediterranean surroundings. Limited experience. A slide show. I am not interested in recording every detail; I am not a botanist. The characters' lives are choking me already. My inexperience is frightening.

Cora and Nancy were hitchhiking. Gnarled trees lined the road, indecisive branches curling and turning toward a stark sky. Olive trees. Cora thought about going to Greece.

"Do you think a guy could grow olive trees in Iowa?" Cora asked.

"No. Too cold."

"I like olives." Cora picked up a small rock from the road and tossed it into the air, catching it as they walked.

"I like corn." Nancy looked over and smiled.

"We got that, I guess." Cora paused. "I used to detassel corn when I was in junior high. You ever do that?" Nancy shook her head no. "Walking between tall rows of corn, all day long, up and down and up and down the field, pulling the tassels out. God, it was hot."

"Why do they do that, anyway?"

"I don't know. I worked for an uncle of mine. I thought it was good money. One year, this lady was my supervisor, probably in her late sixties. She rode a motorcycle to the farm. Wore this purple helmet and red leather jacket and jeans. She used to crack us up. Funny? God, she could tell jokes. She said retirement was too boring.

When I graduated from high school, I invited her to the reception. She brought me a lacy pair of fancy underpants as a gift."

Nancy laughed. "Are you serious?"

"You bet." Cora smiled.

"I always worked for my uncle on the ranch. One summer, I wanted to work at a restaurant in town. All the kids from Birch School hung out there. It was air-conditioned, and I was tired of barns, but my uncle said he needed my help and didn't want me hanging around town all night after work."

There was a silence. Cora threw the rock at a tree and it made a sharp sound as it hit. "Did you go to public school?"

"No. My uncle's sort of strict. Conservative, maybe."

"Was he okay with you traveling alone? Did he want you to come here?"

"Put it this way, I never won him over, but I am twenty-two after all. He just worries. He's always been protective."

"I went to Ben Franklin High School. Early to bed, early to rise. That's Iowa."

"Did you get good grades?" Nancy asked.

"Pretty good. Why?" Cora smiled and looked at Nancy.

"What was your grade point average?"

"High school or college?"

"High school."

"Don't remember."

"College."

"I forgot," Cora said. She shrugged, her smile teasing Nancy.

"Well, I got A's," Nancy said.

"Surprise, surprise." Cora widened her eyes.

"And a scholarship and a certificate of merit." Nancy shrugged.

"Well, I got a jean jacket, a class ring, and a partridge in a pear tree," Cora said. Both women laughed. Cora didn't say she was an honor student too. She preferred to be the wild woman with a few cards up her sleeve. A spare trick or two.

23

OSTIA ANTICA

The ancient city of Ostia Antica looked like a shrubbery maze in the cool green morning. Tall pines surrounded well-preserved ruins; the ancient port was much like Pompeii but on a smaller scale. Thousands of years ago, malaria turned the thriving port of ancient Rome into a ghost city. Preserved by silt and tidal mud which eventually buried the city, the ruins of temples, theaters, and homes were still easy to define.

Cora finished reading her guidebook and walked off in one direction, following the maze's pattern, and Nancy walked off in the other. Patterns of their own were developing. Whenever there was an opportunity, they seemed to separate and experience things for themselves. The closeness was getting to them both, and the need for privacy, or a semblance of privacy, pervaded many of their sightseeing tours.

It was good to be alone, Cora thought. She wondered about the ancient city: what the people did, how they dressed, what was in the boiling pot over the fire? She tried to picture the last days of illness on the canvas of a dark oil painting. She was experiencing so much history through the paintings she saw as she toured museum after museum, she saw things in frames.

Nancy thought about money, and lunch, and where they would eat dinner. She wondered when Cora would leave for Greece and if she should go with her. She wasn't sure that she wanted to.

"Drink?" Cora came up behind Nancy and held out a plastic bottle of water.

"Thanks. This place is strange." Nancy looked around.

"This place is old." Cora smiled. "I don't like thinking about how the people dealt with a malaria plague. Those people who took care of the sick, knowing their time would come. Cooking dinner. Playing games in the grass with the children. It's easier to think of it as a pretend city. No catastrophe." Cora paused. "I'm not so hot with catastrophe."

"I've been thinking about Greece. I am running low on money; I don't think I can afford it. I thought I might start back north when you leave and spend a few days in England before I catch a plane back home. I'm not sure how long I'll be on standby, and I have to have a little money reserved in case it takes days."

Cora nodded. "Makes sense. I'm going the budget route, so if you decide to go, we would be frugal. I hear Greece's very cheap, but whatever you decide."

"It'll be kind of odd. Going, I mean." Nancy smiled, squinting into the sun, her gorgeous face in full sunlight. "Do you suppose we will ever see each other again?"

"Most definitely." Cora was matter-of-fact. "You'll fly to Iowa on your first break from your first show for a nice relaxing week of rest at a cabin on Lake Okoboji. We'll sit around and drink Bordeaux wine and remember when. Then I'll fly out to New York to go to your wedding. You'll be marrying some famous actor or director."

"Right. In the middle of Central Park. In a white gauze dress with daisies in my hair."

"Actually," Cora said, "I pictured a small private wedding in a penthouse overlooking Central Park."

"Of course, how silly of me. If he's famous, we'd have to avoid the crowds."

"Well, you'll be famous too, so there will be security to consider."

Nancy laughed. "Why do you have me getting married first?"

"I plan to live in sin. Or live alone. Circumstances pending."

"My bet is you're all talk. You'll fall in love and get married, and have three or four kids, and send me Christmas cards from Iowa."

"In that order?" Cora was not as comfortable speculating about her future as she was playing make-believe with Nancy's. The past couple of months gave her time to think about the future. What was she planning to do? She had an English degree without a teaching certificate. She was not qualified to do much. Just what was she thinking?

"Maybe, but I won't be in Grace. I can tell you that. I don't have the foggiest idea where I am going to live. I may have to work for a month or two to get enough money to relocate, but I need a destination before I can do that."

"What about looking at a map," Nancy said, "the way we do here? Check out the area, see if the city center is too confusing, get a list of museums and restaurants and go for it."

"Sounds easy enough. Who needs a career?" Cora sat on a flat rock covered in yellow and pale green moss. She took a long drink from the bottle then swatted at her neck, absent-mindedly trying to kill a fly. "Damn!" The insect was a bee and stung her on the hand. Her finger began to swell and tingle. "A damn bee."

"Let me see. Cold. You need to put something cold on

it." Nancy looked around the ruins, as if searching for a refrigerator.

"Italy hasn't even invented ice cubes yet. Forget it. We sure won't find anything out here. Damn, it hurts."

"Try the water bottle; it's cool, anyway. "

Cora stood up and put her hand on a huge rock, on the shaded side. It throbbed. It was hot out, and she was pissed. "Let's get back to the city of circles. I'm starved."

"You aren't allergic or anything, are you? God, don't tell me you are allergic to bees." Nancy was wide-eyed.

"Relax, girl. It's fine. I won't be passing out on you. Have you ever thought about medicine? You have such a calm demeanor." Cora smiled, shook out her hand, and shrugged. "Crisis over. Take a deep breath."

Nancy wasn't as quick to smile. "I got stung on the face once, out in a field exercising Glory. My whole right eye swelled shut. It hurt like hell. Are you sure you're okay?"

Cora nodded. "Let's get going back. We've got a long walk before we reach civilization, unless we can catch a ride."

The two women picked up their day packs and walked toward the road. Cora was wearing a long cotton skirt and sandals. Nancy wore a jumper with a tank top underneath. Neither woman wore shorts much in Italy. Shorts sent out the wrong message to men, and American women had a poor enough reputation the way it was.

The road back into Rome was gravel but well groomed. Cora told Nancy about the time when she and her family got snowbound outside of Sioux City at a relative's farm. She was eight or nine. The drifts in the yard reached over fences and curled up around cars, almost swallowing them completely. Her uncle, the one who was allergic to bees, taught her card tricks and how to play poker. They bet with wooden matches and played late into the night. It was the only time she'd seen her father drink whiskey, drink any alcohol, for that matter.

Nancy listened and walked along. She knew about snowstorms, but she couldn't imagine a father sitting around a chrome and Formica kitchen table, talking tough and playing cards with his daughters and his brother. Couldn't imagine the aroma of coffee and cinnamon in the warm kitchen, her mother snuggled up in a Lazy-boy recliner in the next room, asleep with a book in her lap. Gray wool socks sticking out beneath a quilt of calico squares. Beneath a warm blanket of love. Oh, she knew about love. Dean and Judy had raised her like their own, but she always wondered what might have been if her father had loved her mother enough. If he had wanted her.

Nancy and Cora walked for almost an hour before seeing a car. When the first one appeared, Cora stuck out her thumb. Then, on second thought, she let Nancy stand closest to the road, in simple view. "This one's yours, Beauty. Do your stuff."

Nancy shook her head, smiled, and put out her thumb. No use arguing with facts. The black Mercedes stopped right next to them.

24

SAUNA

The ceramic tiles in the sauna alternate between orange and red. The storybook colors of hell. I say this out loud because I am the only one in here, and I want to hear how the words sound. I expect a weak, misted voice, but it echoes in this hollow oven.

I sit down on my towel and concentrate on breathing. I never feel like I can breathe in here. I imagine I am Gretel, roasting. Hansel is outside the oven tap dancing for the witch — talking her out of adding him to the evening feast. Little feet on the wooden plank floors. Tap, click, tap, tap. Meanwhile, I bake.

I am taking a break from writing. The evening is dreary, and I thought a sauna and whirlpool would be helpful. Get my mind off of fiction. As the story expands, I find myself growing smaller; muscles constrict in my neck and shoulders, my room grows larger around me. At first, I blamed it on typing, sitting at the desk for too long. I bought a better chair with a back support, but it isn't that. There are voices inside me that tell me to get the story right. Pressure me, night after night. The ones with all the petty details, the ones who want to write astounding poetry. They try to take over and crowd my prose. Sometimes I give in, and other times I give up and go for a walk.

The club is within walking distance. I can walk anywhere I need to go. I have no need for a car; I am not planning on leaving. This town in western South Dakota has become my home.

The clock is visible through a thick glass window on the front wall of the sauna. I have one minute to go. I make myself sit here. Sixty seconds is a long time. I may be melting. In sixty seconds, you can push history off course. Turn the boat away, swerve off over rough waves and look to the horizon.

The horizon is a safe place here — jagged hills and pine trees. No long flat line of water pulling on the iris of the eye.

25

ENZO

"Afternoon, ladies." A handsome gentleman lowered the electric window and smiled. He wore sunglasses and a suit and tie. "Do you need any assistance?"

Nancy tossed her hair over her shoulder and smiled. "We are going into Rome, but our interest in a long walk was a bit overly ambitious."

"Would you like a ride? I am going to Roma myself."

Nancy turned to Cora, as if to confer. "Sure, thanks," Cora smiled and opened the back door. Nancy got in front. The car was cool and smelled of leather.

The driver turned to Nancy and extended his hand. "Enzo Aldonti at your service. Call me Enzo."

Nancy shook his hand. "I'm Nancy." She paused.

"And I'm Cora, hello."

"American?" Enzo asked. "Have you been touring

Lido?" Both women nodded. "It is a powerful place. Did you see the stone inscription to Caesar?"

"Yes," Cora said. "I heard Pompeii is similar to this. Is it?"

"More tourists. More commercialism." Enzo was handsome in the true Italian sense. Strong jawbone, fine lips. Dark complexion and hair. His tailored suit was linen. A very wealthy man. "Italian history is my hobby. I teach at a small university in Rome. And you? Are you students?"

"Until recently." Nancy answered the question, since he looked at her when he asked. "We've graduated."

"Where in the U.S. are you from?"

"Iowa," Cora said from the back. "It's in the Midwest."

"Yes, I know. What college did you attend?"

"The University of Iowa in Iowa City."

"Ah, yes." Enzo smiled and looked in the rearview mirror, studying Cora's face. She could feel it, even though he had his sunglasses on. "I am familiar with Iowa. We have a group of students here from Luther College. Do you know it?"

"That's in Decorah, isn't it?"

"Yes. They are on an exchange and will be taking a holiday with a group of my students."

"What do you teach?" Nancy asked.

"Engineering, business and such." He shrugged. "Relatively dull, I'm afraid." He was a charming man. They drove the tree-lined street for a few miles without talking. "Have you seen Rome? Where are you headed next?"

Nancy said "Greece, maybe" at the same time Cora answered "Greece." She turned around and smiled. "We aren't sure yet. Taking it one day at a time."

"Well, that couldn't be more fortunate," Enzo said. "Have you seen any of the coast of Italy?" He paused. "It so happens that we are planning a brief excursion around Sicily starting tomorrow morning. One of my groups from summer school and the students from Decorah will be going, but a couple of students got homesick and headed back early. We still have room for three or four more students, if you would be interested in that kind of thing. We are taking three yachts and plan to be gone for five days. That is, of course, if the weather is good."

Cora was the first to speak. Her fear of water had her shaking already. "We couldn't afford something like that. We are on a limited budget, but thanks. It's a nice offer."

"Oh, it wouldn't cost you anything, except maybe an occasional chore on the boat. We help a little with the cooking. A generous donor to the university is paying for the entire trip. We do this every other year. It is a wonderful time. We stop in Napoli and Palermo. Take our time."

"That would be wonderful!" Nancy was beaming. "We aren't on any schedule, and if it isn't expensive, it would stretch our time in Europe. I think it would be great. How many days did you say?"

"Four, maybe five."

"I'm not sure," Cora said from the back.

"Why don't you think about it? We are leaving from the docks at Lido di Ostia at eight o'clock tomorrow morning. If you decide to come along, just show up at dock number nine. It would be nice to have some more charming women on the cruise."

"What would we need to bring along?" Nancy asked.

"You and your clothes. Whatever you travel with. We will provide food and everything else."

Nancy could sense that Cora was not as eager as she was. They were on the outskirts of Rome when Enzo pulled over at a train station. "This is where I turn. If you'd like to come, we will meet again. If not, enjoy Italy and the Mediterranean!"

Cora and Nancy got out. "Thanks, and thanks for the ride! Tomorrow at 8:00 then," Nancy closed the door. "Definitely a gorgeous man," she said, half under her breath as the car turned the corner and disappeared.

Cora felt a knot growing in her stomach. Things were fraying at the edges; she was losing control. The idea of boarding a boat and spending time at sea made her sick, and yet she could see what lay ahead. She could see herself agreeing, saying yes to Nancy, yes to the fear, to the unknown. She would like to see this as an adventure:

new people and unknown places in a romantic world of desire and wealth. She may never have another chance to do something like this. If it weren't for the sea and her terrible fear, this would be incredible. She could understand Nancy's excitement. She needed to pull in and figure things out. Even then, she knew it was no small decision.

26

LANDLOCKED

Writing about water. The heave and swell of blue green madness. The taste of salt on my lips. The sound of a flat world of water slapping against the hull of a boat.

It may seem ludicrous to picture it. Me, writing this book in a small room in the back of Geralyn Hendricks' house, nestled in the hills around Rapid City. It is snowing lightly now, flakes collecting on the innocent branches outside my window. White wood divides the square panes of glass which frame the tree.

When the heat kicks in, steam forms foggy patches near the corners of each piece of glass.

There is no large body of water for thousands of miles. Lake Superior is as close as one comes, and that is a two-day drive from here. I traveled on boats a few times when I was in Europe. I've been there. Have I mentioned that? I don't get all this stuff out of books. Bits and pieces come from the memories I can still see with my inner eye. The rest is from somewhere else.

Anyway. It's early August and hot and salty on the Tyrrhenian Sea. Two young women are about to discover the horrible gap between appearances and reality. They are in Rome having coffee at a sidewalk cafe near the Forum. They are soaking in the thousands of years layered upon the ground beneath them, listening to horses' hooves on the stone streets of the fifteen hundreds. They imagine the spring blossoms on the fruit trees when the Forum was the center of justice. They smell the strong coffee beans, see the salmon color of a potted geranium on the sill above their heads. They are thinking about their adventure. They are mustering courage. They are making history with their hands tied behind their backs.

27

CRUISE

"But how would he know about Iowa and that college if he wasn't on the up and up?" Nancy tore a thick piece of crust from her bread and waved it at Cora.

"I don't know, but I don't like it. I think we should know more about him. Getting on a boat with strangers?" Cora paused. "It's a crazy idea."

"What about hitchhiking? We do that all the time, Cora. I say we show up and check it out and decide then."

"You can jump out of a car, yell for help if you have trouble." Cora chewed on her bottom lip. "In the middle of the sea, you're on your own."

"Yes. Exactly." Nancy smiled. "Drifting along in an aqua blue sea on a yacht with lots of young people who speak English and some that don't... I'm sorry, I must be nuts, but it sounds wonderful."

"What if I, what if you got seasick?" Cora squinted into the morning sun. They sat at an outdoor cafe having an early breakfast. It was before six o'clock. Their backpacks laid on the sidewalk next to them. They decided the night before to check out of the pensione and make their decision over breakfast. If it wasn't the cruise, they would still leave Rome and both head for Greece, or one would go in each direction. The morning was heavy with decisions.

Nancy raised her eyes. "Then we ask to get off at the next port. I'm sure they would oblige." She studied Cora's worried face. "Oh, come on, it will be our last fling to top off a perfect summer. There is a definite possibility for romance."

"You've just got a thing for professors," Cora said. "If I wanted romance, I'd go straight to Greece. Italy doesn't seem that romantic anymore."

"Please? For me?" Nancy was serious now.

"Would you go on your own?"

"No."

"Why?"

"It doesn't sound like a bright thing to do. I've learned from my traveling companion how to travel smart, you know, in pairs."

Cora felt the web being spun around her. She wanted to believe it would be okay. She did not want to be afraid of the water, of being suspended on a small wooden craft above that monster sea which haunted her nightmares. They say if you fall off a horse, you get back on and ride again, she thought. Ride out of the fear. Maybe she could do that. Looking across the table at Nancy, wanting her to smile, wanting her approval, Cora opened her hands, palms up, offering her answer. "Okay. I'll go to the docks. But if I get a bad feeling, that's it. Deal?"

"Deal." Nancy dug into her pocket for money. "Coffee is on me. Let's get going. You won't regret this. This is going to be a blast."

They reached the port with some time to spare. Boats of every color crowded the docks. The air smelled of seawater, oil, and fish. Nancy asked a man for directions to dock number nine. People were walking around in swimming suits and white cotton. Wealthy sailors, vacationing Italians. Down from the dock area was an expanse of sandy beach. People on beach blankets and under umbrellas. Music from radios. Children playing tag. The early morning already had a carnival atmosphere.

Cora saw the enormous yacht first, all white and polished wood with navy and light blue stripes streamlining the sides. The surrounding boats seemed to be about the same size. The windows were tinted, and a table sat on the deck with several chairs scattered around.

A heavy man in jeans and a white tank top was lifting boxes on to the boat. Enzo appeared from below with a cup of coffee in his hand. He wore baggy white cotton pants and a red shirt. He was barefoot. His sunglasses were on top of his head. He looked like an actor in a television commercial for coffee or anything else he wanted to sell. He was extremely good looking, thin and olive skinned. His hair was long on the top and waved down over his left eye. He looked up and saw the young women as they walked down the plank to the white boat.

"Buongiorno!" he shouted. "Tutto va bene?"

Nancy reached the boat first, and he offered her his hand. "Bene." She replied. "Good morning."

Cora looked at the water near her feet, the movement beneath the slatted boards. She swallowed hard. "Hello."

"Cora, yes?" Enzo asked. She nodded. "Lino, these are the young women I told you about. Cora and Nancy, my good friend and navigator, Lino."

Lino stopped what he was doing and nodded at the women, smiling. "Buongiorno," he said. He had a mustache and a few days beard growth. He looked older than Enzo, maybe in his forties. He seemed uncomfortable; he probably didn't speak much English, Cora thought.

"Where are the others?" Nancy asked.

"They will be along. Sometimes morning traffic slows things up. We will wait. Would you like some coffee? A piece of fruit?" Enzo motioned to a small table on the deck. A thermos of coffee and several cups sat on one side, and a huge tray of fresh fruit, bread, and cheese sat next to it. Out of habit, Cora and Nancy calculated the cost of a peach that size, hard rolls, and fresh butter. They helped themselves.

Enzo pulled up a couple of deck chairs into the sun and helped them with their packs. "Should I put these below?"

Nancy looked at Cora, and Cora looked back. She took a deep breath and picked up a coffee cup. "Sure," she said. "Thanks."

Nancy beamed with obvious glee and winked at Cora. She sat back in the wooden chair. "This is the life," she murmured. "I could get used to this."

Cora felt better. He was a nice man. Things looked okay. The coffee smelled good. And you only go around once, she thought. She sat down and tried to forget about the water.

Enzo came up from below. "There are three sleeping compartments, an adequate galley, and a head, or washroom below. I'll show you around later, when we have gotten underway. The other two yachts are further down the dock; we will rendezvous with them out by a small reef. I just spoke with someone from the other boat on the radio downstairs. The Luther College group met up at his boat. I guess there was a misunderstanding. Anyway, they are all there and we can get underway as soon as two more passengers show up here." He shaded his eyes and then put on his sunglasses, looking up at the dock. "Ah, there is Alessandra now. She is one of my students. And here comes Giuseppe."

Cora saw a blonde woman waving halfheartedly. She had long hair and wore a navy and white polka-dotted halter dress. She carried a small bag and a hat. Enzo went up to meet her before she got on the boat and gave her a small kiss on each cheek.

"Interesting," Nancy said, half under her breath.

"Custom," Cora replied. "Not to worry."

When Alessandra reached the boat, she glanced up at the two women. "Hello," she said softly in practiced English. She had a crooked smile, hiding rotten teeth.

"Cora and Nancy, this is Alessandra. Alessandra, Cora and Nancy are American students. They are joining us."

Just then a young man jumped on the boat, swinging a duffel bag on behind him. Cora couldn't take her eyes off of him. "Giuseppe!" Enzo reached out his hand and shook it, then gave him a kiss on each cheek. Once again, he turned to make introductions. He gestured to each woman as he said her name. "Nancy, Cora, Alessandra. This is my young and handsome cousin from Sicily, Giuseppe." Giuseppe smiled. Black curly hair. Deep eyes. Small, thin hands. He wore a soccer shirt, Levi jeans, and sandals.

"Piacere." He nodded to each woman.

"His English needs work," Enzo said. "This will be good for him."

Lino disappeared below, and the sounds of engines and smell of oil shook Cora from her spell. They lifted the ropes, and the craft was backing out toward the Tyrrhenian Sea. "God in heaven," she whispered, "if you are out there, keep this boat afloat. Please don't let my feet get wet."

Nancy reached across the table and touched her hand. "You okay?" she asked.

"Long story," Cora smiled. "I'll tell you later."

28

MT. RUSHMORE

The first winter here, I visited the monument often; it was always deserted. Snowy stone presidents. No one visits the Dakotas in the winter; tourists like sunshine and crowds. I wandered around outside looking at Lincoln from various angles, trying to get a clue of some kind. I'm not sure what I was looking for.

This winter I've been coming here again. I stand at the railing at the observation area and talk. Try out my stories on Tom and Abe. George seems to be asleep. Teddy isn't interested in contemporary fiction. I tell them about Cora and the men at the cafe in Florence. I ask them if she should be more subdued, move introverted. Does she feel as sexy and flirtatious when she is around a beautiful woman? Does Nancy inhibit her, or does she go to bed with the student from Bologna to spite Nancy? To prove to herself she is attractive? I am already certain she's uncomfortable with her choice the next day. It's inevitable. And what about Rome? Why is Cora acting like a puppet with limp legs? Why does Nancy control things? Why does Cora allow it?

Abe has no comment. The men are good listeners but tight with advice.

I'm stuck chiseling my plot out of stone.

I sit down with a spiral notebook and a thermos of coffee. It's thirty-six degrees. A female clerk from the souvenir shop walks by. The store is open for brief hours, even though it seems no one is ever here. Sometimes, I go inside to warm up and browse at the books and Black Hills Gold jewelry, but I rarely buy anything. It doesn't seem to bother anyone.

The sky is a limp blue. I write wearing my leather gloves. It looks like a ransom note—jerky and urgent. Cora isn't talking today. Her love life is her business. Nancy wants to give me her side, but she is too beautiful. I can't take her seriously when the subject turns to love. She has always been desired except by her mother and father. Nancy tells herself her looks are important because she wants to act. Cora tells herself she isn't beautiful, but she's desirable: beauty based on demand. Nancy accepts compliments and takes care of her body. Cora accepts her body and takes care of everyone else.

29

ALESSANDRA

B y mid-morning, the three young women were sitting on deck chairs facing the sun and blue world of water. There was a breeze, and the waves tossed the boat gently from side to side. It surprised Cora that the motion didn't bother her. It was soothing. Relaxing. She was reading Isak Dinesen and enjoying herself. Nancy was smoothing suntan lotion over her brown, shapely legs. She had changed into shorts. Since they were on the boat, it seemed appropriate here. Alessandra filed her nails and began to talk, to warm up. She took her sunglasses off, as if to study the people around her.

Enzo busied himself with tasks about the boat. He and Giusseppe spoke Italian, tied things down and moved boxes around. Occasionally, they stopped for a beer and a cigarette. Lino was down below.

Alessandra lit a cigarette, leaned back in the deck chair, and blew the smoke up over her head. Her fingernail polish was still wet, a bright pink tip on each finger. She held the cigarette carefully, so as not to touch her nails.

"How long have you been at the university?" Nancy asked.

Alessandra looked puzzled. "Me? At university? Phhh." She made a dismissing sound with her lips.

Nancy shot Cora a puzzled glance. Perhaps she had misunderstood. Wasn't Alessandra supposed to be one of Enzo's students?

"I am study to, ah, cut hair. You know..." Alessandra mimicked scissors with her fingers, the cigarette hanging out of her mouth as she squinted through the smoke.

Cora nodded. "Yes." She smiled. "And how do you know Enzo?"

"Enzo? He is around. Invites me and I think a vacation from this damn shit town would be nice. So, I say yes." She smiled, showing crooked teeth. "You?"

Cora looked around to see if Enzo was nearby, but didn't see him. "We just met. Nancy and I were hitchhiking, and he picked us up."

Nancy furrowed her bow, but forced a smile. "We decided we could use an adventure too."

"Where do you live in America?" Alessandra tossed the cigarette butt into the sea.

"I'm from Montana." When Nancy caught Alessandra's quizzical look, she added, "It's a state out west. Mountains. Big sky. Horses. A beautiful place."

"And I'm from Iowa," Cora added dryly. "It's in the middle of the country. Flat. Big sky. Lots of corn. We grow corn." She smiled. "Not that many horses though, thank God."

"What?" Nancy turned to her.

"I'm scared to death of horses."

"You're kidding! You didn't tell me that."

"I know. It wasn't important. One of my big fears, that's all. And as long as I'm confessing, the other's water."

"No!" Nancy sat up straight. "You don't swim?"

"Not if I can help it!"

Alessandra smiled. She seemed to enjoy observing this conversation and seemed to understand most of it. After testing her fingernails, she pulled lotion out of her bag and began rubbing suntan lotion into her fair skin.

"Then why did you agree to this trip?" Nancy asked.

"Adventure and defiance. I wanted to defy the gods of fear. And, of course, the chance of maybe meeting good-looking men." She raised her eyebrows and winked at Alessandra.

"So, how long do you know each other?" Alessandra asked.

"A few weeks." Nancy shrugged. "I guess we don't know each other well at all."

"Oh, Beauty, don't pout because I didn't expose all my vulnerabilities to you. It's not that important. I don't know your deep secrets or what you're most afraid of, either."

"Shots. Needles at the doctor." Nancy smiled. She looked at Alessandra.

"Me?" Alessandra shrugged. "I don't know. Not so much scares me. Maybe all scares me?" She stared out over the sea.

Cora was growing used to the rock and tilt of the boat. The endless color of sea. "I'm doing okay with the water as long as it stays out of the boat and I stay in it." She looked around. "I'm going to get some coffee. Anyone interested?"

Both women declined, so Cora went over to the small table still on the deck and lifted the lid of the pot. It was empty. She knew a small kitchen was below and went in search of more coffee. Doubts were already growing in her about Enzo's story, the pretenses for the trip, but they seemed insignificant under the glowing sun.

The steps in the boat's stern led down to a dim, but large, kitchen and living area. On the right, a small sofa and chairs fit into one corner. Nearby, a table with four swivel chairs was bolted to the floor. Everything looked anchored down. To the left was the cooking area, complete with a full-sized stove and sink. Oak cupboards, cranberry carpet, gleaming steel fixtures. A large radio sat on a mahogany table in the corner. Money. Giuseppe stood at the sink, smoking a cigarette and holding a fresh cup of coffee. He looked startled and then smiled.

Cora smiled. "Excuse me. I was looking for more coffee."

"Coffee?" Giuseppe turned to the counter and handed her a heavy thermos. "You take it. I make more."

"Thanks." She hesitated. "I'm Cora. I know they introduced us, but I've forgotten your name."

"Giuseppe." He smiled. White teeth. Smooth skin.

"Giuseppe?" Cora repeated it.

"Yes. Very good. Like American Joseph."

"Oh. Hello, Joseph Giuseppe. Thanks for the coffee."

He nodded. "You are welcome... Cora."

She turned to go back upstairs and felt his eyes watching her go. Fear or no fear, this could be an interesting cruise, she thought.

30

SUBPLOTS

Each life could be a story. A multitude of tales centering on the intricate shadows and patches of light beginning in the closets of childhood. The snapshots scattered all the way to the present. I realize it's up to me. I am not ready to sort out what is important from the scraps of life represented on the yacht anymore than I am ready to sort out my stories for Ian. He wants to know all about my past, the things that make me tick. I want him to slow down.

Giuseppe burned his inner thigh from some hot soup when he was seven. He is shy and self-conscious about the scars. He doesn't wear swimming trunks or shorts on the boat. He has never made love to a woman without the room being totally dark. This is for his own comfort. It has nothing to do with the women with whom he has sex. They are simply players in a very old game.

Giuseppe has never been in love. They expect him to marry a daughter of friends of the family in a neighboring village. He accepts this. Tina is shy and okay looking. It is better, Giuseppe believes, not to be beautiful. A wife should be an excellent cook and housekeeper and good with children. She should be okay in bed, but if not, there are always other places to go.

Giuseppe is twenty-four years old and somewhat naïve. Enzo, his mother's brother, invited him to come along on this cruise. When he got on board and saw the three women, he had some reservations. He can feel deep in his chest that this is going to be an experience like none he has known before. He does not know Enzo sees it as his rite of passage into manhood. He does not see it that way. Giuseppe gathers all his beliefs in the same way everyone does, from those around him, from the stories of his youth, from the scenes on the streets outside his childhood home. He is not a bad person when he gets on the boat. He knows right from wrong, but after drinking a lot of wine, he passively participates in the events on the yacht. And then, he encompasses evil as easily as the rest of them.

Enzo has not always been rich. Living in a country with stark contrasts between those who have money and those who do not, he decided at a young age which side of the fence he would be on. He is a businessman, not a teacher, educated and experienced in international commerce. He is on the fringe of organized crime, involved enough to make a lot of money, distanced enough to feel safe in his normal living. He believes he is a respectable man and thinks his appetite for sex is merely a habit, and not even a terribly bad habit. Women who go with him deserve what they get. Good girls do not go out looking for adventure. Good girls follow the script.

Enzo's wife is dutiful. They have been married sixteen years, since they both were twenty and have three children. They live an average life in a large Italian town. Enzo leaves for business often. His wife does not question this. She's comfortable, and their children have all they could want. She knows Enzo lies and exalts himself in his custom-made suits. She knows women find him attractive and thinks Enzo is probably not faithful to her. She's not sure, and doesn't wish to dig any deeper. Some things are better left on the shelf. She still loves him and is certain he has strong feelings for her. The family is important. They will keep it together. There is no doubt of this.

Lino grew up in Salerno, around the kitchen table, drinking wine with his father. From the time he was seven, he remembers frequently going to school drunk. He dropped out and began working at the harbor at thirteen. His mother was an unhappy woman. She had an alcoholic husband and a son who picked up the trade.

Lino's father hit her when they argued. Finally, she left them, left Italy for good. Some said she was working in Germany for a family with four children.

Lino has never married. He is not bright and takes orders from Enzo. He maintains the boat. He drinks. He watches the women and waits with greedy eyes. He is overweight with a belly, but has the enormous arms and shoulders of a weight lifter. Lino thinks of himself as a virile and strong man.

31

FISHING

Near noon, Cora felt edgy. There wasn't much to do, such small flat places to walk on the rocking sea. She was tired of reading and wanted to meet some of the new people they were supposed to rendezvous with from the college in Iowa. The other two boats.

Enzo came up to the deck with a big tray of salami, hard bread, and cheese. There were peaches, and grapes, and three bottles of wine.

Cora leaned forward as he sat the tray on a small table near her. "What time are we meeting the others?"

Enzo tilted his head and paused, as if considering the question. "There has been another unfortunate delay. I was on the radio just now and found out one boat has some motor difficulty. Something broke as they were taking off. A mechanical problem in the engine. And so, it will be late afternoon before they can fix it. We are going to meet them in Naples."

"When?" Cora's voice was strained.

Enzo gave her a polished smile. "Tomorrow, dear. Now can you relax?" He looked over at Nancy and winked. "We will have to entertain ourselves, I'm afraid. Anyone interested in some lunch?"

Nancy leaned back, her hands gripping the arms of the chair. Cora could feel her withdrawing. The hesitancy and fear mulled around in the pit of her stomach. She shook it off. There was nothing to be done but to have lunch and wait.

"Giuseppe!" Enzo shouted. "Come and join these beautiful women and me for some lunch."

Giuseppe walked around the corner, looking sheepish and embarrassed. He stuck his hands into the front pockets of his jeans, waiting until everyone had gotten something on their plates. Nancy just nodded. "I'm not hungry, thanks. Maybe later."

Cora and Alessandra filled their plates and sat back down. Giuseppe smiled at Cora, and feeling a friend there, she smiled back. After he filled his plate, he pulled a chair up across from the women and next to Enzo.

"Is Lino eating?" Cora asked.

"Below," Enzo said. "He is busy with the boat. He will be up later.

Cora felt a need to keep the conversation going. She

wanted to hear the noise, to be involved in thinking about something other than the boat, other than the circle of sea around her. "What is Sicily like?" she asked Giuseppe.

He shrugged, his mouth full of food, and then chose his words carefully. "It is history. Very old. A small island. I live there all my life. It is good place."

"It is a place like a jail. You need to see more than Sicily, Giuseppe. There is more than one deck of cards." Enzo lit a cigarette. "Some chess?"

Giuseppe nodded. The men refilled their wineglasses and turned the small table between them, ending the conversation and beginning one of their own in Italian.

Later, Lino came onto the deck and cast out a fishing line from a huge pole. He caught Cora's inquisitive look. "Dinner," he said with an apologetic smile. "If Lino is lucky."

"What kind of fish do you catch here?" Cora asked. She was walking back and forth on the deck, stretching her legs.

Lino shrugged. "How do you say 'Sogliola'? Ah, a white fish?"

Cora smiled. "Even if you catch one, I won't know what it is; I've never fished in saltwater." Cora continued to ask questions. Lino gave short, polite answers in choppy English. He shrugged his shoulders a lot, adjusting his neck, as if he were wearing a tie, and found it uncomfortable.

"Is this your full-time job, this boat?" Cora asked.

"No," Lino answered, looking over his shoulder, making sure they were alone. "Enzo is my full-time work. Whatever he wants. Drive car. Drive boat. Fix pipes at house." He shrugged and smiled, then looked back out over the water.

"Have you known him long?"

Lino chuckled. "Since we first played soccer at six or seven. We go back." After a long pause of several minutes, Lino looked Cora straight in the eye for the first time, his dark eyes serious. "Enzo is good to me. I need the money. I am not so much lucky all the time." Lino had a beard, and his hair was oily and matted from the wind. He smelled of alcohol. His enormous belly leaned against the side of the boat. Cora stood near him for half an hour, but he didn't catch a fish. "It is not lucky for fish today. We have pasta and wine tonight." He smiled.

When Cora returned to the starboard side, Nancy was asleep in the chair. She had a cap on to shield her face from the sun and a towel spread over her legs. Cora could feel her skin burning too and got a long-sleeve shirt out of her backpack.

When she sat down, Enzo and Giuseppe were still playing chess; only a few ivory characters still stood on the board. Cora watched Giuseppe's long fingers move his knight. He held it for some time before letting it go.

32

MOVIES

Cora got the feeling that it wasn't real. She sat on the carpeted deck in a white lawn chair and then walked around on the deck, looking out across the vast expanse of water. She went below and dragged her fingers along the oak table as she walked past a brass statue of a dolphin rising from the waves. The stove and sink were clean and sparkling. Lino was working all the time. Nothing in her experience compared to this expensive place, this foreign comfort.

After going back up on the deck, she closed her eyes and thought about a girl from her hometown. Doreen's family was well off; she had an enormous bedroom to herself and a canopy bed.

When Cora was twelve, she went to summer camp on a clear lake with white birch trees crowded along the shore. She and Doreen and three other girls from her cabin skipped the morning craft session and walked into the sleepy resort town down the road. It was King Corn Days. They converted the softball diamonds into a midway, but it was mostly deserted at eleven-thirty on Thursday morning. The girls ate cotton candy and rode on rides.

The Swinger, a circle of box-shaped swings on chains, stood empty. A young man with greasy blond hair and a muscle shirt drank Coke from a bottle and leaned on the gate, listening to a transistor radio. "Hey girls," he said. "Want to take a ride? I'll give you the ride of your life."

Doreen was almost thirteen and developing breasts. She had pierced ears with real gold hoop earrings and had a swimming pool at home in her own yard. She said the guy was a carny rat, someone who worked at carnivals. She explained to the other girls that he was a sap, but the ride would be a gas. Doreen decided they should all go. For a quarter, they could swing around and around until centrifugal force leaned them on their sides and pulled the chains tight. They pretended it was a child's ride, and that they weren't enjoying it, but they all were. Cora's stomach lifted as the ride went faster. Around and around, never ending.

Now, on the deck of the boat, she remembered the things the man said as he let the ride go on and on. "How old are you girls? Getting dizzy yet? Boy, there's a look-er." She remembered the ride and the feeling in her stomach and the songs on the radio, one after another, blaring. He sang along. He sang to them and smoothed his hair back, away from his eyes, with his hand. She saw the man and the way he looked at them. Five girls spin-ning. Five young women wanting a ride.

Cora sits there and remembers, but I do not know how her body reacts to the memory. Does she grow tense? Are her hands in fists? I need to study movement, to learn the sequence of events, the physical gestures the women and men display. I need to gain a camera's eye. During the week, I go to matinees at the mall to pay special attention to the visuals. I eat buttered popcorn and try to stay detached from the screen, but I am easily pulled in.

Films can be deceptive. You never know what to expect. You are relaxed, watching some gorgeous sunset over the tops of old trees and suddenly someone is breathing behind you, as if you are in the film, and the next thing you know you are witnessing a murder, or a fight, or a car blowing up. Someone hurting someone else. Grabbing her wrist and forcing it behind her back. Fondling her. Getting a knee in the groin and slapping her face hard. Eyes closed. Eyes open. Hate in her face. Spit. Then he pushes her overboard, like it is nothing. The boat keeps going. She struggles. When they finally circle back to pick her up, she's gone. Flat face of water staring up at the sky. "Only trying to teach her a lesson," he says, "mouthy bitch." He says it again and again, "Mouthy bitch," looking at each face around him, each pair of eyes. The moment is frozen in slow motion. They can do that in the movies.

33

GAMES

Cora sat in the deck chair wearing sunglasses and pretending to be reading a book. She was thinking, surveying the scene around her and trying to grasp what was happening. Enzo and Giuseppe had finished their game, and Giuseppe was fooling around with some small dumbbells that Enzo carried up from below. He was doing curls and drinking wine.

Enzo was the one Cora was watching. He seemed to be withdrawn. Cheerful but calculated. He got a beach towel out and took off his shirt to lie in the sun. In a matter of minutes, he also removed his shorts and was lying naked on the deck, rubbing oil into his legs and arms. He and Giuseppe spoke occasionally, in Italian, and then chuckled. Neither of them seemed even aware of the fact that the women were there. Nancy was still asleep, but Alessandra stirred and lit a cigarette. She too seemed to be watching the "show" and it was quite evident to Cora that Enzo was putting on a show, preening and displaying himself. At first, she was shocked, not that she hadn't seen nude sun bathing before, and it certainly was more prevalent in Europe than back in Iowa, but it was the manner in which he turned and flexed his muscles and responded to being naked that unnerved her.

His tan body was gorgeous, and he knew it. After he was done with the lotion, he lit a cigarette and poured another glass of wine. He noticed Alessandra was awake, and even though Cora had been awake all along, he had not spoken to her since the chess game. He nodded his head at Alessandra. "Did you sleep well?"

Her response was flat and matter-of-fact, as if she were unimpressed with his display of skin. "Si."

"And do you care to join me?"

"No, Grazia. I think I have enough sun for today."

"I am glad you have rested, for the sun will be setting in a few hours and we will have the evening before us." He smiled, a wide, wicked smile. "We always enjoy the evenings on these little cruises."

Giuseppe sat on the ground, his knees up, and put his head down. He placed the weight on the wooden floor and held it with his feet so that it would not roll away. He seemed to contemplate the conversation as well, but took another gulp of wine and shrugged it off. Both he and

Enzo were drinking out of the bottle by this time, and several empties sat tipped on their sides in a crate nearby.

Cora felt her arm muscles harden; she needed to be in control. "There isn't another boat, is there?"

"What do you mean?" Enzo asked with humor in his voice, a bit slurred.

"No college students from Iowa. No professor from the University in Rome." She ran her fingers through her hair, as if to tell him she wasn't shaken up, as if to say she could take care of herself, even though this was not what she felt.

Enzo took a long draw from his cigarette. "Well, that could depend, but I will tell you, they are not here now, and we are not in school, and you wanted this adventure, so maybe you better stop asking questions and start drinking wine." He laughed, stood up, stretched, and walked over to her. He stood naked before her chair. "Relaxing will make the dancing more pleasant later on." He took her sunglasses off of her face, folded them, and handed them back. "And we will be dancing tonight, you can be sure."

Nancy woke up and opened her eyes to the bright light. "What the hell?" She saw Enzo and sat straight up in her chair. "Oh my God!" she said and turned to Cora.

Enzo looked over at her, his face rather scornful. "What is the matter, doll? Haven't you seen a man's body before? Don't tell me you are still a little girl?"

Nancy went to get up, but Cora put her hand on her arm and looked straight at her. She sank back down in her chair. "You mustn't be so shy," Enzo said, glaring at Nancy. "We are all friends here, and there is no place to go. We may as well enjoy ourselves, wouldn't you say?"

Giuseppe stood up and went to the side, his back to everyone. Lino came around the corner and saw Enzo. He did not look a bit surprised or uncomfortable. Cora realized in a sickening minute that this was not the first time. This was a routine. She looked over at Lino while she gripped her sunglasses in her hand. He avoided her eyes.

34

PHEASANTS

I cannot remember what I have created. Each person is a manilla file filled with postcards and scribbled notes. I sit on my porch and sort through piles of urgent handwriting. Geralyn is planting flowers and singing to herself. She doesn't ask questions. As long as I'm pleasant and don't type in the middle of the night, she is happy with me.

I am well versed at keeping the peace. I ask about her garden. I comment on the new Afghan she's knitting. It grows in her lap in the evening when we sit on the porch after dinner. She asks me about my nice young man. She knows his name is Ian, but what's important to her is that he's a nice young man. It's as if she was trying to make sure I knew it, as if I wasn't appreciative of him. He stops by and charms her by picking a flower from her garden and presenting it to her. The next evening, it's in a crystal vase on the dining room table. Geralyn and I have begun eating our evening meals together more regularly. We're figuring each other out.

I can't remember what Cora plans to do with her English degree. I spend most nights writing until one or two o'clock. Then I sleep, or try to sleep, and end up at the desk again. I have lost something minute, like an earring, and I look again and again in the same places, thinking maybe this time it will be there. I am looking for the truth. I am trying to remember what I thought the truth was the last time I sat at my desk. Is Cora going to teach? Does she want to teach, or has she gotten an empty degree like I did with intentions unknown? Maybe I am recreating myself. Like a paper doll, I am the model to hang the thin story on. Little tabs to bend over the shoulders and make her look fully dressed. Little tabs that always wear off before you outgrow the doll... I guess I'm tired.

I make excuses not to write. The story is sinking away from me. The more I fear writing it down, the more elusive it all becomes. I was hoping to finish it by Christmas, but it goes on and on.

I'm raising pheasant chicks again this year. The Department of Natural Resources provides the chicks, and I feed them. Ian and I built the brood house and enclosed pen last year and thirty-one chicks made it. We let them go in Copper Canyon and watched them melt into the gold and brown forest floor. I thought it would be hard to see them go, but it was wonderful. Spiritual.

I believe one person can affect the future of these emerald hills, so now I have four dozen peeping chicks huddled around the heat lamps in the brood house. I feed them and watch for death. I always find four or five small, cold balls of down before the chicks are big enough to go without the lamp. I mother those still living. Ian says I want children. "You don't release children in the fall, Ian. They stay all winter," I say. I do not tell him to mind his own business. I am becoming his business, and he is mine. He can think what he wants.

35

HITCHHIKING

Nancy wiped sweat from the side of her face with shaky fingers. "Cora, it isn't..." she looked around the deck. It seemed hotter, yet the sun was rolling off in the west, growing wide and fat, orange light mixing with the pink clouds and the dark blue water.

Cora sat forward, her hands laced together, her feet flat on the floor as if to show control, a sense of strength. "Yes," she said. "It is."

"But, what, I mean... how?" Nancy's eyes flitted from the water on one side of the boat, around the deck to the water on the other side, like a bird looking for a safe place to land. "What can we?"

Cora sighed. "I don't know. Listen. You've got to get control of yourself. We need to think." Nancy was crying now. Cora's voice grew hard. "Nancy, we're in a car and the doors are locked. Do you understand? We're hitchhik-ing, only we can't tumble out on the pavement because the ride is a loser. We're stuck. Get it?" She paused. "Maybe we can get to the radio. I don't know. Shit. Just help me out here."

Enzo and Alessandra had gone below earlier. Enzo pulled on a robe, spoke to her in Italian and they both laughed, but it was a calculated laugh on Enzo's part. Alessandra simply smiled a plastic, posed smile, stood up, and followed him below. Probably to one of the bedroom compartments. Why? Had Alessandra known this was coming all along? What was her story?

Nancy paced. Cora watched her walk, her long tan legs, her dancer's body. What had happened to the self-confident woman? Cora wondered. Where is the assured and energetic actress? The boundaries were dissolving. Nothing was as it had seemed.

Giuseppe and Lino were out of sight. Maybe they were in the cabin below with Enzo and Alessandra, or maybe this was supposed to be one big dangerous party, everyone expected to play along. The yacht wasn't that big, but neither Nancy nor Cora heard or saw anything, except the skip of salt water against the curved belly of the boat.

36

SILENCES

I've heard of writers getting blocked; sitting down to write and staring at the typewriter. Nothing to say. That is not my problem. There is too much to say, and none of it is true. (All of it is true.) I sit down and end up staring into Ian's eyes, but I'm not looking at him; I'm looking through him. Preoccupied. I'm thinking about a problem in the plot, a problem in the past. How can I justify Nancy's inconsistencies? Why is Cora stronger in the face of danger? What ghosts filled her nightmares when she was young and sleeping through thunderstorms?

I keep having this dream that the ceiling is cracking and falling in on me. When it's storming, I dream that the water is dripping through the cracks and the ceiling's buckling, about to give way. Plaster and lath burying me.

And sometimes, when I open my eyes, still half asleep, I see the cracks and the danger. Only when I am startled awake, do I realize it is the light fixture above my bed. The same light that was an owl with electric eyes the night before. Once, it was a sprinkler system, and I dreamed that an orange blaze surrounded my bed. As in a veritable nightmare, the sprinkler didn't work, and fire licked at my vulnerable toes.

I find myself looking for Brie cheese in the grocery store, wanting to ask Ian if he would ever hit a woman, wanting to ask him if he has, but some questions must never be asked. He would want to know where such a question came from. It would take too much explaining, too much energy. I can only write my concerns down on paper. I have notebooks full of questions and answers, conversations with Nancy and Cora. Lists and itineraries. I cannot include it all. It is necessary to condense and take short cuts and be concise; the story must be interesting.

I know about art and appreciate language and struc-ture. I cannot tell this story; I am drowning in this noise. I write in long hand, furious notes to untangle like fishing line at night, on weekends, and my days off. I am an apprentice with bookshelves of masters staring down at me. Sometimes I hear them laughing. Perhaps they say "How dare you? Stop this foolishness."

Other nights, it is quiet, and from somewhere a voice whispers, "Go ahead. Take your time and write it down. Invite the words in. Listen to your pulse."

37

THREE FATES

Nancy pulled a long string from the terry cloth towel across her legs. Since Alessandra returned, Nancy sat fidgeting in her chair, her hands twisting in her long hair, her toes tapping against the wooden chair leg. The three women sat without talking for a long time. Alessandra offered no explanations; she chain-smoked cigarettes and watched the other two women.

Alessandra smiled when she saw the thread. "My mother was tailor before she died. She... she believed this," she pointed to the long thread still stretched between Nancy's fingers, "this thing had much power."

"Why?" Cora said at the same time Nancy was saying "Your mother is dead too?"

Alessandra looked confused.

"Why is thread important?" Cora asked.

Alessandra thought for a moment. "It is old myth about the gods. Zeus had three daughters and these daughters, ah, control fate."

"I've heard of this," Cora said. "I think I read about it in a mythology class in college."

"In my family, this was important. My mother was powerful; she used this... thread?"

"Thread." Cora smiled. She noticed Alessandra's hands were shaking as she held the cigarette to the side to avoid the smoke in her eyes.

"My mother is dead too," Nancy whispered.

"I have no family," Alessandra said. "No one." She looked at her feet. "But these weird sisters are called Clotho, Lachesis and Atropos from the Greek. My great-grandmother was Greek woman. My great-grandfather, fisherman." She smiled again. "Some yell to Jesus Christ when children do not behave. My mother calls these goddesses and says 'In name of Clotho stop that at once. She will spin your fate!'"

Cora leaned forward in her chair, her eyes wide, her hands in fists. "What were their names again?" Nancy sat with her eyes closed.

"Clotho. She spun string, thread of life. Lachesis measured it. And Atropos cut it when life was to end." Alessandra used her fingers to imitate scissors and snipped in the air.

"Can we talk about something else?" Nancy said, half to herself.

"They have great power," Alessandra said. "For each person, it is said, they control the destiny. And even Zeus cannot change it."

"Was your mother Catholic? Did she believe in the gods along with Christianity or instead of it?"

Alessandra shrugged. "Good is good, and evil is evil. My mother knew of many different gods, as far I know. She went to church, said her prayers, and she is dead." Alessandra brushed the brassy blond hair from her face. "This I call fate."

"So, nothing we do is important?" Cora glanced around her and felt a sudden panic. "Nothing makes a difference?"

"All is important, I think. But yet, there is only one thread, you know?"

Cora sat for a long time, saying nothing. Alessandra fell asleep in a deck chair, the ashes of a cigarette precariously balanced between her fingers. Cora took out her diary and wrote a brief entry. It was a sign of optimism, a step toward the future.

Diary. Read more about ancient myths on the Three Fates. See weird sisters... (as in Shakespeare?) and Clotho, L... something, and Atropos. Atropos is the controller of death and destiny's final hour. Something about thread and the three daughters of Zeus. Alessandra's mother was a tailor. I do not understand Alessandra. With the language problem, it is difficult to talk, but she is an intelligent woman. And troubled. I do not know why she is here. I do not know why we are here.

CD

38

LUCK

C ora was slightly superstitious. At least she wouldn't challenge the odds. She carried a small four-inch-tall brass donkey around in her backpack. It was a packing mule and bore two packs with SALT LAKE CITY printed on the sides. Her grandmother on her mother's side had picked it up on her one bus trip out west to visit her oldest daughter. Cora got the donkey when she was eleven. That year, she also got her own bedroom and a new banana seat bike. She believed, somehow, that the events were connected. From then on, "Salty" was with her.

In college she sat the donkey on her study lamp at her desk. Now she slipped it into a small front pocket of her backpack along with the other essentials of travel. Toothbrush. Comb. A couple of dog-eared novels and a journal. She didn't tell anyone the souvenir's story or talk about her grandma's great cooking and honey yellow kitchen or her sudden death of a heart attack at fifty-five. Cora kept the details tucked away, reaching deep into the pack after doing some laundry when she was rearranging and repacking, just to be sure it was there.

Only once, on the boat, when she was most in need of reassurance, of some religion, did she think of it there with her and scoff at her juvenile games. Nothing to it. A trinket from a junk shop. A toy she should have outgrown long ago.

U nder the blanketed cover of evening, the women sat around a small spool table near the bow of the boat. Stars created a meadow of infinite sparks across the black basin of sky. A warm breeze blew across the calm sea. They could hear Enzo and Giuseppe arguing in the stern, but they couldn't see them. The men had been drinking heavily in the afternoon, but took long naps and seemed to be back at it. Giuseppe walked past earlier, looking irritated and angry, his hands shoved into the pockets of his jeans. He avoided looking at anyone as he passed.

Alessandra was listening. "Enzo says Giuseppe is a sniveling child. He is, ah, how you say, feared? Fearful of the spirits of the night. The ghosts. And perhaps he needs his mommy." She paused and listened again; the men lowered their voices. "Giuseppe is angry that we are here."

"What, what are they saying now?" Nancy asked.

Cora shot her an angry glance. It grew increasingly difficult to calm Nancy down, to keep her in a rational place. Cora felt it was necessary that they keep their heads, but Nancy seemed unable to do so. She quivered and bit her fingernails constantly.

Alessandra looked at the floor. "Damn shit."

"What is it?" Cora asked.

"Enzo says we are entertainment. It is time his nephew became a man."

"That bastard." Cora folded her arms and looked out to sea. "That damn bastard."

"We could jump off," Nancy said. "Take the life boat or jackets or something and jump off."

Cora clenched her fists; the thought of a bottomless pit of water around her legs nearly made her heave. "I can't swim, Nancy. I told you; I am afraid of water. And besides, we are out in the middle of the sea. We would drown or be eaten by sharks, for God's sake."

Alessandra was studying the other two women. "You had no idea, did you?"

"And you did?" Cora was incredulous.

"It is not new to me. I hate my life, so what?" Alessandra lit a cigarette and took a deep draw. "I am not so naïve to think this boat ride was only a ride on the sea. I could do worse than with Enzo. He is a powerful man."

The voices from the back of the boat were subdued. The three women sat looking out at the wrinkled world of water. They did not speak their thoughts.

They drew into themselves and started sandbagging around their fears. Like victims of a rising flood, they could see the water rising. They took stock and armed themselves for whatever battles were ahead.

Alessandra had a second cigarette. She studied Nancy. "Is your American ranch as big as on TV?"

Nancy forced a smile. "It's big. John Wayne style."

"I would like this riding a horse." Alessandra picked at her nails, squinting through the smoke of her cigarette. "Riding damn shit away. Nobody pulling me down. I would ride to keep on going."

Nancy's fingers were shaking as they laid on her knees, but she could no longer calm them. They trembled like chilled kittens. "I want to go home."

"If we could only get off this damn boat," Cora said. "I'm not even so afraid of the water anymore; I'm afraid of them." She didn't say she was afraid of dying, that she had a deep fear of being violated and cast to sea like some unfortunate dolphin caught in the wrong net. Maybe water would fill her lungs, and she would forget to be afraid. She reminded herself that she had jumped from moving cars before. Men were not the only players in this game. She refused to give in to the water streaming down her face, the tears of a young woman drying on the cheeks of someone much older.

40

EVIL

Three men. Three women. A boat, a calm sea, a night captured by the moon. Enzo lit candles in three large pails of sand and placed them around the deck. Later, when it was cooler, they would go below. Lino lingered in the galley after the meal, washing dishes, scrubbing counters, humming to himself as he drank from a bottle. Giuseppe found a cassette player and busied himself with the music. Changing tapes, listening, and smoking cigarettes. He kept his back to Enzo, drank from his own bottle, and said nothing to anyone.

Cora tried once to go to their cabin, but the door was locked. The doors to the sleeping compartments were all locked from the outside. She walked past the radio, but it was a mystery of dials and Italian labels. Then she saw the cord had been removed. The world grew smaller and smaller with each step she took.

Nancy sat shivering on the deck with a blanket around her, following everything with her eyes. She intended to stay in that chair all night if she had to. She thought the chair would save her, thought she could make some of the rules.

Alessandra stood at the thin chrome railing and looked out across the nothingness. She ran her fingers through her long blond hair, pulling out tangles made by the wind.

The evening began this way, each person finding a place to be alone on a small boat, but as the moon crossed the sky, the boundaries between the bodies were erased.

This is not something one writes down. These are not words, but fists beating into fragile facial bones and eyes. Rape is not a sexual act. It is violence and evil incarnate. It is something you can only imagine, and only when you are safe at home, after your windows and doors are locked and the sound you hear turns out to be a stray dog in the garbage or a branch clacking against the window on the second floor of your neighbor's house.

It is only real to members of the club, and believe me, they would like nothing better than to forget it. It is not something a woman, or man, or child will explain in detail to satisfy your curiosity. It is not a fit subject for literature any more than Enzo's hands were fit to touch her neck and back, fit to stroke her, preparing himself, preening and sinking lower and lower into that black hole where the violence becomes habit and fantasy, where his satisfaction lies.

It is only possible to say that it happened. That Enzo and Lino inflicted pain on innocent women, and Giuseppe watched. A theater of cruelty. Evil travels in many forms.

The boundaries between bodies have been erased. We are bought and sold at every marketplace in the world. Shaving cream and soda pop. The human body waved like a flag in front of a raging bull. And some become obsessed with it. They tear and crush the souls of others in search of one insignificant bestial release.

And on that boat, on that day with the blue green circles around the sun, Nancy, Cora, and Alessandra knew what they had only feared before. They knew it and wept, or did not weep, as the cruel seeds of terror, disgust, and guilt grew near each heart. A seed that would harden and never dissolve. A rock which would affect every beat of their hearts, every deep breath they ever struggled to take.

41

WAKING

Cora woke with a cramp in her right shoulder. Her cheek felt swollen and bruised. She squinted to see the small round circle of light streaming into the dark room. A closet? Disoriented, she wondered where she was. As her eyes adjusted and she felt the heave and swell of the water moving her bed, she remembered the boat.

She remembered Enzo, and Lino, and Giuseppe. With a shudder, she recalled the night before. Acid rose in her mouth. She swallowed, pushing back the reality of it, and sat up on the edge of the bed. The door to the galley was still closed. Alessandra slept above her, long blond hair a tangle on the pillow. Nancy was sleeping on the other bunk, somehow repairing the torn fabric of the night before. A needle and thread in her dreams. Montana and Glory, her horse. Her Uncle Ryan. Hay bales. Comfort.

Safety. The theater. Maybe she was dreaming about acting. Last night could have been a play — a terrible scene in act one. The feigned pain and shame would disappear when the curtain fell.

Cora looked at Nancy's face. She was beautiful. Calm and relaxed. She was not having a nightmare at the moment. That was last night. Cora was awake, and it scared her to death. Nothing in her life prepared her for waking up in the cabin of a boat and seeing the horror before her. If only they could all sleep and be transported. Anywhere but here, this morning, on this sea.

Alessandra rolled over and whispered, "You are okay?" Her eyes were half open.

"Not too good. You?"

Alessandra yawned. "Damn shit," she said, holding her forehead. She had gray circles under her eyes. Her tangled hair revealed dark roots on the top of her head.

Nancy started crying. "No. Please."

Cora shook her gently, but she couldn't find words of comfort. There were no words for such a day. "Nancy, wake up. It's a dream."

Nancy opened her bloodshot eyes. There were actual tears. "A dream?" she said. Her lips trembled.

Cora sighed. "Oh, God, I wish it was." The three women sat around the path of sunlight, their eyes adjusting to the fabric of the light.

42

TITLES

I am beginning to feel like a writer. I must whisper this alone at night in the circle of light at my desk. It scares me. I certainly won't announce it in my next letter to my parents. They would worry even more, sitting in their small house in Florida with Uncle Jim and Aunt DeeAnn. Retired and sharing a kitchen. Fred and Ethel, Lucy and Ricky.

They worry enough. They've never been to the Black Hills and think of the whole Midwest as a mythical but boring place. They may even think I'm crazy, but when I started teaching literature classes part time at Black Hills State, they relaxed a little. It was better than waitressing at a strange health food restaurant. I'm not married. I have no career. They are disappointed in me.

The pile of typing paper grows larger. The characters haunt me more during the day when I am serving up pita sandwiches and whole wheat lasagna. (I'm beginning to feel more serious about what I'm doing). I type at night when the world is asleep. Writing a book. Page by page, sentence by sentence; I am taking myself more seriously.

Ian wants to read my book. I've told him very little, but one cannot hide a desk filled with ghost white paper, recipe cards with chicken scratch notes and a map of Italy taped over the desk. I don't remember names, and I can't spell. Something must remind me of my intentions, my imaginary path down the old woman's boot.

I told Ian I was writing a book. "Just a little book," I said. "Nothing really," but he knows when he comes over late at night after closing the restaurant and I have that faraway look in my eyes when he touches me. He knows I'm not all there, but I can't tell him where I am.

Instead, I concentrate on putting the puzzle back in the box. Shutting off the lights and ignoring the smell of sea salt. The sound of water slapping against the side of a boat.

If I ever finish this, I will let him read it. But only after it is done, sealed in wax and protected by its own completion. I am still afraid of outside opinions. I need to protect myself from judgement. One false look and I'm sure I'd take a match to it — turn the whole thing into frail, ashen wings in the bottom of the bathtub.

43

SLOW MOTION

Cora's cheeks were bruised, and her neck was stiff. She couldn't look far to the right, couldn't glance over her shoulder. The mirror showed red finger marks on her neck: the ghosts of hands that hurt her.

When she tried to move her head, she remembered the time in the third grade when she had a stiff neck. She woke up crying, unable to move without pain, calling for her daddy. They took her to a doctor, and he smoothed warm lotion onto her back and massaged it under a heat lamp. The doctor sent her home in a stiff white neck brace and said her neck would heal in six to ten days.

She could go to school and she did, feeling a little like a freak, a little like an important person. Her mother gave her cherry cough drops, not for the pain, but because of it; Cora liked cherry cough drops.

At school she was called to the chalk board to do a math problem. It hurt to raise her arm to the black surface, hurt to form the big numbers. Fighting tears, she asked to sit down. "All right, sit down," her teacher said, "but if you're too bad off to do math problems, you don't need to go out for recess either."

Cora still remembered the shame. Remembered scrambling in her mind to figure out what had caused such a reaction. Was it the candy cough drops? Was it the tears she had tried not to cry? Was it the strange white brace around her neck? While the kids played on the playground outside the window, she sat at her desk and tried to tell her neck to go soft, to feel good again. Tried to tell the clock to hurry and be kind; she wanted to go home.

By mid-morning, the women were on the deck in the sinister sunshine. Enzo had threatened them, told them to come up and eat. Below deck, he barked at Alessandra in Italian and waved his arm.

"He has a gun," she said. "He says if we act like spoiled children, he might lose his tempers. He says we have to eat and get our minds in a friendly attitude, that he is ready for some social conversation."

Enzo smiled at Nancy and finished his sentence in English. "I know American girls are good at conversation and socializing," he said. He turned and went upstairs. He was wearing a swimming suit and holding a cup of coffee, looking relaxed. He was enjoying himself.

Since she woke up, Nancy had been crying and shaking, holding herself, as if to keep the bones of her body together. "I can't feel my feet," she said as Cora held her, stroking her hair. "I can't feel my body at all. I'm sorry. I think maybe I ran away last night... while he was doing that to me... and I can't find myself anywhere." She shrugged, her arms waving about her like birds.

The women made it to the deck in time for Nancy to throw up over the side. She was trying to hold on, trying to keep the walls from falling in around her. Cora felt the same emptiness, the same displacement. She knew how to comfort her friend, so she did. Her own heart kept beating with no help, marking time in a solid, regular rhythm.

For about an hour, they stood near the table laid with the same spread of fruit and cheese and juices they had found so inviting the morning before. Alessandra helped herself to coffee and a piece of bread. Her eyes held a hollow light, like the pictures of people in concentration camps. The same disappeared look.

Giuseppe stayed below, sleeping in or hiding from the blue light of day. Cora could not eat. Acid rose in her throat and stayed there as Nancy heaved again and again over the side. Finally, Enzo came over, a cigarette dangling between his lips, dark glasses shading the truth of his eyes. "You are disgusting," he said to Nancy's back. "Clean yourself up." He tossed a wet towel to Cora and walked to the other side of the boat, leaning over the edge to flick ashes. The wind blew them back on his brown arm.

Lino was drinking again. He had been silent most of the day and was busying himself with tasks on the deck. He avoided Cora's eyes completely.

After half-an-hour or so, when Nancy had nothing left in her but dry heaves, she sat on a deck chair wrapped in a towel. Her eyes were red and puffy. She smelled of vomit. Cora got her a sheet and sunglasses from their room. She shaded her eyes and whispered softly. "Close your eyes; think of home. I will get you out of here, I promise."

Lino stood next to Alessandra speaking in Italian, chuckling to himself, reaching out for her occasionally, a bottle full of wine in his other hand. Alessandra moved away, got herself a cigarette, and found another chair up near the railing of the deck. It was clear that Nancy was not attractive to them now, but Cora wondered with hesitant dread what the day would hold. She would fight back, she told herself, she would kill him if she had to.

Lino continued to mock Alessandra. He reached for her blond hair, held it in his hand until she jerked her head away. Alessandra stood up and moved as far from him as she could get against the slight chrome railing. A balancing act. Cora glanced over at Enzo and turned back to see Alessandra spit in Lino's face.

As if it were happening in slow motion, she turned in time to see Lino slap Alessandra across the face. He had one of her arms twisted, but let it go when he struck her. Alessandra grabbed for the back of a chair, trying to balance herself, but the chair rocked and tipped. She tried to steady it, tried to stand and grab the railing near her, but the swell of a wave moved everything off kilter, and she went overboard, down into the white-capped waves. Lino turned to Enzo to see his reaction. Enzo smiled a cool smile.

"Mouthy bitch," Lino said. "God damn mouthy bitch."

Cora screamed and ran to the side as Alessandra grabbed for air with her hands, blonde hair wrapping around her face. The waves pulled her under, and again and again she came to the surface as the distance increased between her and the boat.

"Help her!" Cora screamed. "Jesus, help her!" Cora leaned over the side, a white spray of water splashing up onto her tan arms. It was cold. She turned again to Enzo, then Lino.

Enzo laughed. "Okay, Lino, turn around and get the bitch. Turn this thing around."

Lino looked from face to face, and then at Giuseppe, who had appeared in the doorway and seemed to have seen the whole thing. "Mouthy bitch," he said again, softer this time. He hurried up to the pilot-house and began the big circle back to the white-capped water near Alessandra.

Nancy could not grasp the reality of the scene before her. She fainted into a soft gray place without danger or consequences. After she lost sight of the flailing arms, Cora looked for a life jacket, a safety ring. "Keep looking!" she screamed. "Jump out there, damn you! You have to find her or she'll drown!" But the sea was a large empty-faced mirror without interruption, except for the waves and their frothy caps. They looked for twenty minutes, maybe a half hour, maybe longer. Alessandra was gone.

44

CHOICES

I write about Enzo jeering from his perch on the other side of the boat; he finds the whole scenario rather humorous. He is macho, and rich, and familiar with crimes of all kinds. But what about Lino? Why is he the one to hit her and send her over the edge? Is it the obvious, easy first choice which grabs me? He is overweight, ugly, and uneducated. He is a servant, doing Enzo's dirty business because the money is good, and he has little ambition to do anything else.

Why not have Enzo be the murderer instead of the rapist accomplice? Or Giuseppe, the handsome naïve lad who is against forced sex, but stands around for a good show, anyway. It isn't a question of morals with him; it simply doesn't turn him on. He even finds Cora attractive at first until he sees what she will do with strange men out in the open on a boat. By choice or not, a decent woman wouldn't get into this kind of situation, he thinks. It makes her less attractive.

Or maybe it is against Giuseppe's morals, and he is a bystander out of fear of his uncle. He knows they are miles from anywhere. He suspects Enzo's involvement with organized crime; he wants to get home alive. Perhaps this is his motivation — to put on a show and flirt with Alessandra, to curry favor with his uncle. Choose the Italian girl, the one without any risk. She is dirt. No reputation, no worried parents at home to follow up on such things.

And what about the rapes themselves? I have rewritten the scene many times, changed the players, changed the time of day, included and excluded various details of violence and sexual vulgarity. I have let Cora and Nancy speak; I have written in cries of horror and pain and taken them out again.

This is not easy. There were three women on a boat in a fictional Tyrrhenian Sea heading for the Strait of Messina, and now there are two. I care about them. I have written them into my dreams and nightmares for over a year now. I want to tell this story the way it would have happened. I want to be honest.

I know Alessandra lost her fight for air; she settled into an underwater grave, drifting down and without hope. Three men and two women were also on board, and they all witnessed the terrible deed being done. Some were responsible, some were irresponsible, and others were merely victims. It is not simple to write them into a corner.

I may need to let the scene sit for a time until someone steps forward and admits to the task. Until someone takes responsibility.

45

AT SEA

L ate afternoon. A sticky web of panic wrapped around the boat. Nancy and Cora stayed below in their sleeping cabin, only half-listening to the angry voices arguing above. The men spoke Italian. They shouted at one another and then dropped their voices to whispers.

Textured tan wallpaper covered the cabin walls. Nancy thought of gunnysacks full of grain back home in Montana. Glory would perk up her ears when Nancy carried a new sack over her shoulder into the barn.

Nancy touched the wall by the bunk she was sitting in with a shaky hand. It looked like burlap, but was plastic to the touch. Her hand was clammy; her face swollen and pale. She held a wet washcloth in her left hand and brought it to her lips every time she felt another dry heave racking her body.

Cora sat on the floor, leaning against the other set of built-in bunk beds, which stood perpendicular to Nancy's. She looked up at her friend. She noticed the delicate gold chains around her neck. The bracelets on the shaking wrist. She looked without feeling or connection. It was difficult to focus. Her hand could not reach out to Nancy's hand, nor did she want to. For a moment, when she closed her eyes, she wished she was dead, transported from this scene, from this uncertain future and this horrible past to a place which required no effort. Cora had lost her strength.

It sounded like the boat was moving faster. The motor was working, the vessel bucking waves and swaying with the swell of the sea. Sunshine sifted in the porthole and lay across the covers of Nancy's bed. She had her back-pack packed again, as if they were getting off at the next stop, as if she had any say in what happened next in her life or what ended it.

Cora held Salty, her bronze good luck donkey from Salt Lake City. A city she had never visited. A gift from a grandma who died when Cora was in the fifth grade. The funeral never seemed real to her. She remembered that all the adults were crying and seemed distraught, but she couldn't cry and felt guilty about it. Death wasn't real then. Someone had simply waxed over her grandmother's lips and put too much make-up on her.

Salty grew warm in her clenched fist. Cora leaned back and closed her eyes.

"They are going to let us go now, right?" Nancy asked in a whisper. She wanted the right answer. She wanted everything from Cora, including safety, and reassurance, and strength.

"I have no idea." Cora's voice was loud, void of feeling. Nancy winced and looked up at the closed door.

"They might hear you."

Cora shrugged. "So? What we say has nothing to do with it, Nancy."

"What do you mean?"

Cora shook her head. "I don't know. What do you want to hear? That we're safe now? That witnessing a murder is no big deal, and they'll allow us to go on our merry way?"

"It wasn't a murder, exactly." Nancy's voice quivered. "I mean, it was an accident. I mean, he hit her, but he didn't mean to have her fall overboard. We could well, we could tell them that, couldn't we?"

Cora turned the small bronze animal over and over in her hand. "An accident? Jesus Christ, Nancy. It was no accident. And what about us, what about what they did to us? These are crimes, you know? And they know it."

"Yes, but we could just tell them we'd shut up if they'd let us go. We could promise."

"I don't think we have any bargaining power here at

all, Beauty." Cora smiled, trying to reassure herself and her friend without avoiding the truth. "I think it's a good sign that we're still here and the boat's moving. Maybe they'll drop us off somewhere."

Nancy cried again. "You mean, you think they might kill us because we saw it?"

"I mean, they might kill us because they are evil people, and we're not important. It seems like they've done this before. Maybe they have a system. I guess we wait and see."

"Oh, God." Nancy turned the small chain around her neck, and fingered it, as if it were a rosary and held some religious answer. "Are you afraid to die?"

Cora shrugged, took a deep breath, and smiled. "Let's do what we can to stay alive. Maybe we could get to the radio. I don't know."

The door opened and Giuseppe ducked and came in with a tray of food. He looked at each woman as if he had never seen them before, his eyes wide. "Food," he said. He laid the tray on the floor and turned to go out.

"Where are we going?" Cora asked. "Where are you taking us?"

Giuseppe stopped and paused, his back to the women. "In," he said and left, closing the door quietly behind him.

Cora looked at Nancy and raised her eyebrows. "The food is a good sign," she whispered. "I think it's very good." She looked down at the tray and took a hunk of bread, tore it into two pieces, and handed a piece to Nancy. "Eat this. It'll calm your stomach. And if they do let us go, we need to have strength to deal with... whatever."

"I'd promise not to tell," Nancy said, her eyes wide like a child's.

"Yeah, okay. Now eat," Cora said.

46

RESEARCH

I should write about South Dakota. The Black Hills have their own exotic feeling. A holiness maybe. I know how each day begins; I understand the lay of the land, the roads that lead from here to there. Many mornings, I go into the hills and walk. The trees crowd around me and keep me company. They whisper ancient words in the Dakota breeze and fill the air with the perfume of spruce and pine.

I have no money to travel to Florence or Rome. I can't remember the minor details I need to make the story real. The original details. What the boat looked like, how rocky the coast was when they pulled into port in the darkness of night. How the air smelled. I should go back and put in supporting details. I've built the rough frame of a house without being a carpenter. I'm not absolutely confident that the walls won't fall in, that everything is level and sturdy.

This is my first story. I thought I knew enough about Europe to make it work. I've been to Italy and Greece too, but I don't remember well enough. Journals and travel books are my only records. There are fragments of exact memories, a few hours at a time when I was totally present in my surroundings. Some of these things find their way into my fiction. Some of the fiction finds its way into my life.

I remember the Caryatids, six stone maidens standing on their hill throne looking down from the Acropolis over Athens, looking toward the sea. I sat in front of them on cool shaded stones and memorized the morning. The sounds of birds in a tree. The smell of diesel fuel from the buses in the city below. The flexible strength of my leg muscles after months of touring and walking from one foreign attraction to another. I wrote a poem about the Caryatids after reading my guidebook and studying their chipped faces for about an hour. It was more like a letter home. It was more a call for conversation with someone who spoke my language.

I've read that they've taken the statues inside to the Acropolis Museum since I was there and left replicas outside to battle the elements. Sulfur rain and smog turned the stone princesses to lepers. Too much pollution. Soon the whole thing will be a copy, a fake.

Should I fashion my fiction after my experience? Should Cora go on to Greece or be forever disappointed that she didn't make it to that paradise she discovered in fourth grade social studies? How do I decide? What role do I play in this plot? It feels like the story has taken over, and I am no longer in control, if I ever was.

And what if some of it did happen to me? I sat on the steps of the Acropolis at midnight when the tourists were gone and drank a bottle of wine by myself. I was not careful; I did not care that I was a woman alone in a strange country in the middle of a night full of stars. I made mistakes. Who cares? I don't know the rules. I guess I am making up my own as I go. You can take what you want and leave the rest. I'm just trying to get to the story.

47

DARKNESS

After Lino had cut the engines, the boat sat in the water for two or three hours like a bobber on a fishing line. Darkness dissolved the day. Cora and Nancy sat below with their packs at their feet. They hadn't spoken for close to an hour; there was nothing more to talk about. They agreed earlier to what they would say, how they would not mention fault, how it was an accident and they would not tell a soul and they just wanted to be set free.

Darkness, father. Our father, father who art in heaven, hallowed be thy name, father be thy name. Nancy quietly repeated the words to herself over and over again, weaving a wish for protection. Her fingers moved with nervous energy. Imaginary yarn knitting an Afghan to hide beneath. A warm, safe place is what she prayed for. Holy Mary, mother of God, holy mother, deliver us from evil, deliver us from evil our Mother who art in heaven. Deliver us, please, from evil. Nancy combed her hair and put on a clean T-shirt. Nothing too attractive, Cora had said. We don't want them after us again. About ten o'clock, the engines started up again, and the boat began to move.

"Maybe they're going to shore now," Cora speculated. "I hope to God they're taking us in."

Enzo opened the door abruptly. He looked from one face to the other. "Come up." His voice was stern and without emotion. "Bring your things."

The women obeyed, glancing first at each other. Cora gave Nancy's arm a squeeze as they filed out. She was saying it would be okay. She was strong enough now to give strength to both of them again. She would manage this one. They were going to live.

On deck, the air was cool and fresh. Lino was up on the bridge, steering the boat. Giuseppe leaned against the railing, looking stiff and uncomfortable.

"We must talk," Enzo said. "Sit down." He motioned to the two chairs before him. He continued to stand as the women placed their backpacks next to the chairs and sat down. Cora felt her jaw grow tight looking at Enzo, his despicable, haughty stance. "We will let you go back to Rome on your own, back to your own homes in the United States, when we drop you off tonight. But you will talk to no one. The license numbers on this boat are fake. We have changed them before and we will change them again. And my name, ladies, is not what you have been calling me." He smiled. Giuseppe looked at his feet.

"You see, we have had these little cruises before. There are always American girls interested in getting something for nothing. Some of them like to have more fun than others. You, my lovely, have been a great disappointment." Enzo reached down and took a strand of Nancy's hair in his hand, then let it fall. "I know many people in the U.S.; I go there often. I have taken the liberty of reviewing your passports. I have connections in very dangerous places. I know your addresses; I know about you. And I will only say, you and the people you love will remain safe only as long as you remain smart and keep your mouths shut. Nothing that happened on this boat was important." He sneered, tossing his head to the side, his hair blowing off his forehead. "Nothing that happened on this boat ever happened. Do you understand?"

Nancy nodded yes emphatically. Cora tightened her fist and relaxed it again. "Perfectly," she said.

Cora and Nancy sat on the deck for some time. Cora watched the charcoal shoreline in the distance. They were following the coastline, following the old woman's boot laces. Shadows crossed the boat now; the water held large dark pools like oil spills. Deep water. Lack of sun. Night spreading and covering the sea.

Would they go through the Strait of Messina? And on to Egypt? To Turkey? Would she see the sandy beach, feel warm flat rocks with the palms of her hands? Would she live to see another sunrise, that burning globe of the gods, back to count another day? She didn't know and hugged herself, her hands cool on her bare arms. She was still here. She could feel her lungs reach and expand. Her heart beat as if nothing was wrong.

Soon the boat motor slowed down, and they saw a shadowy silhouette of jagged hills and rocks against the navy sky. Enzo was running a light at the front of the boat, and settled on a small port about half-a-mile away. As the shoreline grew closer, the women could make out a few houses and buildings, all with dark, gaping windows. There was no light except for those from the boat and the sliver of moon above them.

48

LETTER

I got a letter from my parents today. Hello dear, they said. We are so happy to hear things are going well for you and your boyfriend. (My mother always writes in the plural, as if she speaks for both of them.) We were wondering if you wouldn't like to come down and visit us. If this boy is as special as he sounds, we thought it would be nice to meet him. (This boy. Ian is thirty-six. They confuse me.) Then they said something about marriage plans. Did I have any? What did his family do, etc., etc.

I am losing touch with them. I cannot imagine going to Florida with Ian so he can meet my parents. It is hot and muggy there.

Hi, Mom and Dad. This is Ian. We are planning a small wedding: ivory candles and roses for the head table, red cummerbunds. Do you still have that silver-plated tea set of Great-grandma Hilda's? I thought perhaps we'd have two songs during the service. And should I wear my hair up? Where should we get the cake? Ian's family is from the East. They're curious why anyone would live in Rapid City, too.

Hi, Mom and Dad. This is Ian. We aren't getting married. It's too hot to talk about it, Mom. Where's the bathroom? I'd like to wash my face. Planes make me nervous. Sea sick. I think I have to puke. We didn't bring suitcases. We aren't planning to stay long. We might live together. Why? Is it important? Why is that so important, Dad? I know, why don't you write it down on a piece of paper? Expectations, goals and dreams for our daughter who never got married, or got a proper job, or figured out what to do with her life. You know, list them one by one, so I know what we are dealing with here. Then, on the way home, I can ponder my inadequacies. I think I'll take a bus back. The turbulence makes me nervous. Waves of air batting me around.

I got a letter from my parents today. It was full of holes. Little gaps and hints of confusion. Am I happy? Is this relationship I mentioned in my last letter important to me? Do I want it to be permanent? Permanent. I can't seem to grasp that idea. I don't think marriage was made for people like me. I like freedom. I need space. I won't get married.

49

TROPEA

L ino turned off the boat lights and cut the engine as they slipped up against the pilings of the dock. Giuseppe and Enzo tossed thick ropes around the posts and secured the boat. Giuseppe's hands were shaking. He lit a cigarette to hide his nervousness. The light from the match revealed the eyes of a dazed animal.

Cora and Nancy stood together, backpacks at their feet, standing near the stern, sisters in apprehension.

Overhead, the night sky was a paradise of stars. From horizon to horizon, nothing but blackness and points of light.

The smell of oil. The smell of fish. The smell of a cigarette; a glowing orange ember in one man's hand.

Enzo tied the boat and motioned to the dock. He lit a cigarette and stood there with one hand on his hip. Nancy slung her backpack over her shoulders and stepped onto the extended plank. She climbed down and didn't look back. Cora followed, and with one foot on the dock, turned around and took one last look. Her eyes met with the eyes of each man. They were weak men. Resignation and a bit of fear in Giuseppe's eyes prompted her to smile. "May the three sisters be with you on your sea journey, gentlemen. Was it Atropos who was the Fate of things to come? I forget; Alessandra was the one who knew the tale so well."

She turned then and did not look back. They untied the boat and headed out to sea as the two women walked away from the dock. Cora half expected to hear a shot and feel pain in her back. These were the kind of men who would shoot someone in the back, but she felt good about saying what she did. It seemed important to her to name Alessandra out loud one more time, in that place, in front of those who killed her. And if there was any superstition in the depths of their evil beings, she hoped with all her heart it would haunt them as they headed back into the dark water, as they headed back to their lives.

After their eyes adjusted to the darkness, Cora and Nancy walked onto the beach. Five small fishing boats lined the docked. It looked like a tiny village of less than a dozen buildings. It was quiet. There was a huge rock near the edge of the beach. Nancy and Cora took their backpacks off there and sunk into the sand. Nancy bit her lip to hold back a cry.

"It's okay, Nancy. We are alive." Cora put space between each important word. They sat for some time, holding each other and remembering that fact, wiping out the days behind them as best they could. Cora opened her sleeping bag; she was exhausted. "We'll talk in the morning. Now, I need to sleep." Tears rolled down her cheeks for the first time in twenty-four hours. They stung the bruises on her cheeks. The taste of salt on her lips made her shudder. She took Nancy's hand and didn't let go of it all night.

In the morning, the tropical sun woke them to the reality of a small village waking up. Clearly, they had slept longer than some of the fisherman and seemed to have caused quite a stir among the residents. Cora opened her eyes to a group of four children standing in front of her staring down at them.

One child was a foot taller than the other three, all gangling limbs and brown from the sun. He wore shorts without a shirt. "Buongiorno," he said. He squinted and tilted his head, trying to figure out the strangers.

"Buongiorno." Cora sat up and looked around. A dull pain throbbed in her neck and shoulder. Nancy was still asleep. The boy said something else in Italian, and Cora shrugged her shoulders and smiled. "I'm sorry, ah, non capisco." She turned her hands palms up. The three little girls giggled and began talking among themselves. One of them ran up the beach to a house a couple of hundred feet away. A woman was hanging laundry on a clothes-line that stretched from the house to a scraggly tree. Soon she returned with the child.

"Buongiorno," she said. She was probably in her thir-ties and stood twisting a ring on her finger as she looked at the two young women before her. Nancy was awake now and sat up. "You English?" the woman asked.

"American," Cora said, pleased to find someone who understood.

"How you get here?" The woman looked worried. Her long hair was pulled back, and she fingered the tie at the base of her neck.

Cora paused a moment and shot a glance at Nancy. "We walked. And caught rides with cars. Got here very late last night."

The woman looked around. "Cars, here?" When Cora looked past the woman, it seemed more likely that boats were the primary form of transportation.

"Oh, earlier. We have been walking a long time." She gestured inland, up the only gravel road in sight.

"You want boat ride to Tropea?"

"Can we take a train from there?"

"Si."

Cora's heart raced. "Yes, please. Ah, Si. We would like to hire a boat."

"My husband," she said. "He come at noon. You like coffee?"

"Si, grazie," the two younger women said at once.

THE ITALIAN WOMAN made coffee in a blue enamel pot and served it with fresh bread at a wooden table in the kitchen. A pale blue oilcloth covered the table. Cora would never forget this room; the cups on the shelves, the spices in tins on the windowsill above the sink, the wooden floor. Light sifted in from two small windows, leaving the corners in shadow.

The woman noticed Nancy's and Cora's bruises and red welts. She grew more and more disturbed, scenarios playing out in her mind; she understood more than she acknowledged, more than she could say in words. Her first reaction was to cry, but this gave way to more practical things.

She found clean towels, a small bar of perfumed soap. "Come," she said, motioning to Cora. "Shower for you. You need something, you say. Okay?"

Cora thanked her. She closed the door to the small bathroom and undressed, looking down at her body with shame; she felt contaminated. Cora let the warm water run over her pain. It hurt to be wet at first, but the muscles fought to relax. She lathered her arms and chest with the white scent of floral soap, but she could not get clean. She scrubbed and scrubbed her bruised breasts until she cried, until her skin was red and tender, until she sobbed silently in a warm shower of tears, but it didn't help. The dirt from their hands had soaked into her skin like stains. It was no use. She turned off the warm water and let the cold water shock her; her back went rigid and stiff. She lifted her face up to the wicked water and stood there until she was numb enough to get out.

Nancy sat at the kitchen table. The woman sat across from her, without words, and then got a brush and brushed Nancy's long hair. She was gentle and consistent. Neither woman said a word. Nancy cried. The woman brushed, occasionally resting her hand on Nancy's head. They both listened to the water hitting the tin walls of the shower.

ON THE TRAIN ride back to Rome, Cora and Nancy sat in the same car trying to get as far away from each other as possible, trying to figure out how they felt, trying to understand the feelings they could not explain.

"Do you still want to go to Greece?" Nancy asked.

"I've always wanted to go to Greece," Cora said. "What's that got to do with it?"

"I don't know. I thought maybe you'd feel better."

"Right," Cora said. "Sounds simple. Surgical removal of the traumatic event."

"I didn't mean that." Nancy was on a tightrope and began to fall. "I know. I'm sorry."

They gave up on talking. The pleasant friendship had abandoned them, and it surprised them both. They each wanted a world of their own, one that didn't include the other, the reminder of the horrors at sea. They wanted to peddle backwards to innocence, to a place where guilt did not sit like a stone in the throat, obstructing every breath they took.

50

PASSION

I an sits across from me at the picnic table. He's reading the Sunday New York Times. We're in my backyard and the pheasants chirp in their wire home behind us. Their long legs dance about in the dirt as they peck corn from the dusty ground.

I'm wearing sunglasses and moving the pen across the page. A year ago, I would have been reading a thick novel, my bare toes on top of Ian's, imagining I was Emma or Catherine and this was somewhere else. But now, I am driven to writing everything down, even that which is not important, in case some small fact creeps out of my unconscious mind to join me, some detail about Nancy or Cora which I hadn't known but which might clarify the scene in the deck chairs on the boat, or at the cafe conversation in Florence. I need to understand, so I write things down and wait.

Ian smiles and winks at me over the paper. I think he likes this passion, this drive. He has been spending more time here. More time with me. "This suits you," he says. "The sun, the morning, your preoccupation with that story."

He thinks I'm working on the book. I smile and say nothing. It doesn't matter. He finds it attractive; that's fine. He wants to read the book, and I want to let him. It feels a little like sex. I am able to open up more of myself each time we make love, as if I am reclaiming my body, my life. I have my past, which rests on my back like a ghost. I have adjusted to the extra weight.

Ian wants to understand me. Today, I feel like I am standing at the edge of the line of pine trees near the pheasant pen. I watch the picnic table, as if I am the writer-observer and "she" is the one with the notebook scribbling furiously. She's the one falling in love with Ian. Falling in love. I want to tell her it's okay, that it won't always hurt, that there is room for healing. I want to tell her she can do whatever she wants. Maybe she listens, maybe she simply sits and writes. White pages. Black ink. Sun across her arms.

51

FLIGHT

"I'll never see you again." Nancy was solemn, her face ashen and perspiring. She sat in the Leonardo da Vinci airport in Rome across from Cora.

"Of course you will." Cora knew this wasn't true, knew that the ties which they had broken when they found their freedom from the boat, and Enzo, and the nightmare at sea, were now twisting around their own ankles. They would live separate lives, find their own ways to live with the past. It was not something they could settle. It was an open wound. "Maybe I'll come see you in Montana or in New York."

"I'd like that." Nancy was supposed to fly out of London when she ended her trip, but after they reached Rome, she charged a ticket on her Visa card. Instant money. A safety net.

Cora thought of all the times they had counted pennies, and Nancy sat with a fat bank account at home. She knew her own wallet was the same size it had been when they left land so long ago, except for the train ticket back to Rome. She had three hundred and seventy-four dollars left. If she chose to, she could still go to Greece.

"Will you let me know when you get back home?" Nancy was making small tears in the folder holding her ticket home.

"Sure. I've got your phone number."

"You aren't planning on telling anyone anything, are you?"

"Why?"

Nancy looked startled. "We agreed. I mean, we talked about it. I don't think we should. We can't do anything for anyone now."

"We could put them in jail."

"So what?" Nancy ran her hand through her dark hair. "Then they would get out again. And this is Italy. They'd probably blame us, and if they found those guys, it would be our word against theirs, and we don't even speak much Italian. And if they got out, they'd find us..."

"Maybe." Cora looked out the window. "But Alessandra might have some family somewhere. Don't you think they deserve to know?"

"What? Are you talking about being fair here? What

does fair have to do with any of this?" Nancy clenched her teeth. "I... we've been through enough."

"Then go home," Cora said. "I won't do anything, okay?"

There was a long pause. The intercom crackled; it was time for Nancy to board her flight. She stood up and turned to Cora. "Are you going on to Greece?"

"I don't know." Cora smiled. "I'm not even sure Greece is still there. I need some time to figure out just where it is I want to be."

"Goodbye." Nancy started to cry. "Please stay safe."

Cora hugged her. "You too, Beauty. You too."

When Cora left the airport, the sky had clouded over. She walked along the streets carrying her backpack and looking at nothing in particular. She saw herself in the window of a meat shop, her imaged juxtaposed with chickens hanging from a rack. Cured hams and sausages were stacked in piles in the bottom of the display case. She didn't recognize herself at first. Her brown hair was bleaching out from the sun. She looked thinner than the last time she remembered looking in a mirror.

It was twenty minutes past noon. She needed to find a place to stay for the night before everything filled. It was the middle of August, and tourists were everywhere. She found a shaded bus stop, got out of her backpack, and pulled out her guidebook. Hostels. Pensiones. Cheap and clean. She ran a trembling finger down the white page. There must be some place listed that sounded safe.

52

OPTIONS

I t is a hot, impatient August. Rapid City is full of tourists in the summer. I've been working the swing shift at the restaurant. I'm supposed to be working on curriculum for my fall night class at the college. Instead, I sit near the window and drink iced tea, waiting for a breeze.

I've been waiting for some muse to tell me what Cora decides to do next. She seems to have several options, or is it she has none? I don't know, and waiting doesn't seem to help. Someone told me to talk directly to my characters. I've been doing that all along, but I usually don't write it down.

X: So, what am I supposed to do with you now?

Cora: What, this is my responsibility too? Can't you figure it out? You've written me into a corner already; you get me out.

X: Do you want to go to Greece?

Cora: I've always wanted to go to Greece. What does that have to do with it?

X: Okay. Do you go? Maybe it would be good to remind you that you're alive, that you still have a life, as you said earlier.

Cora: Right. It all sounds very simple, spotless. Surgical removal of the traumatic event. You'd like that, wouldn't you?

X: What have I got to do with it? This is fiction.

Cora: Good try. And truth is stranger than fiction, and you are all about the truth, right?

X: Why are you attacking me?

Cora: You're the one writing this down. Don't point fingers.

X: So, get on with it.

Cora: With what?

X: With whatever it is you're trying to say to me or... whatever it is I'm trying to say to you.

Cora: Now you're getting it.

X: I want to write the truth. I want to record the events as they happened. As they could have happened.

Cora: Fine.

X: I've never been on a yacht.

Cora: Who are you trying to convince?

X: I'm trying to make your decision to go to Greece and sit on the steps of the Acropolis late at night believable. Or your decision to take a train straight back to London to wait on standby for five days while you sit in a youth hostel directly behind St. Peter's cathedral and play chess with a twenty-five-year-old woman from Australia.

Cora: It doesn't matter to me.

X: Why not?

Cora: Because I'm ice now. Get it? I am too cold to touch and too numb to care. This conversation is over.

53

GREECE

Cora wandered through the uneven white streets of the Plaka district the first afternoon she arrived in Athens. She decided to go to Greece because she had always wanted to. She still had a life, she told herself. She was too close to go home without at least seeing the Parthenon and the other ruins on the majestic limestone hill.

Looking for answers, for a sense of clarity, she walked past tavernas full of small square tables with a few people sitting in the mid-afternoon heat. Earlier, she had left her backpack at the YWCA near Syntagma Square. It was a clean, stately building with bunk beds and a lobby where everyone had to check in and out. No men were allowed. A woman's club. A haven.

Her shoulders tried to relax as she swung her arms and got used to the lack of weight on her back. She walked most of the morning looking for another place to stay, checking out the city. Looking over her shoulder. The YWCA was twelve dollars a night, more expensive than she was used to, but she could stay three or four nights. Then she would go out to an island like Crete or Mykonos, where it was cheaper and camp on the beach, or find a youth hostel that charged three or four dollars a night. Or a room in someone's house. A rented room. One with locks on the doors. Or she would go home.

It was unnecessary to plan ahead; it was not possible. She needed to take things slowly: to taste the strong coffee as it slid down her throat in the morning; to feel the pulse of hot water on her back in the shower; to wash and carefully dress a body still obviously in pain. There was plenty of time. Cora's life had shifted course. She was a traveler without a destination.

Around six o'clock, she found a small taverna in the Plaka, the old quarter, with Greek music piped out to the tables in front of the shaded door. A lattice frame overhead supported a web of grapevines and kept the dining area cool. The waiter who greeted her smiled. She felt safe enough. She ate a peasant salad full of fresh tomatoes, cucumbers, black olives and feta cheese. Every sense seemed heightened. She could taste the essence of every bite. Is this what it is like for someone who knows they are dying? Every experience, a treasure and a challenge? But Cora knew she was not dying; she knew she had a long road to recovery, and the road was unfamiliar.

She thought of the Acropolis, that strange and mystic place she had carried with her from the milk carton days of her youth. She was finally here! After dinner, she would buy a bottle of wine and go up the steps to the ancient world. She would sit on the steps of the splendid palace under the stars and know the sea was close by. She would get a new perspective of the old city from the top of the hill of democracy. She would talk to the gods. She would see what they had to say.

Or she would wait until daylight and go with the crowds, climbing the stone steps in the heat with her guidebook and her camera. She would find a shaded spot near one of the great pillars of the Parthenon and sit to write in her journal, but her fingers would shake and she would feel a bit faint. Not from the heat, the time of day, or all the voices swirling around her. Not from the gods whispering the answers to the mysteries of the universe.

54

TALK

This morning, Ian woke up next to me. I was staring at the ceiling above my bed, thinking about finishing the book. He reached over and touched my cheekbone, right under my eye, with two fingers like a sculptor checking to see if the clay was dry.

It was hard to return from that place where I wrote about another life story. My arms felt too heavy to move. My eyes turned to him. He smiled. His eyebrows were bushy, a reddish-brown color. I'd never noticed the flecks of yellow in his eyes. "You're going to melt me," I said.

"I'm trying." Ian smiled.

I raised my heavy hand in front of his face, fingers relaxed like Michelangelo's David. Long and flowing. "Well then, I'm a statue. Rock," I said.

"Sculptured, yes. Ice, maybe. But no granite. That, my dear, is all talk."

"All I've got is talk," I said.

"Then talk to me." He got up on one elbow and pulled my eyes to him.

I looked at his handsome, smiling face, and I started to cry. "Words scare the hell out of me," I said.

"I love you." He said it, just like that, and then looked at me, matter-of-factly. Shock value.

I closed my eyes. On a tight rope between here and there and over a raging river. No balance. No control.

"You can't," I said.

"l do."

He wouldn't give up, wouldn't give the words over to me, so I could pack them into a cardboard box with tissue and old newsprint, so I could store them away and keep them from shattering.

"I can't love you," I said.

"But you do."

"There's too much you don't —"

"History," Ian said. "I'm here, and I'm staying."

And then he held me. He leaned back into the feather pillows and pulled me close to him. I felt the cotton sheets and the hair on his arms and the warmth of his body beside me. I closed my eyes, and Cora was smiling at me from beyond the gray.

II. PHANTOM PAIN

55

STONE MAIDENS

Cora sits on a dark hill, the night sprayed with stars. Above her head the constellations shine, pictures of men carrying arrows, women with buckets of water. Dot to dot. Cora is a ship lost at sea. She looks up through blurry eyes for some hint of direction.

It is August in Athens. The Parthenon rests on its limestone pedestal and glows a gray-white in the moon-light. She sits nears the shadow of the Caryatids, six stone maidens who stand on their hill throne and hold up the roof of a temple with their heads. They stand over the Acropolis and face towards the sea.

The air smells of diesel fuel from the streets below. Cora's skin is covered with a thin layer of diesel and grime. Just as the statues show erosion from the elements, she too is being worn away. She looks at the stone women, their features against the night. She has swallowed a stone herself. It sits in the pit of her stomach. A blue moon. An anchor.

She sits on a hill in the dark, tracing a path through the stars. Looking over her shoulder, she shivers in the warm night, shivers at every possibility. She drinks straight from the bottle of wine in her hand. The Greek retsina tastes foreign to her tongue, tastes of pine and something stronger. She doesn't like the taste, and this pleases her. She is drinking her medicine. She is covering the stone in her stomach, trying to drown that which does not require air.

56

DANCE WITH ME

"Want to dance?" Caitlyn leaned across the table and touched Greg's wrist, then the band of his watch.

"Not really. I'm tired, Cate. We just played eleven innings."

"Dance with me. Please?"

Greg rolled his eyes, finished the shot of whiskey, and drank the mug of beer straight down. "All right. All right."

The wooden dance floor ran the length of the stale bar. Caitlyn thought it looked more like a runway than a dance floor, but she closed her eyes and let the music move through her. She tried to think back to high school, when she felt sexy on the dance floor, when the world was full of promise and she was in love with being young and wild. When basketball games, snowmobiling and beer parties on Friday night were enough.

She tried not to think about anything else.

Greg shuffled his feet in his understated dance style across from her. He was handsome; curly blond hair stuck out from under his Twins baseball cap. His green and white softball uniform was skin tight and showed his muscular legs and small butt. Still an athlete. Still hot.

Caitlyn smiled, but he looked back at her with a bored look on his face.

The music stopped, and he took her arm. "Come on, let's sit down. I'm thirsty."

"Go ahead. I'm going to dance." Caitlyn stepped back and closed her eyes. Everyone else was leaving the dance floor; dancing alone only asked for attention, but she didn't care. Caitlyn closed her eyes and began to dance again.

Her body heard something far away, something inside the tunnel of music, something that began to make sense. Her limbs felt numb. The hot cigarette smoke-filled air smelled comforting. She danced with a child inside of her, danced away from her lover, twirled to the other end of the dark runway, to a place where she was alone and transfixed. She felt like taking off all together, like she was a bird with big wings. Maybe she could fly to a tall tree in the mountains and perch on a limb all alone. Make her own nest. Start over. Or she could dump the nest and climb down and get lost in the tall trees. Anywhere but here. Anyone but herself.

"Cate. Have you had too much to drink? Come on, let's get out of here." Greg's hand cradled her elbow. He understood about being drunk, about getting outside yourself, feeling the license to do and say anything you pleased.

"Fuck off, Greg. I'm dancing." Caitlyn didn't open her eyes.

"Oh Jesus, Cate. Don't make a scene. I'm ready to leave."

"Have another Boiler Maker, Greg. I just want to dance to one more song and get myself tired out."

"You're making a damn fool of yourself."

"Well, good. Let them talk."

"I'm getting out a here." Greg turned to walk away. Caitlyn grabbed his arm, and he turned around.

"You leaving me, Greg?" There was a long pause. "I mean, are you leaving me or what? I want to dance to a couple of songs after sitting all night at your game and drinking with your friends, and I want five minutes. You leaving me over that?"

"I'll be in the car. When you're ready, get your ass out there."

"Okay, honey." Caitlyn smiled and winked at Greg.

He shook his head and smiled, tipping his hat back. He turned and left the bar.

Caitlyn grew invisible instantly. She felt as if she could see through her arms to the tables beyond. Another song started, and she closed her eyes, trying to find the music again, searching for the beat that would give her some pleasure, for the words that would carry her away.

57

THE SHOE BOX WALTZ

When Ray Daneli came home from work, Maureen could tell something was wrong. He parked the pickup next to the basketball hoop and kicked the tires as he walked by. He always kicked the tires, and his wife always watched from the window, but there was something else in his face today, something odd in the way his arms bounced limp against his sides.

"Good afternoon, dear." She muttered out of habit, not that the words held any meaning at all.

Ray let the screen door bang and walked past her, his face a vacant lot. He opened a cupboard door near the back of the kitchen and started pulling out cans and boxes from the shelves. Cheerios, peanut butter, soda. "Where the hell's that box?" he asked.

Maureen paused. "What box, dear?"

"Where the hell's that box?"

"Ray? Dear, what box do you mean?"

"Maureen!" he screamed. Then he turned to her. He was a tall, thin man. It was early September and a humid eighty-nine degrees. The top of his balding head glistened with sweat. Finally, his eyes focused on the woman with whom he had spent forty years. "Oh, there you are."

"What box are you looking for, Ray?"

"The shoebox, damn it. The one full of the receipts. I need the receipts. How am I supposed to run a business?"

"Ray, we don't keep a shoebox in that cupboard." Maureen searched her brain. What he might have meant, what he was looking for, where it could be.

"Well then, where is it?" Ray stopped short and stared at his wife, looking her in the eye for the first time.

"How about if you look in the hall closet? I'll look downstairs in your office." Maureen was always smoothing things over. A calm hand across white linen before placing the china on the dining room table.

"You hid it, didn't you?" Ray flushed at the thought. He walked over to the counter and placed both fists on the avocado Formica, his back to her.

"Hid it? What are you talking about?" Maureen was shaking now. The kitchen felt hot and close.

Ray shook his head. "Jesus Christ," he said and walked out of the room.

Maureen walked down to the basement and scanned the shelves for some box that resembled what Ray was looking for. She found nothing, sighed, and went to the washing machine to start some clothes. If she gave him time, he would calm down and forget — forget what he was looking for, forget that she was there, and things would be back to normal. She sorted the light clothes from the dark ones. She placed her wrists on the white enamel side of the washer, cooling herself.

It was nicer down here, she thought, dark and cool. This was her half of the basement: laundry, a pantry, and racks for out-of-season clothes. Ray's desk was on the other half, sitting on top of an old oval rug. A bare light bulb sagged from the open rafters. He worked at the desk nights, figuring out the books for his small auto parts business.

Maureen walked back upstairs to peel potatoes for dinner. She reached the kitchen just in time to see Ray's red pickup pull out of the driveway. Things had been this way for months, or even longer. She thought about talking to the pastor at church or one of her friends. Even Ray's brother. But Maureen Daneli didn't know what to say. She didn't know what was wrong or how long it had been that way. She only knew that life's noose was getting tighter and tighter, and it was harder and harder to breathe. It wasn't a question of happiness or even love. She had forgotten about such things long ago. But her sense of normalcy was dissolving, and that shook her the most.

It was Friday; the weekend stretched out before her. The best thing to do at times like this, she'd found, was to concentrate on daily things. Peel potatoes. Clean the chicken. Season it. Fry it. Make dinner. He would be back, and he'd want dinner, and he'd want it on time. That might be six o'clock, seven o'clock, or eight-thirty, but when Ray Daneli opened the door to the kitchen, dinner was on the table.

When the telephone rang, Maureen had dinner dished up and ready to put into the microwave. She watched for her husband to drive into the driveway. She arranged everything on each plate like a still-life, noticing color and texture. High school home economics. Family Circle food section. She held the phone in one hand and moved a crispy chicken leg slightly with the other.

"Mom?"

"Hello, dear."

"What's wrong?" Her youngest daughter's voice dropped at the end. She had grown used to picking up hints across the phone lines. Her hope that the conversation would be as pleasant as possible dissolved in her mother's whispering, defeated voice.

"Nothing. How are you?"

"What's wrong, Ma?"

"Caitlyn, I'm fine. It's hot here. I've been frying chicken. How's Greg?"

"Fine. And the boys are fine." Caitlyn paused, put both hands on the receiver to steady herself. "Mom. I was wondering, do you still have that little rocking chair of mine? You know, the orange one that Daddy painted? Is it in the attic?"

Maureen paused. "Caitlyn? I think so. I mean, why would you want that old thing now? The boys are much too old and... you don't have any little..."

"Yes, Mom, I'm pregnant."

Maureen was crying. A grandchild. A soft, innocent baby to hold in a flannel cocoon. A little girl to sing lullabies to while pushing soft, red curls from her damp forehead. A tiny hand like a walnut shell, to hold the hope of the whole world. Caitlyn was living with Greg and his two adolescent sons from a previous marriage. This would be her first grandchild. "Oh, Catie. I'm so happy. Are you okay? Is everything okay?"

"I don't know. I haven't told Greg yet. I wanted the first person I told to be happy about it."

"Well, what will you..." Maureen was shivering now, looking out at the driveway as she spoke, half expecting Ray to pull in.

"I don't know yet. I want to get married, but we haven't talked about that for a long time. I don't know what his reaction will be. We didn't plan this, but I'm happy about it, I think. I am happy. I just wanted to tell you and ask you to look for that old rocker."

"I will. And let me know what..." Maureen paused and looked around her kitchen.

"I'll call you after I talk to Greg." Caitlyn paused. "How's Daddy?"

Maureen did not want to spoil a lovely moment. "He's busy. Seems to have lots of work."

"Tell him hello for me?"

"Certainly."

In 1952, Maureen O'Malley was working as a secretary at the local high school when she met Ray. She had a flat tire on the way home from work, and he stopped in his big gray panel truck and helped her change it. She was twenty-two with red hair and big Irish bones. Ray was twenty-nine and working for a local auto supplier. He changed the tire, gave her a complimentary pen with his business phone number on it, and asked her for her number. They were married eleven months later at the old wooden Lady of Light church in Grace, Iowa.

It was five years before Cora was born and five more before Caitlyn. Maureen continued to work. Her job had worn a groove in her consciousness, and she found the routine comforting. She took care of the daily attendance and absences. Every morning, she knew who had the flu and who was out for a dentist appointment. When the girls were older, she drove them to school with her, and they all drove home together at night. She enjoyed seeing them in the halls, talking with their friends, growing up before her eyes.

They had a good life. Ray got his own business, the girls did well in school, and everyone stayed healthy. Maureen didn't remember when things started to change, or if they ever did. Perhaps she didn't know what was missing because it had never been there. Maybe she was making too much of things. But these days, since the girls had left for college and gone off to have their own lives, she and Ray existed like roommates, telling a friendly joke now and then, putting up with annoying habits of the other, occasionally sharing a tender moment.

Ray drove up. Maureen put the food in the microwave and punched the time. She got the coffee and poured two cups at the table, thinking about Caitlyn's phone call. She wouldn't tell Ray until she knew for sure what Caitlyn was going to do. It was possible she would abort it, wasn't it? Maureen hoped not, knowing how hard it had been for her to get pregnant, how happy Caitlyn sounded on the phone. After all, Caitlyn was almost thirty, but it wasn't her decision. All she could do was wait and see.

Ray walked in, his hands jingling a set of house keys. Maureen said hello, carrying the two plates of steaming food in to the dining room.

"What's for dinner?"

"Chicken. It's ready." Maureen stood behind her chair, smiling. Still a striking woman, five foot nine and thin. Long arms and fingers. Her hair was streaked with white, but wavy red wisps twined around her face.

"Did you find that box?" Ray looked past the table, right into Maureen's eyes.

"No, Raymond. I have no idea what you're talking about." Maureen's shoulders slumped in defeat. The dinner was not enough.

"Yeah, I'm sure you don't. Trying to take my money without me knowing it. What else you got up your sleeve?"

"Ray, please. Can't we eat and talk about this later?"

"Eat? Why the hell should I sit down with you? Where's he eating tonight, huh? You got a boyfriend out there waiting to see you? Is that what all the hurry's about?"

Maureen stopped short. This was a new ballgame. It was as if something had snapped, all the small accusations, all the innuendo out in the open. Ray was shaking and shouting now. "All I do to make ends meet around here, and what do I get from you? I bet somebody else would appreciate the work I do."

Maureen looked at the telephone on the kitchen wall. If she called his brother, he'd come and help her out. Calm Ray down. Help her figure out what to do next. She walked toward the kitchen.

The ironing board was folded up next to the telephone, and before she could reach for the receiver, Ray grabbed the board in his big hands and held it out at arm's length. "So there you are, my lovely. Someone who will appreciate me. Someone who knows how to make a man happy. Shall we dance?"

Maureen was crying and felt like throwing up. "Ray, stop it!" she shouted. "Stop it right now, please. We'll talk. We'll get some help."

But Ray waltzed around the living room with the old wooden ironing board wrapped in his arms. He smiled and murmured at each turn. "Oh, baby, you are so good! Let's get that money and get out of here. Who needs a cheating wife? I can take my money and run. It's you and me. Let's find some genuine happiness. Come on, give me a kiss."

Maureen pushed the numbers on the telephone for Ray's brother. Ray was oblivious to her now, twirling and humming in the next room. Maureen's fingers shook, and her stomach spasmed, as she listened to the hollow ringing on the other end of the line.

She counted to ten rings and then carefully returned the receiver to its cradle. It was getting harder to breathe. Without looking back at Ray, she walked out the side door to the driveway, letting the screen door bang behind her. It was beginning to cool off. Leaves on the old oak in the front yard whispered secrets in the evening breeze.

Maureen looked up into the tree. There was a bird on one of the low branches ruffling its feathers, settling in for the evening. She didn't recognize the bird, didn't know its name or if it was native to the area. Probably just passing through, she thought, headed for somewhere else.

58

FIRE ALARM

My mother died of a broken heart in a crummy little town in Iowa. It was a humid night. The neighbor said she was out on the old wrought-iron bench on the lawn and just sat there. Perfectly still. He was watering his rose bushes and finally walked over to see if she was okay.

Mom looked up and said, "Ray doesn't love me." Then she grabbed her left arm. By the time the ambulance got there, they figure she was dead. Massive heart attack. She and my dad must have had one hell of a fight, because he lost it. Some kind of nervous breakdown. When a police officer come into the house to see if anyone was there, Dad was sitting cross-legged on the floor on top of an old, folded up, wooden ironing board, like his body got tired of doing its job and just sat down in the middle of the kitchen.

They told me later that he just sat there and stared and didn't answer the officer when he talked to him, so they took both my parents away with sirens and flashing lights.

I can almost hear the sirens. A week after I got back from Mom's funeral, the trailer house next to ours burned down. God, sirens and red lights were everywhere. It smelled like burning plastic. I bet if you put your hand on the metal side of our trailer the next morning, it still would have been warm. Nothing but smoke damage to our place, though.

I was pretty nauseated, on account of I'm pregnant. Nine weeks. But I haven't told Greg yet, so I was acting like it was all that smoke. I haven't figured out what I'm going to do, so no use telling him until I get time to think this through. Greg's my boyfriend. We've lived together for three years. Ryan and Daniel, his two kids from his first marriage, live with us. They're ten and thirteen, and it was a shock going from living alone to living with three of them. Boys, I mean. Sometimes I feel like I live in a locker room, after they've been playing basketball or something, and they crowd into this little trailer all sweaty. It's hard to get the air moving.

We stayed at a friend's house the rest of that night, the night of the fire, and camped out on the living room floor. The next morning, we drove home and started cleaning up.

Greg opened the door first. I was sort of afraid of what we'd find.

"Hey, check out these windows," Ryan said. He drew a "Z" like Zorro does on the soot covering the living room windows.

The door stuck a little. "Some panels are warped. I better call the insurance guy," Greg said. Ryan and Daniel followed him inside. I wasn't as curious. I thought about sitting outside all day, but the smoke was even stronger next to the black, twisted mess that used to be Jensen's trailer. When I saw that pink-skinned doll on the floor of what used to be their little girl's room, the hair all singed off, I went inside.

Ryan and Daniel were eating Cheerios because they had to catch the bus to school. Greg walked around, checking everything out. This was his trailer before I moved in. Everything smelled horrible, but looked okay.

"The phone's not working. I'm going out to get a couple of things and call the insurance guy," Greg said. "You boys want a ride to school?"

They nodded with their mouths full, sort of shrugged the way kids do, all boney shoulders and long arms. Ryan wiped his mouth with his sleeve. "I'll get my books."

Ryan and Daniel are talented students. They like school. I never did. Greg was a big athlete at Lincoln High. Football and track, mostly. He graduated five years ahead of me, and I didn't grow up here, so I didn't even know who he was.

The night after the fire, Greg put up three new fire alarms while I made dinner. The boys watched TV. "The insurance guy said they'd clean the furniture and the carpet. They'd pay to have the curtains cleaned, but we have to take them in someplace ourselves. Just get a receipt. You should call sometime and set up for that service to come. I got the number. I think the phone will be working tomorrow."

I thought about the phone call I made to my mom the day she died. I told her I was pregnant, and she cried because she was happy. I sort of wanted advice, but didn't know how to ask for it. I don't know how to ask for anything these days. I just fight down the bile in my throat and try to hide that I'm feeling awful. I flush the toilet a lot in the morning when I'm throwing up. The radio is kind of loud in the kitchen, and nobody seems to have noticed anything yet. Greg stays up late at night, and he's a pretty heavy sleeper.

I thought about the phone and how I'd never be able to call my mom again. I stood over the stove and fried potatoes and cried. I thought about my big sister, Cora. She was at the funeral, too. I hadn't seen her for a while, and she looked different. I mean, I guess we both did. I think your face changes when you're sad. It gets heavy around the eyes.

We both visited Dad, but he was still pretty out of it. He said the drugs made him sleepy. He cried and said he didn't mean to leave the windows open at home. He kept talking about the windows in the house and how it might rain in and would we check them? We didn't talk at all about Mom. The doctor said there would be time for that.

So Cora and I drove home and slept in our old room before I drove back to Sioux Falls. We stopped the mail and the paper and stacked up all those sympathy cards. Cora got somebody to take care of the house until Dad got better. I watched TV and cried a lot.

Cora rode back with me and flew back to Rapid City from Sioux Falls. I didn't tell her about me being pregnant. It didn't seem like a good time, and I wasn't sure yet if I was going to keep it or not. There was enough to worry about. Besides, Cora and I aren't that close anymore.

Cora kept looking in my eyes, but I don't think she suspected anything other than how sad I felt about Mom. She told me to call anytime I needed to talk and to come out and visit her. She lives in the Black Hills; she and her boyfriend built a new house. I've never been out to visit her, but I might call her.

"Hey Dad, you going to get your trophies polished up too?" Daniel looked up at his dad, who stood on a step stool, putting the screws in a fire alarm over the arch to the hallway. Daniel was talking about Greg's high school trophies that set on the entertainment center above the VCR.

Ryan snickered, but Daniel kept a straight face. "My trophies are fine, smart aleck." Greg snapped the batteries in place and put the cover on. He pushed the tester button, and an annoying squeal filled the place.

"Are you sure? I mean, if there's money for restoration, you should get them polished up for free. Can't find trophies like that these days."

Daniel and Ryan don't go out for sports. They're small and skinny like their mother. "Smart little shit," Greg said. "I don't need that from you, okay?"

"What did I say?" Daniel shrugged and held his hands out, palms up.

We sat down to dinner. Everybody was pretty quiet. "You all right?" Greg looked at the small helping on my plate.

"Fine," I said. "Not very hungry, that's all."

I was thinking about babies. Thinking about children with long arms and big hands. Thinking about fire alarms and photos and broken dolls in the rubble. Something started ringing inside of me like an alarm of my own. Ringing and trembling and making my hands shake as I held the fork. The ringing went on and on through dinner and all that tense talking.

Finally, it worked its way to my head, and the pain was awful. I decided to lie down and rest. When Greg came in later, he sat down on the edge of the bed and said he wanted to talk. I thought it was the time to tell him I had a baby growing inside of me. Our baby and what should we do? But he was drinking, and started talking about high school, and how much more fun life was then, when he got noticed for his talents, and people cheered on Friday nights, and how he didn't understand how his boys could be such smart asses. No respect. And worse yet, no interest in the games he loved to play.

He wondered what he did wrong raising them, but kids were damn hard work, he said, and they never even say thanks. Then he told me good night and went back to the living room to watch some cable TV. I heard the announcers call the play-by-play. College basketball. I heard the buzzer, signaling a substitution, calling for a time out. It buzzed again and again until I fell asleep.

59

WINDOW SEAT

Cora

When I sit in the corner of the living room, I can see what is best in the world. The woods outside, running down to a small stream, the cardinals busy at the feeder, the sky a refreshing blue. I live in the woods for more aesthetic reasons than functional ones. Oh, we have a garden that supplies much of our food, and cords of wood that heat the house, and pheasants in back in a coop, pheasants which we grow and give back to the woods, but it is the daily beauty that keeps me here.

Ian and I built this house with the help of our friends from town and an out-of-work carpenter from

Minneapolis who spent most of one summer here. Ian met him in Rapid City the year before, and it all worked out well. It's a wonderful house. Small and warm. Our bedroom is in a big loft with windows that look out on the Black Hills. I never would have believed when I drove in to Rapid City fourteen years ago in a beat up old junker car that I would stay and eventually live in this beautiful place. A holy place, really. But you have to sit in the woods and listen for a long time before it begins to make sense.

I'm sitting in my living room looking out at what is best in the world and thinking about my little sister. In September, we went to our mother's funeral together. We dressed in dark colors and threw flowers over a grave to say goodbye to our mother. We dressed in somber, conservative clothes and tried not to cry. We obeyed the rules and thanked everyone for being so kind. I'm five years older. I'm the one who sets the pace. Caitlyn let me hold her hand, but she wasn't holding mine back.

Something was wrong, I could feel it, but she didn't tell me what it was. Something besides the loss of our mother. Something under her skin. It troubles me.

After the funeral, we went and saw my father who was convalescing in a hospital. Nerves. A slight break-down. He sat and smiled at us and cried and apologized for leaving windows open in the house when he left. The night mother died, he left home too, and neither of them has been back.

We went to the funeral; we went to the hospital; we went to the house, and then I rode several hours in her car to Sioux Falls where I caught a flight back here.

Caitlyn and I were close as children, but when I left for college, she had high school ahead of her and I wasn't there.

The pheasants will be big enough to let loose soon. It's my favorite time of the year. I love to watch them go. Ian always wanted children. I told him I had pheasants, that was enough. He has learned to make do.

I am not sure what to do next. Last night I dreamed Caitlyn was calling me long distance, but she had one of those kid's telephones with the curly cord and a face on the dial, and she was frustrated that I wasn't talking back to her. She would dial again and again, and the little eyes on the phone would roll, and then there would be only silence. I wanted to call her back, to explain that she had the wrong phone, but you can't do things like that in dreams. You must tread water until you are too tired to drown.

I could invite her here. I don't know if she could get away from her job. I don't know what she's running from. I should call her and find out. I should try again.

CAITLYN

Six inches of snow. I'd take the curtains down and let all that white light in, but they keep out some of the draft. It's cold and isn't even November. I'm too tired to go to work. Maybe I should get dressed up and make a snowman.

No, a snow baby. A cold, winter, round kind of baby. Maybe I could show Greg. "Look, honey!" I'd say. "It's a baby. I made it myself. Do you like it? Do you want to keep it? Can we please bring it inside?"

CORA,

I'm at the restaurant. We're weather-proofing all the windows. We may be short on staff over lunch. Call me when you wake up, okay?

Ian

P.S. I fed the pheasants.

P.P.S. When are you going to marry me????

GREG

Does anyone ever ask me how I feel? What do I want? The boys just ask for more and more and expect me to hand it over. Whatever I have. Like I owe everything to them. Like they deserve it all. If that's what being a father is, my old man read the wrong book.

And I wouldn't mind so much if I felt like they appreciated it. Maybe I want a thank-you. Maybe I want a goddamn medal. Maybe I just want to get some room to breathe. A couple of days of fishing. A chance to sit out on the lake and feel the tug of a fish. To smell the pine trees, to talk about old times with my friends. No rides to school, no job, no weepy woman wanting more than I can give. Just a couple of days would help.

CORA

When I first moved in with Ian, he was always trying to figure me out. Always staring at me. "Eyes are the windows to the soul," he'd say.

"I don't have a soul," I'd answer. "I outgrew mine. It shrunk in the wash."

Back then I was working on a book. My first attempt at fiction. It took up a lot of time and I never really put it away. Even when I wasn't writing, I was trying to figure it all out. When I finally let him read it, he quit asking all the psychiatrist questions, as if I had given him the answers in the chapters of that book, as if the character was me, and everything I wrote was absolutely true. He seemed to think he knew me then.

He stopped pushing to get married, stopped asking about children for a couple of years. For a while, I wondered which woman he was in love with. I invented the one on the page, gave her breath and allowed her to say whatever she wanted, whatever I wasn't able to say. I gave her eyes, windows to her soul. She had a soul. I know, I put it there. I wondered who he was in love with, because I didn't believe it could be me.

Maybe Caitlyn is wondering who loves her too. I sit in my living room as the morning stretches into midday and wonder what I can do. I am the big sister. I used to know how to hold hands and make things better, but now we are both adults, and we have no mother, and all the rules are changed. I know something is wrong, something under the skin.

I should invite her here. I can see the Black Hills from my window. We could talk and tell each other things.

CAITLYN

I'm not going to work. I'm not answering the phone. I'm not counting the snowflakes as they bash against the windowpane and pile up on the metal steps outside the door.

The trailer smells like after-shave. After-shave and stale beer. Greg drinks too much. Lately, the evenings are filled with empty beer bottles and blaring TV, and I could just as well be somewhere else. But I'm not. I'm here in my chair by the window watching winter come. My hands are on my abdomen, trying to feel something growing. The silent hourglass has run out. The baby has grown too big to be ignored. I can't ignore it any longer, but I want to. I want to ignore the telephone; it rings twice and then stops. Twice again in a minute, like my sister Cora used to do when we were still at home, and she wanted me to get the phone. Maybe it's her. Maybe it's an alarm going off in my head and there's no one on the phone at all. No answer if I pick up the receiver. No voice to match my own.

60

ACCIDENTS

I stand here looking in the mirror to see if I look okay. I just threw up again. Washed my face. Brushed my teeth. Flushed the toilet again and again, all the time I'm heaving, in case the boys come home from school and hear me. They don't know I'm pregnant. I stand looking sideways to see if I'm showing yet.

I look at my long red hair, then dig in the drawer for some makeup. Lipstick and a comb. My hands are kind of shaking, but I manage to put lipstick on my lips. I got nice, full lips. And I look pretty, I think for a minute, before I change my mind.

Greg doesn't want to get married. He doesn't want any kids, and he'd rather drop this whole thing. He's fishing in a hole in the ice somewhere in northern Minnesota.

I'm fishing in a hole too. I can't breathe, and I'm crying again. Everything hurts. The bumps, the bruises, the stitches. The broken glass deep in my gut where the fawn is curled up and shaking. Looking at me and shaking like a leaf.

We were bowling. Greg was driving, and he'd had too much to drink again. I love Greg, and I know he can't help it sometimes. When everybody else is drinking, it's so damn hard, and sometimes he goes overboard. He likes to joke around with the guys and kind of forgets how many he's had. But when we're out like that, even when he's drinking, he never forgets about me. Like he has one hand on me all the time. Like I'm important. He puts his arm around me and smiles like he cares.

Anyway, he was driving, and it was late and real dark. I decided to sort of tell him. I said I might want a baby, to see what he'd say. I guess it was my fault. I should have waited until we were home. Until he was sober and in a good mood. I should have seen it coming. I should have kept my mouth shut.

He looked over at me and started to laugh. Not laugh, but sneer or something, not looking back at the road. "Oh Jesus, you gotta be kidding," he says. "Don't tell me I'm back at this again. God damn it, woman!" Then he runs his fingers through his hair. He does that when he's nervous. Probably thinking about his ex-wife. Maybe the time she decided to talk to him about children.

Maybe the time she told him she was pregnant with Daniel or Ryan. He must have looked back at the road just before we hit the deer because I was looking down at my hands, and I heard him swear, and we swerved before we hit it.

Then it was dark and silent, and my head was resting on the dash. I thought maybe I was crying, on account of my cheek was wet. Greg was real quiet. I didn't think about anything, like if he was okay, or if I was okay.

I just wanted to lie there. I didn't even want to move, but a car came up behind us, and some man helped me out of our car. I saw his headlights shining on the doe off to the side of the road. She lifted her head and looked at me. My head and my eyes hurt, but I saw that doe's eyes, and they looked right at me. Then I was sick in the ditch.

The guy wanted to give us a ride to town to the hospital. I looked down at my hands and they were all red. I thought I'd thrown up blood. Maybe I'd hurt my baby. "Kill the deer," I said.

"What?" The man had a kind voice. "What did you say, mam?"

"Kill the deer, please."

He took off his cowboy hat and scratched his head.

"Shit, what a mess," Greg kept saying. He was up now and walking around the car.

"That doe. We can't just leave her here," I said. I was shaking then.

"Oh, for Christ's sake, Caitlyn! That damn thing totaled my car. Give it a rest!"

The man took my arm and led me to his car. "I don't have a gun, mam. But I'll call the highway patrol as soon as we get to town, okay? Sir, would you get in the back seat, and I'll give you both a ride?"

He went back to our car and put the flashers on. I got in the front seat and tried not to touch a thing. Greg passed out in the back.

They put in two stitches and used a butterfly bandage on the rest. It's not much of a scar. If a cut is clean and deep, it doesn't leave much of a scar. It doesn't hurt as much either.

I guess the baby's fine. I need to see a doctor or something. I keep dreaming about the deer, and sometimes she's got this fawn, and the fawn gets in the car with me and rides to the hospital on my lap. Greg keeps trying to throw it out the window, but I hold on, and we keep riding and riding into the dark. In every dream, the doe's alive and looking at me. She can't talk, but I know she's trying to tell me something. I wish she would just die and get it over with.

61

THE SWING

I n 1943, Ray reported to the Oahu Army training school. He was a nineteen-year-old Marine in the 4th Marine Division stationed in Hawaii. Because he had some trade school training in mechanics and the Army was running a month-and-a-half long training session, Ray found himself in Oahu, the only Marine in the school.

After the first week of training, he heard about a buddy of his getting shot up and ending up at Aiea Naval Hospital. Ray walked into his room on his first free afternoon. Fred Parker was bandaged up and lying in bed reading the sports page with the one eye without white gauze over it. Ray's face went white. "Well, Daneli! What the hell you doing here?"

"Ah, I'm getting some mechanics training over at Army. Those amphibious tractors got Allison transmissions in them, and they're always overheating and getting stuck. I'm supposed to learn how to service them in the field." Ray shrugged and tried to smile. "How are you?"

"Hell, I'm fine. As long as they don't decide to bomb this hospital; I'm out of here after this." Fred shifted in his bed. There was a long pause.

"And your eye?"

"Ah, the eye will be fine. Can't say as much for the right knee, though. I guess it got pretty much shot to hell. I'll probably have to walk with a cane, but hell, it beats the alternative, don't it?"

"Yeah. It sure does."

"Hey, I met some cousins of yours. They're nurses on this ward. No shit, from back in Iowa. Two Daneli girls."

"My cousins?"

"Yeah. Sophie and Esther. One of them is tall as you are with these gorgeous legs. The other one, Esther, she gives the orders a lot, but they are your cousins all right. I asked them."

"Well, I'll be damned." Ray hadn't seen those two since they were kids. Fred pushed his call button and a tall, blond nurse came over. "Sophie, you know this soldier?"

Sophie smiled and looked Ray up and down. "Well, Ray Daneli! You've just gotten taller and more handsome. What in the world are you doing here?"

Ray hardly recognized Sophie, but when she started

229

talking, he could hear the Iowa farmland in her voice, in the way she spoke with a casual confidence. She had her hair piled on top of her head, and she was almost as tall as Ray.

"Sophie, I wouldn't have recognized you if Fred hadn't of told me who you were!" He reached out his hand to shake hers and held it in both of his. "It's real nice to see you. How long have you been in Hawaii?"

"Here, let me go call Esther. I'll be back in a minute. She won't believe it."

Ray felt terribly homesick at that moment. He looked at his friend in the bed with bags and tubes of yellow liquid coming out from under the sheets. He looked at the window and the tropical trees outside. The clear blue sky.

"Raymond, hello!" Esther was all business. Her hair was short and dark with straight bangs. Her big brown eyes looked straight at Ray as she shook his hand hard. "I didn't even know you enlisted. How long have you been here?"

"Eleven months. I'm here doing some mechanical training for three more weeks." The three of them stood and talked in quiet voices, as there were many men in beds across the ward trying to rest. Occasionally, a doctor walked by and gave a harsh glance their way.

"I'd better be going," Esther said. "I've got a lot to do."

"Could I take you two out to dinner or something after your shift? It sure would be nice to talk a bit more." Ray looked from one cousin to the other.

Sophie just sighed. "I don't know if that would be a good idea," Esther said. "The doctors here are real strict about us fraternizing with enlisted men. In fact, it's against hospital policy."

"Yeah," Sophie said. "Because they don't want any girls dating anybody but doctors; they want all the nurses to themselves!"

"With the ratio of men to women around here, I can't see that I blame them, but we're family. Don't you think they'd make an exception?"

"I don't know, but I can check it out," Esther said. "Why don't you leave where you're staying with Sophie so we can get a hold of you, and I'll see what I can do."

Esther left then, and Sophie gave Fred his pain medication. She got back to her rounds, and Ray sat in the chair next to Fred's bed, just looking around. As Fred drifted off to sleep, mumbling and tossing under the stiff white sheets, Ray looked at the row of beds on the opposite wall. He felt a strange sense of loss just thinking about home. Thinking about the way main street looked at night when the street lamps came on. Thinking about the cars parked out in front of the cafe. The kids carrying their skates to the roller garden. Sophie and Esther lived in another little town, this one in northern Iowa, but they were family and a close to home feeling washed over him every time they talked.

Sophie and Ray were dancing a slow one at the U.S.O. club. Ray liked the slow dances because they could talk better. He liked hearing about his uncle's farm outside Burgus Springs. The latest letters from home. "Esther is thinking about signing on again. She's head dietician now, you know. I think she likes this service stuff. Me, I don't know. What about you, Ray?"

Ray looked over at Esther, who sat at a nearby table sipping a rum and Coke. "I just plan to do my hitch and go back to trade school. I'd like to own my own garage or auto parts place someday. Right now, I'm guaranteed a job at a local station. It would be a place to start. They do a good business."

Ray had a beer bottle in his hand behind Sophie's back and took a drink over her shoulder. "You got a steady girl, Ray?" Sophie asked.

"No, mam."

"Well, you should. You're a nice guy, even though you did push Esther and me into that muddy old creek after the family picnic. God, and then I got those blood suckers on my legs! I could have shot you!"

Ray laughed. "I guess I owe you an apology for that. We were just little kids, after all. I didn't know better."

"You were fourteen and should have known better, but I'll forgive you if you buy this nurse another screwdriver." Sophie walked over to sit by Esther, and Ray went up to the bar.

The band started up a Glen Miller song and Ray asked Ester to dance. "No thanks, I've been on my feet all day. I'd rather just watch. You two go."

Ray looked at Sophie. "One more?"

Sophie smiled. "I never turn down an offer to swing. Let's go, Ray!" When they got to the dance floor, she whispered in Ray's ear. "She's never off duty, I swear to God. She's head dietician now, and I think she's going for lieutenant the way she's acting!"

Ray just smiled and took Sophie's hand. He'd had several beers and felt pretty good. It was easy to be around these women, no rules, no uncomfortable lapses. They'd grown up together and swam in the creek, looked up at the same Iowa sky, knew the same smell of cut alfalfa and fresh silage.

Later, during another slow dance, Ray spoke into Sophie's ear. "I want to own my own business," he said. "I want to make my own hours and take a day off if I want to and not have cows to milk or corn to plant. I want to make a name for myself." Ray was feeling the numbing sensation from the beer. His muscles relaxed from the dancing. Suddenly, he was aware that someone was tapping on his shoulder, cutting in. He turned to see an officer standing there.

"My dance, soldier," the officer said.

"No, sir, I don't think so, sir." Ray slurred his speech. "You see, this here is my cousin from Burgus Springs, Iowa, and we're having a dance."

"Evening, Dr. Webster," Sophie said in a monotone voice. She turned to Ray. "It's okay, Ray. We'll dance the next one. Why don't you go keep Esther company."

"I'm dancing with you, and that is that." Ray reached for Sophie's hand again, but she hesitated and then pulled it away.

"This isn't a good idea, Ray. Now please sit down."

"Soldier, you're making a jackass of yourself. Why don't you listen to the lady and have a chair."

With one turn, the doctor had Sophie in his arms and was moving away. Ray, in the elapsed moment, made a fist and struck at what he thought was the officer's chin, but it turned out to be empty air. He spun off balance and ended up in Esther's powerful arms; she had come up to get him. "You're damn lucky he didn't see that, Ray; you'd be in the stockade. Now come on, sit down."

"I wanna dance. I wanna dance," Ray said over and over again until he thought of Fred and his shattered knee, until he thought of his unit getting ready to go back into the field, until he thought something like tears would stream from his eyes at any second if he didn't get control and stuff it. He swallowed hard and asked Esther to order a cup of coffee. He went into the bathroom and leaned against the wall, trying to remember how he was supposed to act, trying to remember who he was, trying desperately to remember what a man did if he was strong.

62

THE WONDER HORSE

T he girls took turns in the backyard bouncing on "Flash, the Wonder Horse." Maureen kept an eye on them through the kitchen window while she finished up supper dishes. Cora was seven, too big for the spring toy, but she folded her long legs and bounced on. It was the only horse she would go near. Out at the farm, her parents still had a couple of old mares, but Cora was petrified. Maureen had always loved to ride.

MAUREEN O'MALLEY WAS as tall as most men before she even considered herself a woman. Her maturity snuck up on her; she was more concerned about riding horses and shooting baskets than trying to find a boyfriend for the homecoming dance at Keosauqua High.

Her parents lived on a small farm west of town. Maureen had two brothers, and since no one expected girls to do farm work, she spent much of her time daydreaming down by the creek as the Pinto munched the rich green grass. Her mother could have found mending or cooking for her to do, but she seemed to prefer solitude and rarely asked for Maureen's help. In fact, it seemed to Maureen, her mother resented it when she came around asking for things to do. Ever since she stretched up, she felt out of place, as if there was too much of her and no place to put it.

She got the height from her father. Both brothers were tall and played on the high school basketball team. Girls' basketball was already big in Iowa, but Maureen didn't play. She went out her freshman year and felt awkward and exposed in the uniforms. Red hair, pale skin, freckles. She didn't want people to watch her, so she spent her time in the corn crib back home where her father had rigged up a makeshift basket. When they weren't using the cement crib at harvest time and throughout the long winter, she could practice as long and often as she wished. She liked the feel of the dusty ball in her hands, the scuffed leather as it lifted off of her palms and bounced against the rim before finding its way down through the battered old net. The sound of the ball in the net. The swish.

Maureen shot hoops with her brothers, too. A little game of two on one, but it wasn't as fun as practicing alone with the sun held prisoner between the slats of the crib.

When Maureen walked into the house, all sweaty from shooting baskets, her mother often greeted her. "Maureen Mary O'Malley, when are you going to take an interest in girl things?" Mrs. O'Malley stood with her hands on her hips at the ironing board. She sighed and shook her head. "Yes, you may go riding. But be back by four-thirty. The boys need to be in town at a quarter to six, and you need to help me with the dishes."

Looking down at the sink full of soap and dirty dishes, Maureen felt as if that was all she'd done for the past twenty years.

"GIVE ME A TURN, you little brat, or I'll twist that nose right off your face." Cora stood with her neck out, gritting her teeth at her little sister. Caitlyn sat with her pale little hands clutching the handles on each side of the horse's head. Caitlyn had her mother's complexion and wavy red hair.

"No. My horse."

"Cora, stop that right now! If you can't talk better to your little sister, you can go into the house. Caitlyn, you share with your sister. Your turn's almost over."

Maureen rinsed out the sink and wiped her hands. She got a Coke from the refrigerator and went into the back-yard to supervise. Sitting in the shade in the old folding lawn chair, she felt she had better control of the girls.

"Can I have a pop too, Mom?" Cora squinted into the sun. She was growing up, going to be in third grade in the fall.

"Go get two plastic glasses. I'll share this with you girls."

When she was seventeen, Maureen had thought she was pregnant. She met Harold at a horse show in Ottumwa. Every summer, Maureen and her brothers competed in a couple of Western horse shows just for fun. They could show off the horses and do some trading if Mr. O'Malley wanted to buy or sell a horse or two that year. It turned out Harold was from Eldon, just down the road from Keosauqua. He'd graduated a year earlier and was farming with his dad. Maureen and Harold spent the day together when they weren't riding and went out to a movie that night after the horse show.

After that, and for the rest of the summer, Harold would drive his gray Ford pickup across Country Road 6 and out to Maureen's place to say hello and maybe take her into town to see a softball game.

One evening in late August, the dust followed Harold's pickup into the yard, and Mrs. O'Malley came out, wiping her hands on her apron. She always had a big smile for Harold. Maureen figured it was because she was finally "interested in girl things."

"Where are you children going tonight, Harold? Mrs. O'Malley asked.

"I'm not real sure, mam. I hear there's a softball game. Otherwise, I thought we might see a movie in Ottumwa. If that's okay."

"Certainly. Just have her home by midnight." Mrs. O'Malley smiled and went inside, letting the screen door bounce closed behind her.

When Maureen got in the pickup, she could smell Lava soap and warm, clean cotton. Harold was blond and tan. She liked to hold on to his arm when they walked, to feel the muscles when they moved.

"My parents took a bull up to my uncle's farm. They're staying the night. Some kind of card party, I guess. Want to go over to my place?" Harold kept his eye on the road, as if the question held little weight, but Maureen knew he hadn't asked anyone else the same question before. Living at home had its drawbacks. Harold said one day he'd build his own house on the place, when he got a little money saved.

"Sure." She wanted to know what that white body looked like underneath his Levi's. Sometimes, when it was hot, and he wasn't wearing a shirt, he'd take a breath and she'd glimpse some white skin right around the waist of his jeans. She wanted to see everything.

Later, when she was counting the days on the calendar, she wondered why she'd done it. It wasn't like she loved him or anything. She just wanted to see under those jeans.

She got her period the same week Harold enlisted in the Army. "I need to see a bit before I settle down. Dad doesn't need me yet. Three years from now, I'll be back here to stay." Harold coughed, cleared his throat. "I'll be on that farm forever. I'm going to try to get stationed in Germany. I hear they got excellent beer over there."

"Oh, I'm not pregnant," Maureen said. She hadn't told him she thought she was, but wanted to tell him, anyway.

"Oh, good," he said. "That's good." He slid his arm around her. "You going to wait for me?"

"No," Maureen looked out the windshield of the pickup to the front light of her house. "No, I guess I'm not. You have a good time in the service, Harold. It was nice knowing you." Maureen got out of the pickup and walked up to the house. There was no reason to be kissing him now. She was free again. Her life was starting over.

"Mommy, we're tired of that dumb old horse. Can we run through the sprinkler? Please?" Cora smiled, her pretty white teeth all in a row.

"Sure. Just wear those shorts, I'll get you dry ones after you play." Maureen turned on the faucet and an arc of water shot up across the grass. How could she have known back then that it would be hard for her to get pregnant? That she and Ray would be married five years before Cora was conceived and another five long years before Caitlyn? Her two precious daughters. Her gifts from a mysterious God.

Her infertility problems didn't seem to hurt their marriage much. Yes, they were both disappointed. It was most obvious at times like Halloween, when children would arrive at the door with shining faces, asking for candy, asking for the world. But Maureen and Ray were both silent people. They both worked full time and got lost in the garden or the garage workshop in the evening. When something isn't going quite right, you work harder, work through it. It was the way they were both raised, so they didn't talk about the dissolving hope, the helplessness. And then she got pregnant with Cora. Maureen grew round and content, and her life seemed to take on a deeper meaning.

Ray walked into her room after the delivery. "We have a daughter, Ray. A beautiful little girl." Maureen folded back the baby blanket to show off Cora's face.

"How about that?" Ray's voice was a whisper.

"Would you like to hold her?" Maureen held up the little bundle in front of Ray. He shoved his hands into his front pockets. "Oh, no. Not yet, dear." He paused awkwardly. "I better wait a little."

Maureen laughed. "Okay, Daddy. When you feel ready, you let me know."

Ray was a good father, always finding time for the girls, always making a place in that quiet heart for the things that mattered.

63

THE CRUEL WAR

Cora and Caitlyn Daneli sit on the long wooden dock throwing pebbles into the water. Cora, ten years old, sits near the shore where she can still see the rocky bottom of the lake beneath the pilings of the dock. She does not trust Lake Superior. She does not trust the power of its pull.

Caitlyn is only five and trusts everything. "I bet I can throw two of these rocks in the air and have them land in the same place. Make the same rings in the water, you know, those ripples. Wanna bet?" She looks up, squinting into the sun, her long red hair blowing around her face.

"I bet you could do it a hundred times and they wouldn't land in the same place once." Cora shakes her head.

"I'll show you." Caitlyn goes to gather more small

rocks on the beach, and Cora reaches for her book. She is reading *Pippi Longstocking* and imagining she lives alone in a cave on a tropical island. Pitching pebbles should keep her little sister busy and out of her hair.

There is a warm breeze. Maureen Daneli bangs the screen door of the cabin, a lawn chair in one hand and a magazine in the other. She is wearing shorts over a swimming suit and has on dark sunglasses. Her white legs are long and thin.

"Girls, how are you doing? Shirley and I are going to have some iced tea; do you want anything?" She sets up her lawn chair, puts *Good Housekeeping* on the grass and heads back to the cabin. Cora looks up but doesn't answer.

Soon Shirley walks down from the next cabin carrying her own lawn chair. She is wearing a skirt and nylons with sandals. "Well, girls. Catching any fish?"

Cora looks up. Squints and looks out at Caitlyn to see if there is even a fishing pole on the dock anywhere. She looks back at her book.

Maureen walks up holding two glasses of iced tea. "I told Ray that if he didn't get the car fixed this weekend, we'd have to call a tow truck to come in here and get it, but you know how Ray is with cars. I hope the muffler holds until we get home at least. The thing is starting to sound like a Sherman tank."

Shirley looks serious, looks away at a Sitka spruce in the middle of the small yard. A bird bath sits under it. "Funny to have a bird bath right next to a lake," she says. "Always have thought that was odd."

"Sorry, Shirley. I wasn't using my head." Maureen reaches over and touches Shirley's arm. Cora is paying attention to the conversation, although it looks like she is reading. There is something about the Johnson cabin, Shirley and Garret Johnson, that intrigues her. Her parents use soft voices when they discuss them at night. Every year for five years they have vacationed on the North Shore of Lake Superior, and every year the Johnsons have rented the cabin next to them. They're from Cedar Rapids. Home folks. He runs a hardware store, and she teaches nutrition at the vo-tech. This is the first year Jim isn't around. Fishing and playing beach volleyball with a bunch of kids he's met from up the shore.

"What's the latest news?" Maureen turns the watch on her wrist around and around as she asks the question.

Shirley shrugs, "Nothing out of Washington. He's still MIA."

"Hey, Cora!" Caitlyn shouts. "I got two almost in the same spot. Look!"

"Well, he's in our prayers and so are you," Maureen says quietly.

"Doesn't count," Cora says. "Has to be right on top of the other one. You got two sets of rings."

246

"I worry about Garret," Shirley says. "He can't seem to concentrate anymore. Sits looking at the store's books at night and never even turns the page."

"Cora, look at this jewel!" Caitlyn is standing over her, holding an agate in her palm. She is barefoot and her cut-offs expose her long legs. She is going to be taller than Cora, no question.

"Wow." Cora puts the book down. "May I look at it?"

"Sure." Caitlyn smiles and hands it to Cora.

"Well, I just can't imagine," Maureen says. "I really can't."

"Let's see if we can find some more of these," Cora says. "You go on one side of the dock, and I'll start on the other."

"Okay," Caitlyn's eyes are wide. "Want me to go get a pail to put them in?"

"Sure." Cora looks at the dry rocks near the lake's edge, careful not to get too close to the water.

It is early evening on Sunday, and they are driving through Iowa and heading home. Maureen dozes in the front seat. Cora and Caitlyn are best friends now, out of necessity, due to the proximity of the back seat. Cora is teaching Caitlyn a new song. "The Cruel War is raging. Johnny has to fight. How I want to be with him, from morning till night. I want to be with him, it grieves my heart so, won't you let me go with you…" Cora looks expectantly at Caitlyn.

"No, my love, no," Caitlyn sings in her small voice. Then she looks puzzled. "I forgot the next part."

The car sputters and slows. Finally, Ray steers it off the shoulder near what looks like an old schoolhouse. There are poles for a swing set out back, but no swings.

"Well, how about that," he says quietly, almost to himself, as he tries to start the car again. It moans and dies.

"I told you we should have stopped in town and had them take a look," Maureen says quietly, shaking her head.

"Oh, for Chrissakes, Maureen. I think I know about as much about cars as anybody. Just give me a minute to peek under the hood."

"What's wrong, Dad?" Cora asks.

"Won't know till I take a look. Doesn't sound too serious."

Maureen sniffs and looks out her window.

Ray has his head under the hood for some time. "You women may as well get out; we aren't going anywhere for a while. Maureen, will you hand me that map?"

The girls climb out of the back seat, happy to stretch their legs. "If you see any cars coming, you give me a holler, okay?" Ray says. "I may need a lift into the next town. So that's your job. Being lookouts."

"Can we go explore this place?" Cora asks.

"Sure. You watch your sister. Maureen, we're going to need to get the suitcases out of the back so I can get at the toolbox. Looks like we got a problem with the connection and the brushes. You don't have a rubber band or two on you, do you? How about one of those binders you use for the girl's hair?"

Cora and Caitlyn find an old merry-go-round out behind the building. They give each other rides until they both feel queasy.

Maureen spreads a blanket on the ground, fixes some peanut butter crackers, and slices a few apples. She and the girls nibble at the food as Ray tries the car, and it starts. "All aboard," he says, sounding cheerful. They grab the picnic and push it into the back seat, afraid the car will kill again, so they need to hurry.

Once on the highway, Maureen studies the map. "There might be a station open in Simcoe. We'll get there in about half an hour."

"Oh, no need to stop now. It'll hold until we get home." Ray is confident again, his shoulders square after his success with the rubber bands. He laughs. "See, the problem originally was a short in the starter motor. A couple of bare wires. Your fingernail polish took care of that just fine. I coated the wires to provide insulation, but then the problem was the brush springs lost their tension and were slipping. It should be just fine now."

"Wonderful. It's growing dark and you're trusting the car's mechanical ability to some nail polish and rubber bands."

"Nope. I'm trusting my mechanical ability." Ray looks straight out at the highway. "Twenty-five years," he mutters to himself, shaking his head. "I know about cars."

As late afternoon turns to dusk, the landmarks become more familiar. They pass through town after small town where everything is closed up for the night. Ray drums the steering wheel. "Well, what's going on this week?"

"Not much." Maureen's voice is quiet and distant.

"I'm thinking about getting a new section of fence for behind that garden. What do you think?"

"Fine."

"How are the tomatoes coming along?"

"Fine."

Ray resigns himself to the highway, to the pavement and the dark shoulder. The occasional flash of a pair of eyes in the long grass of the ditch.

As they reach the county line, Cora and Caitlyn are awake, on their knees, looking out the back window at the stars. Caitlyn finds the Big Dipper. "The cruel war is raging," Cora begins.

Caitlyn joins in, confident of the words now. "Johny has to fight. How I want to be with him, from morning till night."

The two girls sing the song over and over again. By the time they reach Grace and can see their house, Maureen is singing too in a soft, reflective voice.

64

BARBIES

"I thought we was all going to play. You let me play that one time before." Caitlyn twirled her long braid around her finger and wrinkled up her face to make herself look mad.

"We were, not we was, you dope. And I never said you could play today, so get out of here." Cora stood up and put her hands on her hips. She was eleven, five years older than her sister. "I'm telling Mom if you don't scram!"

Ellen and Doreen sat on the cement floor arranging their little cardboard boxes and spool furniture for their doll's houses. "Ah, she can stay, Cora." It was Ellen's house. She was an only child. She always gave in. "She can play with my Penny Brite doll."

"But she can't go to prom," Doreen said. "Penny Brite isn't old enough to go to prom." Doreen had a real

Barbie house and a car and twenty-seven outfits. She lived on the other side of Grace, over by the post office and the new golf course. The course wasn't finished yet, and there wasn't much grass, but they were building all the little ponds and bridges and planting trees. Someday she'd live near the country club. Doreen had a swimming pool in her own backyard, but most of the time she rode her bike over to Ellen's or Cora's, and they played Barbies in the cool basement.

Cora didn't like to swim, anyway. "If we're going to play prom, I want the real Ken doll this time."

"It's my Ken. Why should I let you play with it?" Doreen looked at Cora, but Cora ignored her. Doreen continued, "I'm getting pierced ears this week. My mother said I could."

"You're going to let somebody stick a pin through your ear?" Ellen winced.

"It doesn't hurt, silly. They do it real fast and then you have earrings. Mom said I can have real gold ones if I promise not to lose them."

Cora sat back and thought about what it would be like to have pierced ears just like her Barbie doll. Barbie's earrings were little blue dots, but Cora's mom didn't even have pierced ears, so Cora probably couldn't get them either. Besides, she thought, the needle part didn't sound so good. She'd wait and see how Doreen liked them, if they got all infected and made her ears turn purple or something. "Well, if I have to pretend I have a date for prom again, I don't want to play. I'm tired of getting her all dressed up to go to a dumb old dance where I pretend she has a partner."

Ellen sniffed. "I suppose they could have a picnic in the backyard."

"Hey, what about a swimming pool?" Caitlyn approached the group cautiously after standing back and listening. "We could dig a hole in the backyard and fill it with water, and then they could go to the pool and swim and have a picnic."

The three older girls looked at each other. Finally, Cora shrugged. "That might be fun. Might be boring, though."

"I don't think we could dig a hole in my backyard," Ellen said. "My mom wouldn't like it."

"Well, we could ask our dad," Cora said. "He's working in the garage."

"I'll bet we could dig back by the garden under that tree. I bet he wouldn't care." Caitlyn's voice was excited now. She was happiest when she was planning some new activity.

Ray Daneli was at the workbench, taking apart a carburetor. He smiled when the girls came in and wiped the sweat from his brow with the sleeve of his chambray shirt. There were large blue circles under his arms. "So, how are my girls today?"

"We want a swimming pool, Dad," Caitlyn said. She leaned her chin on the bench and looked up with big green eyes.

Ray laughed. "Oh yeah? Should we put in a guest house too, while we're at it?"

Cora rolled her eyes. "No. A little one. For our Barbies. I'd dig it myself out by the big tree where nothing is growing anyway, and I won't make a mess, and I'll put the shovel back."

"Now just how big of a pool are we talking here?"

"Just big enough, sir," Doreen said. "A kidney-shaped one like ours would be fun."

"Well, you take that spade out there and see what you can do. I need to put this thing back together, and then I'll help you out if you need it."

The girls all shook with excitement. They took a spade out around the garage to the shade of the old red maple. The Barbies were in their bathing suits, and Ken wore his terry-cloth robe, since he would be the lifeguard.

AN HOUR LATER, long after the girls had given up on digging in the hard soil and gone in for Kool-Aid and chocolate chip cookies, Ray wiped his forehead on his bandana and stood over the girls resting in the shade of the maple. "So, you want a swimming pool, do you?"

"Yes, sir." Doreen played with a strand of her long hair.

"I tried to dig it, Dad, but that shovel isn't any good." Cora stood up and walked over to the spot where they had tried to break up the dirt.

"Cora wouldn't even let me try, Daddy. I bet I could have done it." Caitlyn put her hands on her hips and returned the face Cora was making at her behind her father's back.

"Well, let's just see what we can do here." Within half-an-hour Ray had dug a kidney-shaped pool about three feet long, two feet wide and a foot deep. The girls were busy smoothing the sides so that no roots or lumps stuck out. It was hot, and each of them had dirt smeared across their faces. Ray was mixing up cement in a wheel-barrow when Maureen walked out to put a basket of laundry on the clothesline.

"Hey, Mom, look what Dad made for us! A Barbie swimming pool." Caitlyn jumped up and down. "It's going to be a real one with cement and fish and every-thing." Maureen walked up and looked at the hole, then at Ray.

All the girls' eyes were on her. They lay on their stomachs, their hands in the hole, patting against the sides. "Well, will you look at that?" She smiled. "Looks like your father has another talent I wasn't even aware of. You want a cool drink, Ray?"

"Nah, I'm fine. Almost done here."

The Barbies sat in a row in their bathing suits, stiff, thin legs before them and the girls sitting behind them, as Ray smoothed the cement up over the edge and formed a thick lip to the pool. "Now you need to leave this alone until tomorrow. By then, it should be okay to put water in it."

Once the pool was completed, the girls headed back to Ellen's basement to plan the next day's activities. "I'll have my mom take me to Woolworth's to get a couple of goldfish for the pool," Doreen said.

"I'll ask my mom if I can have some old washcloths to cut up for beach towels," Ellen said.

"We can make beach balls and a table and lawn chairs for by the pool," Caitlyn said.

"Out of what?" Cora asked.

"I don't know."

"You have to have an idea before you volunteer such a dumb thing." Cora said.

"Your guys' dad made the pool, that's enough," Ellen said. "I think that's enough."

"We'll think of something." Cora glared at Caitlyn. "Or I will. See you tomorrow."

For days, the girls sat around the small pool, tanning the plastic legs of their dolls, watching the small fish dart through the water. To cool themselves, they dipped their hands into the pool and splashed it up on their faces and smoothed it over their foreheads like holy water. They talked about Barbie and Ken and starting back to school in the fall. How Doreen's mother was going to have an operation and had to quit smoking. How it made her grouchy. They planned a sleepover in the backyard in Daneli's tent the weekend of the Fourth of July. Then they could watch the fireworks together.

Eventually, the water in the pool got too warm, and the fish died. Caitlyn found them belly up and buried them in a matchbox behind the peony bushes. The water grew dank, and mosquitoes swarmed around it. The girls weren't interested in scooping the stagnant water out and putting in new. By that time, the game had changed to something else. Barbie and her friends were skiing in Switzerland. As the summer passed, the pool dried up and then filled with rain. Birds took baths in it, squirrels drank from it, but mostly everyone just forgot that it was there.

65

THUNDER

I was eleven the night we sat laughing inside that pup tent, telling stories and waving the flashlight around on the green canvas ceiling. Outside, the sky pulsed with silent flashes of light. The sort of lightning one sees on a hot Iowa evening. There was no thunder, no real threat of rain. The tent was in the yard behind my grandparents' old white farmhouse. A small garden with leaning hollyhocks and painted daisies separated our tent from the farmyard.

"I ate six apples once." Jake sat on top of his sleeping bag.

"At one time?" Caitlyn was wide-eyed. She's my little sister and was six at the time. Easily misled.

"Liar, liar, pants on fire." I pulled my gum out of my mouth and stretched it until it broke in two.

"Did too, ask Grandma." Jake squinted his eyes and

nodded toward the house. He had a butch haircut and a farmer tan from his baseball cap. Jake's my cousin and six months older. "It was right here in this yard. The apples were off that tree by the windmill. You just ask her. She knows it's true."

"Hope you got sicker than a dog." I smiled and popped the gum back into my mouth. Jake and I were in love with being mean.

"Mom says you ain't supposed to have gum in bed, Cora." Caitlyn sat with her thick red hair pulled back into a ponytail with one hand. "You know what happened that one time."

"Shut up, squirt, or you can just go into the house where babies belong. If you want to sleep out here, you better stop acting like such a little tattletale." I blew a bubble and looked mean.

"Well, I ate 'em. All six of them. I didn't get no stomachache neither. Well, not a bad one anyway. Bet you couldn't do it."

"Bet I wouldn't be so D-U-M-B," I said.

There was a low rumbling sound off in the distance. "Hear that?" Jake asked. "Thunder. Means it's going to rain like hell. We're going to get soaking wet."

"Oh, shut up." I unzipped the tent, tossed my gum, and had a quick look around. "Doesn't look like rain to me. And if you can't take a little rain, you better go inside with baby Caitlyn."

"You ain't supposed to swear, Jake," Caitlyn ignored my put down. One problem at a time.

"Rain don't bother me. You guys will probably be in the house before midnight. Girls can't handle rain, and the dark, and stuff like that."

"What do you know about girls?" I asked. "You got a girlfriend? You like girls, Jake?"

"Not a chance. But I've got three sisters, and they're all wimps just like you guys." Jake took off his canvas tennis shoes and started pulling out the laces.

"Seems to me we're sleeping in this tent too," I said. "I'd even make a bet about who will chicken out and go inside tonight. We'll stay, won't we, Cate?"

Caitlyn nodded. "I'm not afraid." She paused. "Well, not much, that's for sure."

"What's that sound?" Jake asked. "I wonder if they caught that prisoner who escaped from the penitentiary last month. Some said he was heading this way."

"Real funny, dumb boy," I said. We climbed into our sleeping bags. It was getting a little cooler, but it was more for protection than anything else. Crickets chirped outside against the silence. "Is there really a bad guy out there?" Caitlyn asked.

"No, dummy," I said. "Jake is trying to scare us into the house. Don't worry about it. And you better shut up, Jake Anderson, or I'm going to tell Grandma and Grandpa you scared the pee out of Caitlyn."

"Ah, they won't do nothing." Jake slapped a mosquito. He was the first grandchild and could do no wrong.

"Then I'll beat the crap out of you, so leave her alone!" I laid down on my pillow. "I'm hungry. Any popcorn left?"

Jake handed me the paper bag. "What was that?" he asked.

"Jake, I said knock it off." I ate some popcorn. Caitlyn pulled the covers over her head.

"No, I mean it! I mean, I think I heard something this time." Jake was whispering now.

I stopped chewing long enough to listen. Not like I believed him or anything, but then I heard it too. A snorting sound, and bumping and moving gravel, like someone was stumbling up the driveway.

We sat up and instinctively reached for each other's hands, trying to identify the sounds coming from outside the tent. The dragging gravel and snorting sounds grew louder. We could hear cows out by the barn bellowing and carrying on, but the new sound was close and getting closer. "Let's get the hell out of here," I whispered.

"No, I don't think we can. I mean... I think it's between us and the house." Jake leaned toward the zipper to look outside. My hands quietly searched for the flash-light. Caitlyn started to cry.

"It's okay, Cate. We're safe in here, don't worry. We'll get to the house, won't we, Jake?"

Jake pulled his head back in just as a loud bellow came from outside the tent, over near the dog house about fifty feet away. "Shit!" Jake turned to us. "You guys, it's a bull. It bumped into the doghouse. His head was down and he ran right into it!"

"Shut up," I whispered. The bull was sniffing, standing still. We could hear its heavy breathing. The cows continued to bellow out by the barn. We sat still and tried hard not to breathe.

"I want Grandma," Caitlyn cried in a soft, terrified voice. I touched my fingertips to her lips and put my arm around her. The bull answered the cows. His angry bellows seemed even closer.

"Jake, do you think we can get out and run around the house the other way?"

"Bulls chase people," Jake said. "They're really fast." By this time, all three of us were crying softly, trying not to make noise.

We heard the screen door from the house slam shut and then our grandfather's voice. "All right, you old son-of-a-bitch! What are you doing in my yard?" The sound of his voice comforted us immediately, and we peeked out of the tent. Grandpa, in his underwear and T-shirt, stood holding a gun. The bull stopped and turned toward the sound. "Don't move, kids," he shouted. "It's going to be all right, but you got to sit real still and be quiet. Do not move."

A pickup truck pulled into the driveway and slid to a quick stop near the front of the house. A man jumped out and pulled a pitchfork out of the bed of the truck. The bull started to move toward Grandpa, but Grandpa darted out of the way. "God damn devil!" he shouted. The man got closer to the bull, stuck his pitchfork out, and started jabbing at him.

"Sorry, Joe. I don't know how he got out." The man shook his head. "Move over, you crazy bastard, get home." The bull was bellowing and foaming at the mouth.

"Let's try to get him out into the barnyard area." Grandpa stood with his gun in one hand and a broom he'd picked up next to the steps in the other. "I got three grandkids in that tent over there."

"Jesus Christ!" the man said. "We can try it, but if he's gotta go down, he's gotta go down."

Caitlyn and Jake and I stared out at the wild, muscled beast. He had foam dripping from his huge mouth, and he pawed at the ground.

Suddenly, Grandma appeared from the other side of the house, barefoot, in her robe, her gray hair in long braids. She ran straight to the tent. "Come on, kids. Hold my hand and run." We circled around the back of the house. I stopped on the front step and glanced over at the bull just as it smashed into the front fender of the man's red pickup. The metal folded in like paper. Grandpa handed his gun to the man, and he raised it to his shoulder and pulled the trigger before I could look away.

The bull sank to its knees and landed with a labored sound on the gravel next to the truck. It lay there, twenty feet from the front steps of the house. Grandma grabbed my wrist and gently pulled me inside. "Come on, dear, that's not for you to see."

"What happened, Grandma? What was wrong with that bull?" I looked into the living room. Caitlyn sat on the sofa. She was pale and still shaking, but she'd stopped crying. Jake stood there with his hands in the pockets of his jeans, looking out the living room window.

Grandma pulled the shades. She was a large woman and winded from our run. "He's the neighbor's Angus bull, and he's blind. Must have got out and gone kind of crazy when he heard our cows. Looks like he'd bumped in to some things on the way over here, and I think it made him mad." She sighed. "Are you kids all right?" She hugged each one of us and then looked us each straight in the eyes, holding each head in her soft, plump hands, as if the answer were held in our eyes. "Well, praise God you weren't hurt."

"What was that sound?" Caitlyn asked.

"A gun," Jake said. "They shot it. Geez, was that thing ever big!"

"Is the bull dead?" Caitlyn looked at Grandma, then at me. I felt sick to my stomach and looked away. Grandma sighed again.

"Yes, dear. I think it was in a lot of pain. Now it ain't. How about if we do something fun to take our minds off of it? I can't think anyone is going to sleep for a while."

"Like what?" Jake asked.

"I've got some apples in the kitchen that would make a wonderful pie. We could peel them and bake one up. I even have ice cream. Do you suppose you could eat something that sweet this late at night?"

"I think I could," Caitlyn said earnestly.

"Great." Jake smiled at me. The adventure was continuing.

"Grandma, did Jake really eat six apples once?" I asked.

"As far as I can figure, he did, and he was sick for the whole weekend, but apple pie won't make you sick. Let's go to the kitchen and get started."

We sat around the gray Formica table watching Grandma peel the bright green apples. The circular fluorescent light hummed above us. Flies and moths bounced against the outside of the screens. We heard Grandpa still out in the yard talking with the neighbor. The scent of cinnamon and apples and coffee filled the kitchen.

"Grandma, what would have happened if you hadn't

heard that bull and Grandpa wouldn't have come out to help us?" I ate a long, twisted peel from the tart fruit.

Grandma paused for a moment, holding the paring knife away from the apple and titling her head slightly. "Then you probably would have saved yourselves and run around the house the way we did."

"How come?" I frowned. "I mean, we were afraid to do that and thought he'd chase us, and what if he'd of come over to our tent?"

"Well," Grandma wiped her forehead with the back of her hand, sighed, and began peeling again. "I don't think that was a possibility. You would have made the right choice if you'd been forced to. The human will works hard to survive. I think we was meant to make this pie tonight. It was the bull whose luck run out."

Now, years later, whenever I eat warm apple pie, I remember the process of that evening: peeling and slicing the apples, rolling out the crust, adding the cinnamon and sugar, then waiting in the warm summer kitchen. I remember more than a feeling of nostalgia, of an adventure turned brown at the edges like an old sepia photograph, more than the death of that bull. I remember how it felt, and how it tasted, and how it was to be alive.

66

ROSES

The snow was deep and a pale blue under the full moon. I sat behind Danny on his Arctic Cat and hugged him through his snowmobile suit. The air smelled like engine exhaust and love. Three other machines trailed behind us as we rode the ditches out past the sale barn, over Milson Creek and south toward Pigeon Falls.

It was Friday night. I was fifteen. Danny and I were back together. Everything was possible. It was easier to get the snowmobile than the car, and the snow was deep that winter. Perfect conditions. Most weekends we rode together like a pack, racing around, stopping at the bowling alley for something to eat, or going to one of our houses if the folks were gone. That night we rode about ten miles, found a drift over a barbed wire fence, and turned into a field. Danny stopped by a shelterbelt and the other three snowmobiles formed a half-circle, the noses all pointing to the middle.

I pulled off my helmet and shook out my long hair. The air was still. When everyone turned off their machines to talk, it was so still it felt as if we were in some kind of vacuum; steamy breath, moon shadows, and crisp stars in the cold sky.

"Where too?" Danny was the ring-leader. His father owned a snowmobile and boat sales business on the edge of town. Nate and Susan rode on one of his other snow machines because neither of them had one. Joel and Doreen each had their own Scorpions.

Joel pulled the woolen ski mask up over his blond hair. "Let's ride awhile. Maybe look for an old abandoned farm. I helped myself to a pint of whiskey from my old man's cabinet. We could check it out."

Doreen kicked snow up at him with the toe of her boot. "Nice idea, but where's the Coke to go with it? And I suppose you want me to drink out of the bottle." She smiled her coy little smile. The one that was so rehearsed. The one she'd grown up practicing.

Danny shrugged, started his motor up, and spun around. I leaned far to the right with him, out over the seat, feeling the rush of speed as we straightened out. Then I pulled the helmet down over my blowing hair.

Twenty or thirty minutes later, Joel led us into a long driveway lined with old pine trees. A small dark farm house and two dingy old barns stood on the property. One barn leaned to the right. It looked like it would tip over if you gave it a shove. We stopped in the driveway by the door of the house. Everybody got off and stretched, stiff from the long ride.

There was an old green Chevy parked near the garage with a flat tire. A case of beer bottles set near the house. It looked like someone lived there. Joel opened the front door and walked in, shouting as he went. "It's open, come on."

Doreen followed behind him, then Nate and Susan and Danny. I hesitated until Danny turned and reached out his hand. "Come on, Cora. Let's check it out."

Inside the front door, Joel turned on a light in a small, warm kitchen. We all stood in the middle of the linoleum like a half dozen space men in their fat suits and helmets. Coffee pot on the stove. Potted plants on the windowsill. Slippers over near the door.

"Hey someone does live here," Doreen said. "Someone with super bad taste." She looked at the starched doilies on the kitchen table and small knick-knacks made of pipe cleaners and sequins stuck to the refrigerator.

Joel picked up a piece of paper from the counter and read out loud. "Water flowers good the tenth. Lock up when leaving. Back on the fourteenth. Thanks Carol and Murl."

"Hey, what's today? The twelfth? We got ourselves a place to party!"

Everyone shrugged and started unzipping the heavy suits, hesitating only when someone else did. I stopped short. "This is nuts. There is no way I am staying here in someone else's house. Are you guys crazy?"

"Probably," Joel smiled. "Sorry, you want to wait outside? Come in when you want to warm up."

"Very funny, Joel." I looked over at my best friend. Susan shrugged.

"We could just sit here inside the door. We'd see a car if it drove in, and we could say we just stopped to use the telephone. We just got here or something." Her voice dropped off at the end.

Danny came up behind me. "Ah, it won't do no harm. We won't hurt anything. Let's just warm up, okay? Finish that bottle and head back into town."

Everyone else nodded and slipped out of the arms of their suits, sitting down on the floor. Their boots left water and mud all over the place.

Before long, Nate and Susan and Danny were watching television on a huge old black and white set in the living room. I wiped up the kitchen floor with an old towel. I heard Joel and Doreen laughing from somewhere in the back of the house. They'd found a bedroom. They always found the bedroom. I'd known Doreen since we were both four years old, and she'd always acted years older. She always took giant steps and left me asking "Captain May I?" In grade school and junior high, I even thought she was the captain.

I stood there in stocking feet with my hand on the doorframe and looked into the small, square dining room. The wallpaper was old and faded, an off yellow color with black sketches of horses and carriages and umbrellas running across it. I noticed a built-in buffet, and that's when I saw the roses.

I guess I was curious. I knew I shouldn't be in the house, but I thought I was in love with the boy in the other room watching T.V. I was naïve enough to think that being with him was worth it. That he'd take care of things. He was a man. I didn't have to make decisions. I could just go along for the ride. I walked over and looked at the wilted flowers. Eight roses in a cut crystal vase. A card on the table next to it read, "More than ever, darling," in small, careful cursive.

My eyes blurred. I put on my snowmobile suit and hurried outside. The air was crisp and felt light. It was the first time I remember that I figured every family was not just like mine. All feelings weren't slow running water on the bottom of a frozen creek bed. All unpleasant events did not reverberate in the silence of the room until they dissipated and went to hide in their own corners.

Danny and I had been together off and on for over a year. I never told him anything. We talked about basketball games and the top forty songs of the week. Things like that. The roses inside that old farmhouse were not from the movies or a romantic advertisement for perfume; someone gave them to someone else without fanfare because they wanted to, like each flower was some kind of unspoken promise.

I sighed and took a deep breath. I knew how to file things away into my nice little dark box. That's one thing I had learned all right. Keep things neat and tidy. Safe. Deep breath. In and out. "Sentimental crap," I said out loud as the door opened and closed behind me.

"What?" Danny walked over to me, but I turned away. "Nothing."

"Cora, are you mad because we're here?"

"Sort of. And where'd Nate get that beer I saw in his hand? We going to steal and trespass?"

"You want to go? We'll go." Danny walked over to the snowmobile and sat down.

I followed him, stood in front of the skis and wiped a tear from my cheek with the back of my mitten. Trying to act cool. "Do your parents like each other? I mean, do they act like they like each other?"

"Yeah, sometimes. Most of the time, I guess." Danny paused. "Don't yours?"

"Do they kiss in front of you? Do they ever go out?"

"Ma doesn't like to go out as much as Dad does. I

mean, he'd go to every Hawkeye football and basketball game if he could. But the farm... you know. He's busy."

"Do they fight?"

"I don't know. Sometimes. Talk, yell, you know, like everybody does."

"My parents have never raised their voices in front of me. Ever." I kicked the snow.

Danny sat quietly for a minute. "What's so bad about that?"

I could feel inside my stomach that it was bad, that something was very wrong, that it had always been wrong. "When I was eleven years old, a firecracker blew up in my hand. There was blood everywhere. Dad drove me to the doctor. He told me he loved me three times that day. Once in the car on the way, once when the nurses were bandaging my hand and once when he tucked Caitlyn and me into bed that night. At bed time he told Caitlyn he loved her too. I don't remember him saying it to me since."

Danny sat there in front of me in the odd light from the full moon. He sat and listened. "I mean, I know he does. And I know he loves my mom and my sister. But it's like ..."

Nate and Susan came out the door of the house, pulling on mittens and zipping up coats. "We got to get going," Nate said. "I hollered at Joel and Doreen, but I don't know if they're coming."

Susan walked up to me. "Are you okay?"

I shrugged.

She smiled. "I'm hungry. Let's go get some food."

"I'd better get the sex monkeys. I'm not sure we should leave them here. I'll be right back." Danny went inside and returned in about five minutes with Joel and Doreen.

"Danny, lock the door behind you, would you?" I hollered as they closed the door.

Doreen got pregnant when we were juniors and moved to Iowa City to finish high school and live with an aunt and uncle. Joel ran his snowmobile through the ice on Pigeon Lake the following spring and had to be fished out by the fire department. His Scorpion is probably still on the bottom of that lake, a jumbled mess of rusted metal. Danny and I dated until the middle of our senior year. Nate and Susan remain friends, and I get a card from her once or twice a year from Madison, Wisconsin. Nate is somewhere in Colorado practicing medicine.

I could say none of it is important. An old farmhouse, some dead roses, a couple of stolen bottles of beer. A night when I was young and the moon and adventure seemed to be enough. But now, looking back, I understand that it was important. That each piece of the puzzle makes the picture clearer. I mean, I asked Danny to lock the door, didn't I?

67

PAINT

When I came home from Europe late that summer, Dad was painting the house. He picked me up at the Greyhound station and we made small talk on the way home. I was tan. I looked healthy, he said. How was the food over there? He had paint speckled across his Levi's and canvas tennis shoes. Pale yellow paint. White primer.

I kept my voice steady. No emotion. I'd been practicing for three weeks. I'd been sitting on a beach on Crete practicing my English. Some days, I wandered around important archaeological sites and let the sun bake the poison out of me. As if there were germs. As if I was contagious. Some days, I made up stories about my trip through Europe. I wove them in between the actual events and the ones I no longer allowed to exist. I was my own tour guide. I was holding the hand of the lost.

"We've been painting the house about a week now. Got a string of rainy days and the business has kept me busy, but it's coming along."

Dad pulled into our driveway, and I saw my home with a tourist's eyes. Black pavement. Oak tree spreading cool shade. They had scraped the paint off of the house where I'd grown up, and it was patched with white and yellow paint like a calico cat. Tears rolled down my cheeks as the pickup stopped.

Mom stood on the step, wiping her hands on a white cotton dish towel. My little sister, Caitlyn, walked out the door seconds later, waving. Dad looked over as he took the pickup out of gear. "You okay, honey?"

I put on a practiced smile and took a deep breath. "Just happy to be home, Dad." I wiped the tears from my face with the back of my hand and opened the pickup door. Mom felt thin across the shoulders when we hugged. Older. Her hair had a little more gray, but it smelled the same.

"Welcome home, Cora." Mom was crying too.

Caitlyn walked up slowly, awkwardly, with her arms out. "Hi, Sis. Welcome back."

I wondered if they could feel it in me as we hugged. If they could tell my bones were softer, my shoulders less certain. I wondered if they could feel my heart beating in my throat, the enormous lump I could not swallow. After several months of traveling around Europe, I was home. I had seen a world foreign to central Iowa. I witnessed both beauty and deceit. I felt the violent blows of evil.

"God, you've got some muscles there," Caitlyn said. She seemed taller than when I left, my head at her shoulder.

"You still growing?" I asked.

"Nah, these are high-heeled tennis shoes." Cate smiled. "Let me get that bag. I even cleaned all my clothes out of the closet in your room."

OVER THE NEXT FEW DAYS, I practiced walking through the house without looking over my shoulder. I took food out of the refrigerator whenever I wanted and filled my glass with water a second time. I took long baths, washed all my clothes, and put my backpack up in the attic. After three days, I was ready to help paint.

Dad stood on a ladder next to mine. We worked toward the middle, painting even strokes of pale yellow across the old wooden boards. Yellow and white. Green grass. The only blue was in the sky.

I stopped hearing water slap against the side of the boat — except at night, when I couldn't sort out sleep from fitful tossing and turning. Sometimes I dreamed about it, sometimes I played back the sickening tape again and again to see if I could have done anything differently. I told myself what I needed to hear.

Dad looked at the brush and kept painting. "We enjoyed your cards and letters. What place did you like the best?"

I tried to remember my trip, the time before I got on the yacht with an American friend, three Italian men, and her. Alessandra. I tried to recall the streets of Paris, the port in Copenhagen, but nothing came to mind. It was as if the book had been burned, and I could only remember the flames. Could only see the ashes and curled pages where a story used to be.

"It was all so different," I said. "I don't know where to start."

"Would you do it again?" Dad asked later, after a long pause. "Go, I mean."

"Yes," I said. "Since I was a child, I've always wanted to see Greece." Tears gave me away again. They were one thing I could not stop by practicing. I casually wiped my cheek with my T-shirt sleeve.

Dad stopped painting, his brush poised on the board for a long time. Finally, he looked directly at me. "If you ever want to talk about it, I mean, about anything, you know your mother and I are here."

"Thanks," I said, because no other words would come.

When I was in grade school, I was a historian. I read Greek mythology and daydreamed about the aqua Aegean Sea. I practiced sailing boats using sheets on the clothesline and jump ropes to steer us across rough water.

I studied Ancient Civilizations in high school, studied literature in college, and planned my adventure for years. Nothing could keep me in the flat predictability of Iowa once I was grown. I left after Christmas, after graduation from college, and arrived in the gray softness of a Stockholm winter.

The country I left was not the country I came back to. Now Caitlyn was headed to college, to start that journey of her own. In two days, I would be the only one at home with my mother and father and their ritualized, separate lives.

There was nothing in Grace, Iowa for me. I walked downtown one evening, the day cooling and smelling of cut grass. The local restaurant was open, and I walked in. Red carpet. Velvet swirled wallpaper. The smell of alcohol. I stood in the doorway of the place where my family had eaten breakfast on Sunday mornings for years. I saw the pool tables in the back room, the cigarette machines, the telephone.

I saw furniture bolted to the floor of a boat, a radio for emergencies, round portholes opening to a dark, watery night. I saw three men on a boat with three young women who had no choice and no power. I saw two of the women's faces, but Alessandra, the Italian woman's, was turned away. She ran in the opposite direction, as if there was any place on the boat to go. As if she had any say at all about what happened to her body. As if there were any rules. She kept running and screaming, and I followed her with my eyes.

All the way back to my parents' house, she ran ahead of me, darting behind trees, dodging through the lazy traffic of main street. She pounded on the door of my parents' home with two fists. She stood outside the pale-yellow house screaming something in Italian I could not understand. She was trying to escape, but she was still on the boat. Not yet a panicked face under the surface of a wicked sea. Not yet a sick feeling in the pit of my stomach which would turn to stone and then become a part of me. A part of me as I sat in the foreign city of Athens in some white-walled taverna, trying to make sense of being alive. Trying to figure out what was supposed to happen next.

So, Alessandra had found her way back to Iowa with me. She appeared in the shadows, in a glimpse of mahogany furniture, in the smell of stale cigarettes and wine. She exploded in my stomach and screamed through my arms and legs at every breath. She stood at the door of my parents' home pounding as if to save herself.

I stood there pounding with her. Pounding on the door of the freshly painted yellow house in Iowa where I grew up surrounded by safety, where I never knew that such things could happen to young women, that such things could happen to me.

When I saw my mother at the window and that awful shocked look on her face, the glass between us took on the qualities of water, and I knew that I would never be able to swim. She was drowning, or I was drowning, and no one, no one, could save us.

68

POW-WOW

Everything was falling apart. Falling off the trees. Red and yellow leaves drifting to the ground and giving up. Life in the Black Hills grew serious in the fall. Animals dug holes and made nests for sleeping through the long white winter. Birds told each other off and flew away for warmer trees near the scent of the sea.

Cora tightened the straps on her backpack and checked the front pocket to be sure she had her wallet and Sandy's number. It was time for a vacation. Just packing a small pack brought back the memories of hitch-hiking around Europe after college that summer that changed her life, and she became acquainted with the world outside of Iowa. A world she sometimes wished she'd never seen. Living in the soft hills of South Dakota, she felt at home. But it was October, and Ian was busy with the restaurant.

She needed to loosen the kinks out of her life. She needed to get away for a few days.

He would feed the young pheasants and make sure they had fresh water. They were going to let them go after she got back. Already they left the door open for part of the afternoon, but they all came back for the food and the warmth of the coop when night fell. They would take the fence down and close up the coop, encouraging the brave ones to make a go for it. They would still offer the food, but by the middle of the winter, most of the pheasants would have scattered over the hills and found cover elsewhere. By spring, they would forget the feeling of domesticity and fly off with a strange wild need pulsing inside their hearts.

Ian encouraged her to go. "Take a book along and your camera. Tell me all about it when you get back," he said. "You deserve to get away."

You need to grieve for your mother's death is probably what he meant. You need to have some time to think and figure out how to live the rest of your life. Ian was good at giving space. Otherwise, their relationship never would have made it.

Cora drove to a pow-wow at Red Scaffold on the Cheyenne River Reservation. Sandy White Cloud had spent the summer in Rapid City working for the tourist trade, selling jewelry and moccasins. She was a vegetarian and ate at the restaurant a lot. She and Cora became friends. "You got to see a real pow-wow sometime. Not like the ones at the Civic Center, but outside under the stars. You come and see me. I'll show you a good time."

When the postcard came in late September, inviting her again, Cora decided to go. The thought of traveling alone frightened her, but it was time to work past that, she thought. Time to move on.

She drove the old pickup north on I90 out of town and toward Sturgis and Vale, and then east to Faith. "From there, the roads turn to gravel and gumbo," Sandy said. "Gumbo is like a mixture of mud, clay, and quick sand when it's wet. Just hope it's not raining. Call me, and I'll come and get you. Show you the way to the third world."

Cora stood in the Amoco station drinking a Coke when Sandy walked in. She was smiling, her hands pulled up inside the sleeves of a big Harvard sweatshirt. Her long black hair hung out beneath a Twins' cap. "Cora. How was your trip?"

"It's nice to get out of the truck. I've never been to this part of South Dakota. It's pretty."

"If you like brown grass and rolling hills. Not many pine trees."

"I get enough of those at home."

"Come on, my family's waiting to meet you. It's about thirty miles. The roads are pretty good."

Following the dust of Sandy's Blazer out of town, Cora drove up and down hills, past an old trailer house with three junked cars in the yard. At first it looked abandoned, but then she saw some kids chasing a skinny dog and a couple of boys playing catch. The further from Faith they drove, the more she saw old houses and trailers scattered along the countryside. The sun was just disappearing when they reached the top of a hill that overlooked a little village. There was a white church, a brick building that looked like it could be the school, and some trailers. Three rows of small prefab houses branched off from the road out past the church. Most of the houses were painted bright blue. One white. One brown. In the other direction, back behind the school, were some older buildings in need of paint. Dirt yards and skinny dogs everywhere. People's heads turned as they saw Cora's truck pass. She began to feel uneasy. A foreigner once again.

They parked in front of one of the blue houses. Three bikes lay on their sides on the dirt in the front. A dog barked and then stretched, arching its back. "Come on in." Sandy opened Cora's door.

Once inside the living room, Cora's eyes adjusted to the light from the TV. An older man and woman and two kids sat on the sofa. A woman came in out of the kitchen. She smiled like Sandy. "Ma, this is Cora from Rapid. Cora this is my ma, Adel White Cloud."

"Nice to meet you."

"Nice to meet you," Cora said. "Thank you for your

hospitality. I've never been to a pow-wow outside of Rapid City."

Adel nodded, still smiling. She turned to Sandy and said something in Lakota. "Ma wants to know if you'd like some coffee."

"Yes, thank you. That would be nice."

They spent the evening in polite conversation. Sandy's grandparents watched television along with some brothers and sisters and cousins. It wasn't clear how everyone was related, but at about seven-thirty, Sandy's daughter, Lillian, woke up. She was two-and-a-half. She sat on her mother's lap and stared at Cora, two fingers in her mouth. Large almond eyes studied the visitor.

About eleven o'clock, several people filed into each bedroom, and Cora rolled her sleeping bag out on the sofa. A full moon illuminated the furniture and shadowed the room. A picture of an old native man holding a baby hung on one wall. Next to it was a shelf displaying two small trophies, each with a basketball player extending the ball to the hoop. On the wall going to one bedroom was a poster of Janet Jackson in black leather. Above the television, an oil painting of an eagle hung next to a dream catcher.

Filled with renewed contentment, Cora sighed. She had forgotten how traveling could soothe her. It awakened her senses and reminded her of the incredible diversity in the world. She was about a hundred and fifteen miles from Rapid City in the middle of another time.

Cora thought of Sandy, still living with her mother, now a mother herself. She thought of her own mother. What would Maureen think of this place? Would it frighten her? Would the difference in cultures be a barrier too big to cross? Maureen had always talked about going to Ireland. One day, she would pack her bags and do it. But it was too late. Now she was gone, and she never left the United States. She saw the West Coast twice, but never made it to the East Coast. Cora closed her eyes and hoped the night would be without dreams.

The pow-wow began the next day at noon. The household rose early, and Cora smelled coffee before she opened her eyes. The sun pushed in the kitchen windows and heated the small rooms. Three young children, all in shorts and bare feet, stood before her, giggling. Her heart jumped for a moment, thinking she was in another part of her life, on another beach, again a foreigner. But in the time it took to catch a breath, she remembered where she was, who she was. She was safe, and it was okay to smile back. "Morning," she said in a weak, sleepy voice.

"They don't see many wasi'chu," Sandy said. She held Lillian on her hip. "White people," she added as an afterthought. "Except on the TV. Lots of your folks on the TV." She raised her eyebrows and smiled an impish smile.

"Cut it out, Sandy," Cora said. "I haven't had my coffee yet."

"Well, come on. We got some right here. I even made some muffins."

The site for the pow-wow was a large circle in the middle of a flat plain on the edge of the town. A permanent wooden structure formed a fence on the outer edge of the space and had a small three-foot awning over it to provide shade. It was a warm seventy-five degrees. Some elders already had their lawn chairs set up in the shade and were sitting talking among themselves. Cora scanned the crowd. There was one white man over by a pickup truck. She was the only white woman.

"Is it okay?" she said. "I mean, that I'm here?"

"Sure."

Several tents stood set up on the periphery, and some people were tailgating. Tarps and blankets stretched out over campsites for a scrap of shade. An old bus from Wounded Knee sold pop and popcorn; a small trailer offered Indian tacos and iced tea. Campfires and the smell of coffee and bacon filled the air. Some fancy dancers were putting on their costumes. Children ran around laughing. It was like the first day of the county fair.

Sandy was going to dance. She slipped a white buckskin dress over her shorts and t-shirt. The bead work was all blue, white and yellow. She braided her hair and put on long beaded earrings like she had sold in Rapid City over the summer. "You look like royalty." Cora reached into her pack for a thermos of water. "Am I in the company of royal blood or what?"

Sandy looked a bit embarrassed, almost pleased by the compliment. "You want to watch over there while I dance? The Grand Entry will start pretty soon."

"I'll find a spot. Don't worry about me."

"You hungry? Pete's Indian tacos are the best. That yellow tent over there by the Bronco. I won't eat until after the first dance and the giveaway."

"Okay. Thanks for the tip. I think I'll find a spot in the shade and sit down with a taco. It's getting hot."

Cora slid down against a post, resting her fry bread on her knee as she slid her backpack off of her other shoulder. An older man with white braids came with a green folding lawn chair and put it down close to her. He nodded as he sat down.

"Hello." Cora smiled and finished her food.

After a few minutes, the man looked at her. "This is your first time to a traditional pow-wow. You will learn many things."

"Yes, I'm looking forward to it. I live in Rapid City, and I've been to a few pow-wows there, but Sandy, my friend Sandy White Cloud, says this is different." Cora paused, not certain of the proper etiquette.

The man held out his hand. "I'm Floyd Iron Horse. Nice to meet you."

"Cora Daneli. Nice to meet you."

"I knew you were coming," the older man said, shifting in his chair. "I knew two days ago."

Cora thought he was related to Sandy, or the news of her visit had spread quickly, but he continued. "You're having a difficult time with your life. Letting go of those who have passed and reaching out to ones left behind."

Cora's face was flushed, her throat dry. "Did Sandy tell you that?" She took a drink from the thermos.

"No one told me. Some things you can know by paying attention to the earth."

Cora was silent, not sure what to say next.

"I am not a medicine man," Floyd continued, "but I study ways of medicine and healing and try to help people. It is what I have done all my life. I never went to the white man's school. I learned your tongue from my children and grandchildren. It still makes my mouth thick to speak it."

Cora was out of her element now, truly without a foothold. She sat politely by and sipped at the water in her thermos.

"You want a Coke?" Floyd said, reaching into the small cooler beside him.

"No, thank you."

"I would like you to have one. It is the Indian way to share when we come to celebrate at a pow-wow."

"Okay." Cora smiled. She took the cold can and held it between her hands.

"Your visit was meant to be. You were not sure if you wanted to come, but the power of earth was stronger and you came." Floyd took a drink from his soda and put on a pair of sunglasses from his front shirt pocket.

What a bunch of malarkey Cora thought. Does this guy hit on all tourists or what? Maybe he should be in Rapid City in the summer.

"Rapid City is not where your problems lie. That is your sanctuary. Your safe place," Floyd said, as if picking up on her thoughts. "Your problems are at your birth home where your mother left you, and everyone else went into themselves like turtles into shells. And you still hold storms inside of you from some place much farther away. Some country not your own."

Cora looked up at the stranger telling her these things. Things even Sandy didn't know. "Who are you?" she asked.

"Just an old man who can read what is written on your face. On the grass before your feet. On the backs of the grasshoppers as they dance their dance."

"Why are you saying all this?"

"Because you want to hear it. You've been listening for

a long time, but you don't trust your ears. You must call on your strength to reunite with your people. Your family. The man who shares your life." Floyd looked out at the dancers, drums began, and the Grand Entry proceeded. "We Oglala know about reuniting. We have been doing it for hundreds of years. Since the spirits were shot through with your people's guns. Since we forgot who we were."

Two young men stood in the middle of the circle near a center pole holding some dried sage in a small bundle between them. The older man of the two, probably in his late twenties, asked someone for a lighter, and the bundle was started on fire. It soon began smoldering, and he gestured in the four directions as he spoke in Lakota. The younger man was being honored.

Cora's stomach fluttered, and she looked away.

"I do not tell you this to make you sad and weak. I tell you so that your strength can come back, so that you can remember who you are."

Several women brought bags and baskets of blankets and handmade star quilts into the circle. They spread them out on the yellowed grass along with some bowls and cooking utensils. They presented gifts from the host family of the man being honored to people from various families.

Suddenly, the drums started again, and the singers joined in with an honor song. The beautiful earthy songs sounded as if they had been there all along and were only echoes coming back around.

About fifty dancers began curling around the grassy arena, bells shaking at their ankles and the hems of their skirts. They entered one by one, solemnly, slowly. The singers joined in with the drumbeat, sending shivers along Cora's arms and down her legs. She watched Sandy dance, saw the look of reverence and pride in her face, watched the light touch of her moccasins on the worn dirt of the circle.

The dancing continued throughout the afternoon and evening. In the ninety-five-degree heat, men, women and children danced on. Some dancers wore long buckskin robes or trousers with layers of beads or feathers over the top of them. Some dancers wore jeans. Occasionally, a dancer incorporated a brightly colored bandana or scarf into the costume. One woman wore her feather in a sun visor. It was a constant, charming mix between the present and the past.

In the early evening, Cora saw some little kids break-dancing in the grass near the edge of the dancing circle. Dancing to the insistent drum beat. Dancing with one foot in each world.

And later that night, listening to the drums and laughter of people visiting and dancing, Cora sat with Sandy and looked up at the Dakota sky. It was a vast

bowl of stars, a circular glimpse at the heavens and everything beyond.

69

NO OTHER TOOLS

Ray was good with his hands. A mechanic most of his life, he knew how to use his hands like tools when no other tools could reach the problem, when no other tools would do. Even in the hospital, he sat looking out over the hills at the Grace Country Club, and he thought of the sink dripping in the bathroom next to his bed. He told the nurse he could fix it; all he needed was a couple of wrenches and maybe a new seal. He couldn't tell until he took a look. Probably didn't even need a seal. Could probably fix it with one wrench. A couple of minutes. That's all it would take.

He looked out toward the manicured greens. People were golfing in cardigans and sweatshirts. It was getting colder. He never did try out that golfing stuff. He always thought it looked kind of silly. A waste of time. Maureen used to say that people who golfed didn't have anything better to do than walk around trying to wear out those silly shoes.

Maureen would be disappointed in him. Still in this small-town doctor trap and nothing wrong with him. She should have gone to the doctor. She was the one with the sick heart and they never even knew it. Maybe he should have known; maybe he should have done something, like tell her to get a check-up. People were supposed to get check-ups every year at her age. He should have seen it coming. Should have been able to tell by her color or something.

Ray knew that it was not his fault. The doctors and pretty therapists told him that day after day. Afternoon, Ray. How are we feeling today, Ray? Are we ready to talk about something new?

The night Maureen died was still a black spot. The funeral happened, they told him, but he couldn't go. Maureen was his wife for forty years and he was too sick to tell her goodbye. They never used the word "sick." They said he was tired. Even his two daughters, back to take care of all the details, told him he needed to rest and then he will be able to go home.

All he wanted to do was sleep. Sleep or fix that damn faucet. Drip. Drip. No one thought he could do anything. That was clear.

70

PHANTOM PAIN

So, you walk to the door of the Greyhound bus station and see your little sister standing there next to the cigarette machine, looking lost. She is pale and taller than you remember, yet you saw her only a few months ago at your mother's funeral. Caitlyn's come to visit you for the first time. Traveled across South Dakota on a bus. She isn't good at giving answers to unasked questions, and you aren't any good at asking. You're both adults now. You push the glass door open and walk inside to meet her.

She looks up, startled. "Cora. Hi." There's a smile. It looks like she's happy to see you, relieved that you've shown up and saved her from waiting alone in the terminal. Happy to be here at last. But the smile also looks pained, as if her head hurts or something deep in her bones won't stop throbbing.

"Welcome to the Black Hills," you say before giving her a hug, and you mean it. You put your sun-browned arms around her big shoulders and hug the same way you did back in Iowa when you both buried your mother. "My pickup is out front. Come on." You lift up her suitcase and notice how light it is. How like Caitlyn to underestimate her needs. "I've taken the next few days off so we can look around. I can show you the Hills. Ian's at the cafe. I thought we'd stop in there. Tell him hello and maybe have some lunch. Have you eaten?"

"No." Caitlyn looks out the window, away from you. This is not what you expected. Being the big sister, you thought the hug would melt any difficulty, a little cheerful talk and things would be okay. You're used to holding hands and making promises. You're thirty-five, five years older than this woman in the cab of your truck who called crying in the middle of the night and asked if you would like some company. The sister who felt like a part of yourself growing up, a limb, a right arm maybe. An echo in the predictable beating of your heart. You turn the corner and pull up to the cafe. It's mid-afternoon and there are half-a dozen cars.

"Ian's been looking forward to seeing you." You pull the keys out of the ignition and turn to Caitlyn. "And so have I. I'm glad you came."

The cafe is small and well-worn. Everything oak and pine. Everything a part of the forest. Plants grow on the windowsills. Large windows line the walls by the green upholstered booths, each one like a small room, the backrests extending almost to the ceiling. Ian stands, smiling, with a towel in his hand. He's been your lover since you came to Rapid City over a decade ago. The year you fell off the edge of the world. "Caitlyn, damn, it's good to see you." He gives her a big hug, less cautious than yours, more greeting than consolation. He spreads his arms wide. "Welcome to the Black Hills. What do you think?"

"I like what I've seen so far." Caitlyn's smile reminds you to be less serious. Like those old mood rings when you were a kid, she responds to the surrounding warmth. Ian makes people smile.

"We've got some killer eggplant lasagna left. You two have lunch?"

"That would be great, hon," you say. You and Ian run the cafe together.

You've made a life of this place. Healthy food, healthy air, and a good man. You feel proud to be standing there, showing off your life for Caitlyn.

After a while, when the talk turns more relaxed, you eat the hot food and talk about your father. "I think he's holding up pretty well, considering," you say. "Have you talked to him on the phone lately?"

"I wrote to him this week." Caitlyn's hands shake when she reaches for her glass of iced tea. You want to wait until the two of you are home to have this serious talk, so you talk about your father instead, about the hospital, and how he expects to get home soon. How the doctors say he was just run-down. Needed a mental vacation. Needed to work through the loss.

Caitlyn folds and refolds her napkin. Smiles that camera smile. Nervous and polite. Too polite for your sister. "I took three days' vacation. I could have waited until Thanksgiving, but with the weekend, it isn't so bad. I didn't mind the bus much."

"How's Greg? The boys?"

Caitlyn shrugs. "Okay. I don't know."

A woman with three kids comes in. Two walking and one in a stroller. She tells you hello and gets a small table over by the window. The girls crawl under the table and giggle. The woman unzips the baby's snowsuit and kicks the last bit of snow off the stroller's tires. "Girls, get up here this minute or we're heading home." Her voice is steady and calm. She pulls off her parka and rolls her eyes, smiles at you and Caitlyn as you look her way. "Cora, just be happy we come in before the dinner rush."

You laugh and tell her she's welcomed any time. You put a bite of lasagna to your mouth and notice a tear running down Caitlyn's face. "How about we go out to the house," you say. "I'm eager to show you around."

Later, you sit in the living room of the house you and

Ian and a bunch of friends built by hand. The room is long and has a vaulted ceiling. All the wood is rough and exposed. Wool rugs cover the floors and a red Navajo blanket hangs behind the couch. The outside wall is all windows and a sliding door out to the yard. You sip coffee and brandy and look out at the snow. A spotlight angles off into the pines, and it's as if a stage is set and you are both waiting for the actors to appear. You pull your feet away from the warmth of the fire and curl them beneath you.

Caitlyn's eyes are clear now. She seems relaxed. Her long fingers curl around a big mug. "I'm pregnant," she says. Her face shows no emotion. You pull in your breath and lean forward. Put your cup on the table in front of you. Look across the firelight into her face.

"Pregnant? Caitlyn, congratulations. I mean... are you happy? Did you want this?"

She forces a smile. "Time to make up my mind, huh? I mean about if I'm happy or not. And if I'm... shit."

You sigh. Collect yourself and shift gears. You've always been the trouble shooter. Your instinct is to try to solve the problem logically. Your emotions submerge until it is safe to surface again. You choose your questions carefully. "And what about Greg?"

"I haven't told him yet. Three-and-a-half months go by. I throw up every morning; I'm always tired, and he sees nothing. I try to bring up maybe having kids, and he yells at me. Tells me I'm trying to trap him."

"Trap him?"

"Yeah, you know. Make him marry me. He says he already done that once, and the two boys are weight enough for that chain. Says it right with Ryan and Daniel in the next room watching TV. Then he goes out and gets drunk and doesn't come home."

"Is his drinking getting worse?"

"It's not getting better." Caitlyn smiles now. "I feel like bad luck following trouble sometimes, you know?" She pauses a minute and looks out the window. You wait for her to continue. "You were always the smart one," she says. "The one who could figure out what to do next. I just hoped sooner or later I'd get it right."

"It seems to me there are lots of things to talk about. I mean the pregnancy, of course, but also the whole thing with Greg. If he's still drinking so heavily…"

"I love him, Cora. I don't know why, but I can't imagine not waking up next to him in the morning."

There is a long pause, and you listen to the logs crackling in the fireplace. The smell of burning cedar mixes with the liquor and coffee. You sip the drink and wait her out.

"I love him, but it hurts to be with him sometimes. I don't think he loves me as much. Maybe he likes beer and TV basketball more. Like I'm convenient, you know?

Then I think maybe I'm crazy to stay around. Some nights when he's real bitchy from drinking and he's telling me all I did wrong that day, I sort of get out of my body and sit up in the corner of the room and watch him yell. Like my body doesn't even belong to me. I just look right through him... I don't love him then."

You begin to feel something strange within yourself as your sister tells you this story. You feel sand falling away, slipping back into the blackness and then more and more, like a silent landslide. You feel as if your defenses are dangerously low. You get up and get another cup of hot coffee. Skip the brandy this time. "And how do you feel about this baby?"

"I called Mom. She knew about it. I called her the day she died."

You feel great sadness hearing your mother talked about as if she were alive. Hearing that she knew about this baby months ago. You feel a little left out and empty. "What did she say?" you ask, your throat thick with pain.

"She cried. She was happy and said she wanted a grandchild. She didn't get time to tell Dad because I hadn't decided if I was going to keep it."

"Have you decided now?"

"What, abortion? Fat chance of it. You ever try to find somebody to talk to about it? I mean South Dakota. Shit, I don't think there's a doctor in the state that does it anymore. Guess I waited too long to make that choice."

Caitlyn wiped her eyes. "When I heard she had a heart attack, I thought maybe I had something to do with ..."

"No. Not a chance. Heart attacks don't just come out of the air from one piece of exciting news, Cate. The problem builds in the heart for years and years. You had nothing to do with Mom's death."

"I can't trust Greg. I mean, I can't when he drinks." Caitlyn looked away.

You hear the word trust, and you know you're going to talk. You see out across a great expanse of water, that familiar horizon of blue meeting blue, and you start to feel the heave of the waves. "I'm not the one to give advice about trust, Cate. I'm not very good at that myself."

Caitlyn looks over at you, studies you and sits quietly. After a time, she asks, "Why didn't you ever marry Ian? He wants to, doesn't he? Don't you ever want kids?"

You smile. Those questions must have been simmering awhile. Caitlyn has never asked you about marriage or children before. "I haven't married Ian because I like the way things are. It's hard for me to even think about it."

"What about kids?"

You feel dangerously exposed. On roller-skates. A gradual hill. Bend the knees. "I've never told you. There's something I've never told you." Already your voice begins to betray you; your eyes well up with tears.

It is amazing how much power the memory still has over you. "That year that I went to Europe, my life changed. When I came home, I was someone else. I am someone else."

"Something bad?"

"Yes." You run out ahead of the conversation and try to figure out what parts to tell, what to leave out. You edit again and again in the silent gap that follows, but none of it makes much sense.

"That summer I met Nancy in England, and we were traveling together. In Italy, we met this guy when we were hitchhiking. He picked us up in a fancy car and told us he was a professor at the University. He invited us on this trip a bunch of students were taking from the school and from a college in the States. Three yachts and a bunch of college kids, he said. A free trip. He told us two of the students were from Luther College, in Decorah. I mean, he even knew the name of the college in Iowa. Anyway, he said two of them were homesick and went back early. They had these two spots and we could have them."

"You know how I hate the water. I was petrified, but Nancy was so persuasive and so beautiful and so smart. I wanted to be her. I wanted a glamorous life. I'd seen a bit of Europe and was almost embarrassed to be from Iowa. I knew nothing about art or history or fine food. I said yes, I'd go."

Caitlyn nervously twists a long strand of her red hair and leans back in the overstuffed chair. You start editing again. "It's a long story, but when we got on the yacht, we were supposed to meet the two other boats at the end of the harbor. There was one other woman and three men. And then the story was that we were supposed to meet them in Naples. We were near Rome." You look out at the snow, think the white drifts look almost like waves. You see shadows in the trees and think they are moving.

"There were no other boats, Cate." You can't keep the tears back now.

You think maybe this is inappropriate. Caitlyn's the one with the problem. She came to you and here you are. It all comes back in violent, salty blows. You will never have a baby. You will hold scars in the place where others begin life.

Caitlyn moves over to the sofa next to you. "Oh, God, Cora." She cries and wraps her arms around you. "Why didn't you tell me? Oh, God." She strokes your hair and you feel like a child. Thunderstorms rage in your head; you are afraid of the noisy dark.

"I'm doing the best I can," you say.

The fire dies down, and the two of you sit waiting for words. "Did you ever tell Mom?" Caitlyn finally asks.

"No. I stayed home that fall when you left for college, but it didn't work. I felt like I didn't belong anywhere. That's when I packed up the old car and headed out west.

When I ended up here. I met Ian right away, but it took a long time for me to let him be my friend."

"Did you ever, you know, talk to anybody?"

"You mean a counselor or something?"

"Yeah."

"No. I mean, I talked to my doctor here. A couple of years later, when Ian and I moved in together. I found out... I found out I couldn't have kids." You try to say it lightly, without too much investment, but it comes out the way it feels to you. Your voice withers and dries up.

"Oh, shit!" Caitlyn says. She is scowling and is shaking. It surprises you and takes you off guard.

"Cate, I don't mean, I didn't tell you this to make you feel... oh, God, I'm sorry I said anything. I'm so sorry." You put your hand over your mouth to try to stop the emotion. It's too late.

"No. It's all right." Cate says. "Don't you see? I'm mad as hell at those men. This isn't about me or about my baby. It's about you. My sister. And I never knew. It helps me to understand why I lost you when I left home. It isn't fair."

You hold each other until your shoulders stop the silent shaking. Until you feel more relaxed. "It was your tone of voice, that desperate sound that brought it all back, Cate. Not that you're having a baby. It was when you said you didn't trust Greg and then you asked me about kids. I don't know. It's still hard. It feels like they say amputees feel. You know, that they can still feel their fingers, or their leg itches when they have no leg? It still hurts so much sometimes."

"Did Nancy..."

"Yes."

"Did you go to the police over there?"

"No. There was more to it. I don't want to talk about it."

"Okay." Caitlyn is quick to agree. "I'm sorry I made you feel bad."

"No, sis. Those men made me feel bad. You just asked a simple question. Sometimes those are the hardest ones."

THE SUN TURNS the snow a blue-gray as it rises. Ian came home hours ago and slipped quietly upstairs into bed. He knows about space and the importance of long, patient talks. You doze off, leaning against Caitlyn. She shivers and wakes you up. "I'm frozen. We need more wood on the fire."

"I'll get it. Let's pull out this sofa," you say. "You need to get some sleep."

"No. I'm starved." Caitlyn smiles.

"Okay, I'll make some scrambled eggs and toast. Good protein, huh?"

"Sounds good. And maybe some orange juice and bacon? You got any bacon?"

"We're vegetarians, sorry. But I could whip up some great blueberry pancakes to go with the eggs."

"Now you're talking," she says.

You look at her green eyes and see something like hope again. You feel that familiar echo in your heart, the one that belongs to her.

71

IAN

When I was almost fifteen, my brother and I watched our house burn down in the middle of the night. My father, a Unitarian Minister, was over at Boston General comforting the family of an old friend. Mother stood in the dewy grass in her blue chenille bathroom and bare feet, and held each of us by the hand, as if we were still three and five years old. We let her do this, because it was comforting, and because it was dark, and no one would have seen us anyway.

After an hour of watching the huge hoses spray water on the tunnel of fire, we sat down on the bench at the bus stop across the street. By that time, neighbors were out and offering to take us in, placing cotton blankets over our laps, bringing hot tea and cool hands trying to comfort.

When Dad drove up, there wasn't much left. Lights circled the yard, bounced off the old oak trees that now stood alone on the lot, surrounding a skeleton of black, jagged timbers and half-walls. Everything smelled of burned plastic and chemicals.

I don't remember crying. And I don't think Mother or Martin cried either. Perhaps it was the shock. Perhaps we thought the others were trying to set an example. When Dad pulled up in his VW wagon, his face was white in the swirling lights. Mom screamed to him right away and a police officer brought him over to us. I saw the tears on his cheeks, and I knew he was crying out of joy to find us alive.

We salvaged an old tin-lined trunk of photographs from the basement and whatever was stored in the detached garage. Sporting equipment and tools. The rest was gone.

At fifteen, the world was a difficult enough place. I was living in a hotel with my family, wearing strange new clothes, trying to recall each thing in my bedroom so that we could claim it on all the insurance forms and try to get it replaced.

Martin, my younger brother, found it all even harder. In his mind, nothing could be replaced. His life was gone, stolen in a single evening, and it was as if he searched in dark corners for a hint of who he was now. What could he possibly be without those things he called his own, those things which defined a thirteen-year-old? His sloppy old tennis shoes and worn jeans told him who he was. He couldn't sleep at night and started taking long walks and showing up late at school. He seemed to need an incredible amount of freedom just when our parents felt like suffocating us with love, because they felt so lucky to still have us. Their caution was their way of coping.

My family always talked about our problems. Since Dad was a minister, we had grown up being honest and open about what concerns we had. We saw a therapist for a time to help with grieving the loss of our home and belongings, but after Martin was first arrested for shoplifting, he refused to go, and it all fell apart.

My parents were beside themselves. Their rational minds told them to endure, that the world was a good place, that Martin was going through a grieving process all his own, that we just needed to support him. And they were right. But I was fifteen; I saw the shadows growing under his eyes. I saw the monster climb onto his back and throw his balance off; I knew that the fight was his alone.

I hung around the hotel more than I used to. Martin liked to play pool and foosball. We spent afternoons in the lobby shooting pool and not talking. His hair got longer. His face broke out. His hands started shaking. I figured he was doing drugs, but I didn't know what kind, or what to do about it, so I concentrated on the eight ball in the corner pocket. I kept my ears open and my mouth shut.

Eventually, he came around. He started to talk, and it seemed like he didn't stop for about three months. Then it was spring, and the carpenters were rebuilding our house. Martin and I got to plan our bedrooms: where we wanted the closet and the door; what kind of carpeting we wanted; how big a window we should have. I got my license, and he and I drove to Barlow Square to shop for furniture. Mom and Dad relaxed and things slowly got back to normal. Like a change in the seasons, I couldn't put my finger on the turning point, what made him decide to join the family again, to join up with his old life and go on, but I do know we played a lot of pool in the meantime, and I listened to all that he would tell me and most of what he couldn't.

I found out then how easy it is to turn a corner. How easy to slip and never make it. Martin was on the edge, and somehow, he got the space he needed to turn around. That's what I try to give to Cora. She still has nightmares and wakes up wanting something I cannot give her. She wants me to tell her it was just a dream, that none of it happened, but I can't. All I can do is love her and let her know I'll keep loving her. I am good at being patient. I'll play pool and keep my mouth shut. I don't want to lose her.

72

TELEPHONE CALL

No, we're not going to make it to Dad's for Christmas. Things got a little tied up here. What? No, nothing big. I just... Well, I can't come, that's all.

Cora, sometimes I think I'm getting the hang of it. Like I'm figuring things out, and I can tell what I should do next. And then some damn thing or other happens, and I'm back to square one. Sitting here with a fat body, and dirty dishes, and Cheerios all over the floor.

The boys are spending a week with their mother. Having some quality time for the holidays.

Greg's probably out trying to figure out how to get me out of his life. I just mention kids, and he loses it. I mean, I haven't even told him I'm pregnant. I mean, Jesus. How many times have we made love, and he doesn't notice the extra fifteen pounds? I know he touched my stomach. I remember expecting him to say something.

No, he's not wasted every night. I mean, he has a couple of drinks after dinner, for sure. Well, you know, it hasn't been that great lately for us. I figured it was my hormones or something. I mean, he's usually pretty fast to roll over and go to sleep and we aren't talking all that much, but... it's not like that. It's not fair to make him out to be just some drunk or something. I'm just pissed. First, we had this car accident and then —

Well, we hit this deer last night, and now Greg's been gone since early this morning, and he's lucky the state patrol wasn't there because he'd be spending some time in jail drying out. Anyway, I don't know when he'll be back.

He doesn't want a kid. I don't think he even wants me anymore. So, what do I do now?

Thanks for the offer, but I can't just pick up and move out. I don't know. I mean, you hardly know Greg. Last time you were in Sioux Falls, I'd just moved in with him. You walked around the trailer like it was a museum or something. Like it was some kind of strange place to live. Almost like you were above it.

No, I'm not blaming you. It seemed that way, that's all. Ever since you started writing, you seem to be taking notes.

Okay. Okay, you don't. I'm wrong. Anyway, Greg doesn't want this baby. I don't even know if I do.

What do you mean? What do I mean? Isn't it clear? Yeah, sure. I screwed up and should have aborted it before when I could. Well, what then? What should I have done? Okay, shit. I'm sorry. I just don't know what the hell to do anymore. I can't do anything right for anybody. Maybe what I need is to just go have a long chat with Mom and call the whole thing off. I mean, just check out. No. No. Of course, I don't mean it.

Look, I know I never finished college. I don't have all the answers like you do. I'm angry because I'm drowning and don't have a goddamn clue about how to swim! Don't you understand?

God, I'm sorry, Cora. I'm just scared. I've been scared for a long time. I know. I know. No, I'm not coming. Greg leaves the day after Christmas for his fishing trip. I want to stay here and figure out what to do. Alone. I'll be all right. I just need some time.

No, isn't your fault. You're just the big sister. It's what big sisters do. He's going to be gone a week. I'll call you. I'll let you know what I've decided.

Yes. Yes. I'll make an appointment for a check-up. Yeah. I'll put it on my list.

Tell Daddy hello. I'll call Christmas day, okay? I won't. I won't. I will. All right. I promise.

Day One

Caitlyn called about three o'clock and said she wasn't coming. I'd been expecting her all afternoon. I flew into Sioux City last night and rented a car. Dad was waiting up for me, standing at the picture window in his white T-shirt, holding a cup of coffee. This time, Mom wasn't standing next to him; she wasn't sitting in the rocking chair by the fireplace reading her Good Housekeeping. Christmas seemed like some kind of trial by fire one needed to just get through. And now, Caitlyn wasn't even coming.

Ian flew to Boston to be with his family. He might stop a few days on the way back out. It depends how things are going at the restaurant. It depends on how long I stay here.

Dad seems the same. Maybe a little quieter. More nervous. I think we both are. He's tried so hard: cleaning my old room and Caitlyn's, placing fresh sheets and a stack of towels at the end of the bed just like Mom used to do. And now Caitlyn's going to stay home. She sounded so, so dramatic. I don't think she's serious. I can't run her life for her. She hasn't even told Dad about the baby yet. I suppose she thinks that's my job too.

Thursday

Cora got here about eleven-thirty last night. She was driving a '92 Ford Escort that she rented at the airport in Sioux City. I was a little worried about the roads, but kept telling myself she's a big girl now. Lives in another state and has another life, I said to myself. She gets along fine on her own now.

I guess Caitlyn isn't coming. She must be too busy at work or something. I was looking forward to all of us being together. Well, you know what I mean. I still have to do my Christmas shopping for Caitlyn. Maybe Cora will help me tomorrow; she knows more about that stuff. I never had much trouble thinking of things Cora would like. I don't know why. Maybe she never did like the gifts and just didn't complain about what I got her. Maybe. Maureen did most of the shopping when they were growing up, but I always tried to get each of my three girls something special just from me. Something that let them know I knew who they were. I knew what kinds of things they would like. Maureen used to like to wear those pins you put on your lapel. Those little jeweled things. She had a jewelry box special for all those little glittery things I bought each Christmas. I don't think she ever wore them much, but I know they meant a lot to her.

Day Two

Dad bought a fake silvery Christmas tree for the living room. "Is it all right?" he said, as if I held all the answers, as if I knew what to do.

"It's fine, Dad. Do you know where the decorations are?"

We spent the morning awkwardly placing red satin balls and lights on the little four-foot tree.

"What do you think Caitlyn could use?" he asked. "I haven't picked out her gift yet. I thought maybe you could go with me. I... I haven't seen much of her and I don't know..."

"Sure Dad," I said. "I can help." I couldn't decide if I should tell him or not, but when we were wandering around Vogel's department store, looking at sweaters and coffee-makers, I took his arm and walked down the aisle to the baby department. I put my hand on the first stroller I saw. "This," I said. "This is something Caitlyn could use." I was matter-of-fact. This wasn't my job, and I wasn't about to try diplomacy when she didn't have the guts to use any herself.

"Caitlyn?" Dad said. "But ..."

"Yeah, I know. She hasn't told many people, but she should have told you.

"Is that why she's not coming? Does she think I —"

"I don't know, Dad. I don't pretend to know what she thinks or why she's staying in Sioux Falls alone. Maybe she needs time to think."

"Well," Dad picked up the nearest boxed stroller, strength and determination replacing the anxious look of insecurity. "Well then, we need to get this to the post office and get it mailed, so she has it for Christmas. Come on, they'll be closing soon." I smiled, took his arm and followed him to the check-out register.

Friday

I'm going to be a grandfather. I should probably call her up. I don't know how to be a grandfather. What if I'm not good at it? Maureen would know what to say on the phone. She'd have the right words. Sometimes I think my brain is shorting out. Like I could be getting that damn Alzheimer's stuff. Then what the hell would I do? There's nobody here to… I don't want to be dependent. I didn't live my life to end up a burden on somebody.

Maybe I should call her up. Tell her it's okay. Tell her she's welcomed here. Ask her if she wouldn't want to come home. Maybe just for the weekend. There's still time.

Day Three

Ian called. He and his brother just got back from playing racquetball. Martin's taking a job in Seattle the first of the year. They've talked about driving a U-Haul cross-country together. Martin would stay with us for a few days and then go on to Seattle. He starts work on the fifteenth.

They're drinking cider and playing poker. Ian says his mother's winning. Jesus. The Norman Rockwell normalcy is overwhelming. I spent the morning throwing old Avon cosmetics out of the medicine cabinet. Touching bottles of perfume to my wrists, holding them to my face and closing my eyes. Trying to get close to the dead.

Christmas Eve

I tried to get Caitlyn's present there on time but they can't guarantee next day mail the day before Christmas Eve; the guy at the desk said it had to be there by noon to be guaranteed. I guess I can't guarantee anything. I could tell Cora thought I was getting upset. She worries about me going over the edge again. Her nutso dad, so I shut up. It doesn't pay to explain myself. There's nothing to say that will clear things up.

I had just taken my medication and sat down in the Lazy-Boy in the living room when the music started. "Silent Night" right outside the picture window.

"Is that music?" Cora walked into the room holding a dish towel and a glass of wine.

"Carolers," I said. Probably from Divine Redeemer Lutheran Church two blocks down. I'd heard from Madeline Heart they were going out this year. She's a neighbor two doors down. She stopped by with some cookies last week. Asked if I was going to be home for the holidays. Where would I go? I joked. We both laughed, but neither of us sounded convincing. She's been alone for almost twenty years now. I turned on the outside light and looked out the picture window. Seven or eight bundled up neighbors sang and waved. Madeline was in the back row and gave me a smile and a nod.

Cora came over and stood next to me, her arm touching mine. They sang "Joy to the World" and "We Wish You a Merry Christmas" and then trudged through the snow to Tobersons. We stood at the window until the telephone rang. It was Caitlyn wishing us a Merry Christmas.

Day Four

I gave Dad his present after scrambled eggs and muffins. It was a llama's wool cardigan sweater from Colombia. I bought it at an International Market they have every year at the Civic Center. Dad always talked about his time in the service when he was stationed in Hawaii. I got the impression he would have liked to have traveled more if he could have afforded it, so every year I gave him something unusual or exotic.

Sitting on the airplane, I held up the sweater and thought it looked too small, but it fit. Dad seems to have grown smaller. Now it is the house that seems almost large.

Christmas

I get the feeling Cora won't be staying long. She's begun to pace around the house, refolding Afghans and straightening towels on the rack. She never could sit still. We've had a nice time though, I think. It's been wonderful to have someone in the house, to hear human activity and not notice each time the refrigerator kicks into the defrosting cycle.

My first Christmas without Maureen. The first time my family has not all been together. And what of next year? How do I get Caitlyn back? You know, after Cora went to Europe, she was never my little girl again. I could never quite reach her. Sometimes I think she saw the rest of the world, the sophisticated stuff, and we weren't good enough. Other times, I think something went terribly wrong over there. I guess I'll never know.

But today on the phone, Caitlyn had that same hard quality to her voice. She didn't tell me about the baby. I waited for her to, but she didn't, so I said that I knew. I said that Cora was excited and let the secret out, so she wouldn't think we were plotting against her or anything. She said the right things: that she was about to tell me, that the news was to be sort of a Christmas present, that she would have told me earlier but she wanted to make sure everything was going okay with the pregnancy first... All the right words but nothing in the voice. Somehow, in the course of living, everyone we love slips away. Some faster than others, some with words and others with the silent sound of a breaking heart.

74

THE ANGLER

T he ice cracked deep down below the surface, and it sounded like the moan of a dying animal far off somewhere in a cave. Greg tapped the toe of his boot against the crusted snow to keep his foot warm.

"Well, I don't believe it. What kind of damn queer thing is that to say anyway?" Daryl reeled in his line and checked the bait. He shook his head.

"I've known him for twenty years. Twenty frickin' years. I mean, we were on varsity, for chrissakes."

Greg took a deep breath. The fish house was warm, but there didn't seem to be enough air to breathe. He and Daryl were alone. The other guys had walked up to the cabin about half an hour earlier, after Thomas dropped the bomb and left. To go for a walk, he said. Greg stood, stretching out the kinks in his back, and walked outside with a beer in his hand. The shadows were long and inky black beside the pine-covered shore. He glanced up the beach looking for a big jacket, a male form, something moving. The ice buckled the night before and left huge, jagged slabs pushed against a small arm of land. It looked like a bulldozer had pushed them there. Broken slabs of concrete. A road they were building over.

The air was cold, and Greg had left his gloves inside the cabin. He felt a pain around his heart and imagined it was an attack of some kind, not the cold air. He was a young man, didn't smoke much, liked a beer or two, but wasn't the profile for a heart attack victim. Thirty-five years old. Divorced. A father of two. He thought of Caitlyn and her recent interest in a child, in marriage, in the whole damn movie all over again. Maybe that was the mysterious pain. A small steel trap with jagged teeth trying to grab him by the chest.

He walked back into the fish house, rubbing his hands. "This was supposed to be an R&R kind of week. What's going on, anyway?" He looked at Daryl when he asked, but it wasn't as if he expected an answer. It was only Wednesday. Four more days with the five of them. Four more days away from the rest of his life. "I wonder why he told us today? Why didn't he wait until later?"

Daryl shrugged. "Hell if I know. What did he think we'd do? Jesus, that's great, now we can go on a date? Weird. Too damn weird for me."

Greg took a shot of schnapps from a pint sitting on the ice between them and reeled in his line. He threw the limp minnow back into the black hole in the ice; it floated belly up in the water.

He'd known these guys since junior high. Every year they made this trip, got drunk, caught fish, played cards, and talked into the night. They talked about wives and girlfriends. Jobs. Professional sports. Even the death of Mike's daughter a few years back. They were tight. "Maybe he was giving us some time to get used to it. Couldn't be that easy to tell us. It's kind of creepy, though… when you think about it."

Daryl scratched his red beard and shrugged. "Well, he can find a new bunkmate. I ain't getting naked with a queer in the room." He looked at his watch. "I've had it; they ain't biting. Let's go in."

The two men walked out across the blue ice and snow toward the cabin with the square, yellow windows. A tendril of smoke climbed out of the chimney. Greg could smell the fire before they got off the lake. The burning cedar mixed in with the northern Minnesota air. His hopeful eyes scanned the long beach. A downed tree or an enormous boulder looked like other things. It was almost dark.

Where would Thomas go? There wasn't another cabin for at least a couple of miles. Greg's stomach turned, thinking about the cold — a timber wolf with gray eyes.

Stalking, keeping a few steps behind your thoughts. Ready whenever you weren't.

"Throw it on the grass when we drive by." Tom shifted the green Impala and turned onto 12th street. Daryl and Greg sat in the back seat, the naked mannequin pressed between them. Their white T-shirts and canvas sneakers caught the streetlight as they passed. Three boys rode in the front. Short hair. Converse high-tops.

"Coach's light is on. Let's forget it."

"Drive on by."

"Oh, you chickens."

Tom turned off the lights and slowed down. "On three, you guys, and don't break her. Get out and lay her on the lawn."

It was ten-thirty at night. The boys found the mannequin sticking out of a dumpster behind Wolfe's department store on main street. Cruising main after a game of three on two.

Greg and Daryl stumbled out of the car, and one of the dummy's feet hit the door as they pulled her out. Toes broke off and landed near the curb. It surprised Greg how fragile the thing was.

Everyone was laughing when they drove away, envisioning her in various compromising positions. The five of them slept in a tent in Greg's yard, and no one else found out about "the gift."

The next day, going in to an early football practice, they drove by the coach's yard. At first glance, Greg thought it looked like one of those lawn ornaments, a deer laying down in the grass, but as they drove by, he could see the bald thing face down on the sod.

"Hey look, she's mooning us," Tom said.

"Coach will probably keep her. Prop her up in the living room for company." Mike took a swig out of a bottle of orange juice.

"I bet he'll keep her in the bedroom," Daryl said. "Coach seems a little off."

The boys piled out of the car and into the locker room for the day's first practice.

"WHO'S FRYING THE FISH?" Wayne tore open a bag of pretzels, poured them in a bowl, and put it on the table. He swung his long leg over the back of the chair and slid back into it. He was six foot four, a great first baseman back in high school with that long reach. Now he worked at 3M in the accounting department.

"I cleaned them." Daryl grabbed a pretzel and studied his cards.

"I'll do it. Who's eating?" Mike looked around the

room, scratching his head, fingers lost in thick raven curls. He wondered where Tom was, but didn't say it out loud. Thomas. He wondered where Thomas was. Things change. People grow away. Change their names and walk down the beach without another word. How long had Thomas known? Had he kept it a secret all this time? Wasn't it something you were supposed to know just by looking at a guy?

Al, Wayne, and Daryl were playing poker. Al's muscle-bound arms perched on the table like two separate animals. "I don't see why he brought it up, anyway. Pass." He folded his cards and laid them in a stack in front of him.

Daryl threw three white chips into the anti. "Damn weird, if you ask me. I've known him twenty years."

"I wonder if all that time…" Wayne threw in three chips. "Call. I mean, does a guy always know that, or does he decide, or what?"

Mike stood at the stove and dropped the first walleyes into the hot grease. The fish sizzled and spattered, making everyone realize they were hungry.

"Who cares anyway?" Greg said. "I mean, he's been our friend for so long. What difference does it make?" No one answered. The room was silent except for the wet logs crackling in the fireplace and the sound of frying fish.

Greg looked at the faces of his friends, but he wanted

to answer his own question. He wanted to understand what difference this all made. How Thomas must feel. How they would all act from now on when they were together. Any secret kept that long was bound to crack the foundation of a friendship, wasn't it? But how long had Tom known? What was there to "know" anyway?

Greg walked outside onto the front step and shut the door. His breath caught in his throat. It was damn cold. There were stars and a grapefruit moon. It was six-thirty now and dark. Tom had been out there almost three hours. There was no place to go, and the temperature was dropping.

Greg shook his head and ran his fingers through his hair. He was graying at the temples, getting older. He thought about Caitlyn and his boys back in Sioux Falls and wondered how cold it was, and if they'd gotten any snow. Caitlyn was so good with the boys. So patient. Better than their own mother was. Better than he was. It didn't make sense that he and Caitlyn fought so much these days, but she kept pushing him, always trying to change him into someone else.

Greg took a deep breath and screamed, "Tom! Thomas!" The sound echoed in the intense cold. Before long, all the men were on the porch in their stocking feet and flannel shirts screaming, a jumble of cries.

"Thomas!"

"Hey, Tom!"

"Dinner, man. Thomas! Come on in. It's time to eat."

"Hey, Tommy, where are you, man?"

Greg got the keys to the snowmobile, grabbed a hat, some extra gloves, and a down sleeping bag and came back out on the porch. The others were still standing there, their hands in their pockets, frosted air coming out of their mouths like steam. "I'm going to go have a look around. If he gets back, blink the porch light, would you?"

"Sure. You want me to come along?" Mike asked.

"No. If I find him, he can ride back with me."

The "if" of that comment sat heavy in the air.

"He can't be far away," Wayne said.

"Nah, he's fine." Daryl's voice was subdued and hesitant.

The men filed back inside when Greg started the snowmobile and headed down to the shore.

BACK IN HIGH SCHOOL, Greg and Tom were the closest. Greg thought about the time they painted the art teacher's house as a summer job. An old three-story Victorian up on the hill near the prison. It took all summer to scrape and paint that thing. They made a little money, but they had time to talk and screw around. Miss Magney was young and single, and it intrigued both boys to be around her house, working near the windows, looking in on her private life. She listened to classical music all day and sculpted in a studio in her attic. She made all of her art from stuff found in nature: bones, feathers, driftwood. Sort of primitive and spooky, the boys thought then.

Supposedly, she fell in love with a man who was sent to the prison, and she moved into that house to be near him. Rumors were always raging about the young teachers.

GREG THOUGHT ABOUT THAT SUMMER. Had he and Tom ever talked about girls? They must have. None of the guys dated much in high school. There was always too much to do. Football, basketball, baseball, or track. There was always some practice, some game. They were a close group of boys who liked a quick game of two on two, a weekend fishing at the lake, a bike race to the Pizza Shack across town. They thrived on athletic competition so much that they were almost seniors before they discovered girls. Then Greg was married and divorced before many of his classmates had finished college.

Tom was a joker, always daring others to do some ridiculous thing. The leader. The get-away car. He was never the one taking the risk, except for the time he climbed the water tower and wrote "Let It Be" with purple spray paint.

Greg scanned the shore. It was snowing again. He rode about a mile-and-a-half from the cabin, then the shore curved to the north. He followed some tracks but was losing them and needed to decide if he should follow the shore or turn inland.

He turned off the motor and sat for a moment to think when he saw the footprints again, up the beach, leading into a small moonlit clearing.

"Tom? Thomas?" His voice was soft, hesitant in the shadowed, dark envelope of night. He stood up and tried again. "Thomas!" This time, it echoed. There was a long pause and then a reply.

"Over here."

Greg turned and saw his friend fifty feet away, sitting on the bottom branch of an old pine, his feet tucked up under him. "God." Greg sighed with relief and sat back down on the seat of his snowmobile. Finally, he got up and walked over toward the tree. "You scared the shit out of us, you know. What are you doing here? You okay?"

"Fine. A little cold."

"A little dense. You want to freeze?" Greg felt comfortable now, seeing his friend and slipping into the old roles. "Get out of that tree, would you? You planning on spending the night or what?"

Tom shrugged. "I thought I'd bag a wolf and then ride it back. I've been hearing a few howling."

"Yeah, and they're talking smorgasbord on a Scandinavian white boy." Greg shook his head and smiled. The moonlight made it easy to see. Thomas slipped out of the tree, stretched his arms and legs. "You think I'd come out looking for you?"

"Not really. Why?"

"What were you going to do?"

"I was sitting and thinking, man. Do I have to report to you or what?"

"No." Greg looked at the ground, then at Tom's thin gloves. "I got some choppers along. Want them?"

"I'd give you a crisp fifty for them about now."

"You could have come back, you know."

"Yeah, I know, but the birds ate all the bread crumbs I'd trailed. Couldn't find my way." Thomas paused a minute. "What are they saying back there?"

"Not much."

"Liar."

"Okay. There's a little talk. Some confusion. Some surprise."

"And a hell of a lot of discomfort," Thomas said.

"I don't know. Everyone was worried about you out here."

"Right. That's the reaction I saw on all the shocked faces when I told you."

"What did you expect? We didn't know. We were surprised. Is that so awful?"

Thomas didn't answer. He shoved the thick buckskin mittens over his thin gloves and pushed his hands into the pockets of his parka.

"I left all of them standing out on the porch in their stocking feet screaming their heads off calling you. Telling you to get your ass inside. Telling you to come back."

"And what are you thinking?" Thomas looked right at Greg.

"I've been thinking about painting Magney's house the summer after our junior year. How we sat up on that scaffold and talked for hours. About the time we dumped the mannequin on coach's lawn. About the times we rode our bikes out to the pit to go swimming." Greg stopped. "I've been thinking about my friend. Wondering what all this means. How long have you known you were gay? I mean, is it something you decide or something you just find out? I've been wondering if you're happy. If this is going to change all of us. How I'm supposed to act."

"I don't know." Thomas' voice was softer now. He wrinkled his brow. Frost covered the fox fur around the hood of his coat. "I only know I couldn't keep it a secret anymore, even if I lost all of you for friends. My life's almost half over. I just want to be myself."

"I've never known anybody who's gay."

"You've known somebody who's gay for over twenty years, Greg."

"Yeah, I guess I have." Greg smiled.

"You don't have to worry. You're my friend. You've always been a friend. That's all I'm interested in."

"I don't know about the guys. I think…"

"You don't have to think for them. I'll talk to everybody myself. I just wanted a give you all a few hours to think about it. But I tell you what, I'm cold. You going to give me a ride back on that snowmobile, or what?"

"There's fresh walleye for dinner," Greg said. "I caught them all myself."

"Yeah, right. And ten bucks says I catch the most tomorrow."

"You got a bet." Greg started the engine. The light of the snowmobile penetrated the tree-lined shore. The pines and birch stood tall and crowded together. A sort of shelter. A fortress from the cold.

75

AISLE FIVE

I was working the four to twelve, getting carts in from the parking lot, when I first saw her. It was cold, sort of snowing, and I didn't pay much attention at first. I thought she forgot where she parked her car, walking around like that.

Vern, that's the manager, kicked butt if we didn't hurry when we got the carts, and I'd forgotten my gloves. It was freezing. Friday nights were the worst. Everybody in town was buying groceries and stocking up for their parties; it was New Year's Eve. Anyway, I saw her out in the lot. She was holding her coat shut around her. She was real tall, that's what I noticed first, and she had this long red hair that was blowing around in the wind and snow. I went inside.

I was stocking aisle five when I saw her again. Five is the diaper aisle, and she stood down at the end near the stacks of pink Pampers. She was wearing black stretch pants; I guess I noticed her long legs. I don't know how old she was, and it's not like I was going to hit on her; I was just taking a look. She was standing there and the next thing I know she's crying. Kind of quiet like and not making a big show, but she was crying all right. I opened a carton of newborns and tried to mind my own business. I was feeling sort of weird about it, like I felt sorry for her or something.

Lately, when people cry, it makes me feel like I'm in a hospital, and there are monitors everywhere and all that beeping. Blue screens, yellow lines. Green screens, white lines. Red blinking lights. Beep. Pause. Beep. Who would have ever thought a seventeen-year-old guy would spend a whole summer sitting in a hospital room watching his best friend's body fight back? Now Kyle has a new heart, and we drive out to the mall on Friday nights, and I'm back at work. He wants to play catch and go biking, but I don't trust his heart as much as he does. I always talk him into a movie. Say I'm tired from working or something.

So I emptied two more cartons, and she was still standing there. "Can I help you?" I asked. My chest felt tight, and I was kind of uneasy.

She jumped, like she was startled or embarrassed. "No, but thanks."

Then we both just stood there. I didn't know how to leave, and she didn't seem to want to, so I looked at the floor and then straightened a couple of rows of pull-ups. "You got a kid?" I asked. I don't know why I said that. She didn't want any help, but I looked right at her. She kind of smiled.

"Sort of," she said. "I'm pregnant."

"Hey, great." I smiled and felt my face get red. Pregnant women embarrass me. It's like I can see through their clothes or something, like I've just heard about the details of their female anatomy. Kind of like saying the word "breast," it doesn't feel natural. I shrugged and thought about walking away.

"Yeah. I suppose." She smiled a little again and brushed the hair from her face. Long red hair. She was really pretty.

"Well, if there's anything I can do…" I was so damn stupid. I sounded like… I don't know what. I remembered that she'd said earlier she didn't need any help. I shrugged and headed down to the other end of the aisle, pulled a couple boxes of baby shampoo off the cart, and started shelving again.

When Kyle first found out he needed a new heart, we were juniors and had just started football practice in the fall. It took ten months to get a heart; I mean, to find a donor. Some guy on a motorcycle got hit by a car, and Kyle was on the table hours later getting his heart. It seemed gross at first. I guess I hadn't thought much about life and death and all that. And then I spent almost an entire summer in the Sioux River Hospital sitting in a maroon chair near a steel bed, surrounded by machines. Kyle's father's dead and his mother works, so I stayed there. He's my best friend. I read the sports page to him every day and Sports Illustrated cover to cover. We watched game shows and talked about friends from school. We didn't talk about the guy on the motorcycle until this Christmas. Even then, when I saw him cry for the first time, I worried it was too hard on his heart. I know I shouldn't worry. They say he's just fine, but I can't help it.

"You okay?" She was standing next to me. I guess I was standing there like a dolt, looking at the shelves. My face felt hot. I shook my head. "Yeah. God, it's been a long day."

"I'm Caitlyn. Happy New Year." She held out her hand.

I shook it; I didn't know what else to do. "I'm Tim."

"Not a great night to be working, huh?" She smiled again.

"It's not so bad." I didn't mention the time-and-a-half. I didn't figure it was cool to talk to a customer about money. She stood there a while, and I couldn't think of a thing to say. I just wanted her to leave. I felt uncomfortable and couldn't figure out why she was there. She didn't even look pregnant. Then I got this idea that she was shoplifting, like with a partner, and she was supposed to keep me busy. "Excuse me," I said and did a quick aisle check. I didn't expect to see anyone; it was almost twelve, and the place had emptied out except for a few stragglers picking up more seltzer and soda for their parties. At least I expected her to be gone when I got back.

I had two boxes left to empty, then I could clean up and go home. I just wanted to leave. Luckily, when I got back to aisle five, she wasn't there. I tore down the boxes and walked in back for my coat. After I punched out, I walked past the registers to leave, and she was standing in lane three. She paid for a box of newborn diapers and was holding the bag close to her chest. I walked out first and didn't look at her.

I was scraping off the windows of my truck when she walked by. "Have a nice night," she said. Like she knew me. Like she was my mother or sister or something. I didn't answer her. I didn't know her, and I didn't want to talk anymore. She walked out of the lot and turned up Willow towards the pricey housing development.

All the way home, I thought about her long legs and that baby growing inside of her. Two hearts beating in one body. It was snowing pretty hard, and the wipers were batting away the snow. I stuck in a tape and sang to myself, but I couldn't forget how it felt to see her cry.

I kept making up stories, giving her a story of her own. She was rich, and her husband didn't want the kid.

She was poor, and she didn't want the kid. She was rich, and the father was poor. She was sick and shouldn't have a kid. The kid was sick and shouldn't be born. The woman wasn't pregnant at all; she was a scam artist, shoplifting food. She was pregnant, and she needed a friend. She was twenty and looked older. She was thirty and looked twenty-two. She thought I was handsome. She thought something was wrong with me — standing like a zombie staring at baby shampoo. Wondering if my best friend was going to have too much fun this New Year's Eve and make his heart work so hard that it stalled out on him. Wondering if the biker who had the heart first was a strong guy. Wondering what a strong guy was. Wondering how strong a heart really was. Wondering how much was muscle and how much was something else.

76

BABIES IN THE TREES

Dream. Cora wakes in a groomed English garden. The kind of shrubbery maze often found in the palaces of English aristocrats, with little to do and large lawns to do it on. Tall green hedges surround her. Neat grass beneath her bare feet. She stands in a thin cotton nightgown and wakes with a start, as if she'd been sleeping on her feet. The feeling of foreboding is a shady umbrella over her head.

"Just start moving," she thinks to herself. "You'll figure it out. How hard can this be?" She is trying to convince herself. (Cora is fairly good at this.)

Her father is watering the trees, pruning branches, touching the bark like braille. Loving the trees. He is the gardener, oblivious to Cora standing near him.

Maureen stands in the middle of an expanse of lawn, a gingham apron tied at her waist, white sandals on her pale legs. Caitlyn stands near her, towers above her. Stands with her head tilted to one side as if admiring an oil painting.

The shrubs turn into olive trees. They grow and melt and move like claymation sculptures. Gnarled branches reaching every which way. Suddenly, the cool moist garden turns into the dry coast of Italy. As is common in dreams, the scene changes, and Cora accepts the new backdrop. Enzo pulls up in his polished car, swerves around Cora's mother and sister. Stops. Opens the door. "Want a ride, Lovely?" He smiles his handsome, murderer smile. Then he disappears.

Only grass and olive trees and Cora, unable to move. A wax figurine.

"What are you doing, dear?" Maureen asks. "Come and play with your sister. It's time for dinner, Ray. Would you like to go dancing?"

Cora slowly realizes that her mother is dead and cannot go dancing. It is a curious realization. Cora studies her, wonders what it is like to be dead. Maureen smiles and takes Ray by the hand.

Cora looks up into the branches of the towering trees. Babies are wrapped in pastel flannel blankets, perched in the crotches of several of the huge, old branches. They cry, and Cora reaches out, but one after another disappears between her fingers. "No! Come back! I won't make you cry."

"Here, you can have my baby," Caitlyn offers. She holds out a bundle. She smiles.

"I don't want your baby; I want my own!"

Cora wakes with a start. There are raccoons out in the garbage cans. They string the food out and make a mess. She watches them from the window, not angry but numb. She sees their childlike antics, their little masks.

"What's the matter?" Ian is standing behind her in his robe.

"Raccoons." Cora manages to sound calm. "Just some raccoons."

Ian turns the outside light on and off twice and the animals hurry away. "Come here, you're shaking."

He wraps his arms around her, and Cora takes a deep breath. She can smell the two of them. The familiarity comforts her. "I love you." She turns to Ian and finds his eyes in the half-light. "But I can't marry you."

"That's okay. I've already married us. One night at midnight, don't you remember? I spun a web around the bed and asked you if you loved me. You said yes, although I think you might have been asleep. And then, though you were still sleeping, you asked me if I loved you. 'Yes, yes, of course' I answered and then you said 'Well I guess that's done' and I said 'Yes, I guess it is.' Don't you remember that? I don't think it was a dream. And if it was, we were both dreaming it, so it's okay."

Ian pushes Cora's long hair away from her forehead.

He says, "Just live with me. Just be my friend and lover forever, and that will be enough. Okay?"

"Okay. Then you won't ask again?"

"I might. I don't know. I enjoy asking you. Do you really want me to stop?"

"No. I guess not." Cora snuggles closer to Ian, to the warmth. "I had a bad dream just now. There were babies in the trees."

Ian puts his arm around her and turns off the lights in the backyard. "Come back to bed. I'll hold you and propose to you with such beautiful language and emotional intensity it will knock your socks off. And," he says after a pause, "it might help you get back to sleep."

"Okay. But in English this time. I hate it when you speak French. You know I don't get a damn word."

"Just say oui. That's it."

"Yes, Ian. Of course, Ian." Cora crawls under the wool blankets and flannel sheets. Her eyes feel heavy. Tears slip down each cheek and make her face itch as they dry. Ian reaches up and runs a finger across her face. "Tell me again," Cora says. "Tell me about the spider web."

"Well, I think it was late fall. We'd just had a fantastic dinner and had taken a long walk in the Hills so we were both tired..."

77

CHECKERS

I am at this party at my boss's house and it's a little hard to breathe, so I decide to slip out and take a walk, which I do, down to the Super Value. It's open all night. I don't mean to go to the grocery store, but I'm walking around looking at these big houses and Christmas tree lights, and I come to the store and decide to go inside. I don't know.

It's New Year's Eve. My boss isn't a Christian, so we don't have a Christmas party every year. Instead, we live it up on New Year's Eve at the law firm's expense. Party at his house while these maids in little black dresses with white aprons pass plates of shrimp and these stuffed mushroom things.

I'm a secretary. I've been there ten years, and the pay's okay for a town this size. Anyway, I'm feeling kind of queasy, on account of I'm pregnant, and things aren't going so well right now. But I walk into this grocery store and end up looking at the Pampers. Rows and rows of these smiling baby faces staring down at me. Over ten bucks a box. And then you throw them away.

I stand there and think about diapers. Then this kid asks me if I need any help. A real fresh kid, you know, clean cut. Fancy haircut, pimples, big high-top shoes. A high school kid.

"No thanks," I tell him. No help for me. I'll do this thing alone.

Greg doesn't know I'm pregnant. I told my mom though, on the phone and she died of a heart attack later that day. Seriously. Awhile later, I rode a bus out to the Black Hills and told my big sister and she said I should have said something at the funeral. At the time, it didn't seem like such a good idea to me.

I still don't show much. I can wear a big sweater and stretch pants and nobody's got a clue. I'm five-foot-eleven and I guess I've got lots of room for a baby inside of me. It's outside, in my life, that I don't know about.

So, I buy these diapers and walk back to the party, the brown paper bag tucked under my arm. A guy in a black suit takes my coat again and looks at me kind of funny. I don't smile at him. I should, I mean, I'm not normally a snob or anything, but I can't find a damn smile anyway.

I take the bag upstairs to the bathroom and lock the door. The bathroom is as ritzy as the rest of the house. All black-and-white tiles. Walls of white tile around a black square tub. Squares on the floor like a huge checkerboard. Only there are no red squares, only big red towels and red and white flowers in a black glass vase. Fresh flowers. In the bathroom. I put one foot on the black square and one on a white one and lean over the toilet, but this time I don't get sick.

I pee again and wash my hands again. I stand here and look in the mirror, look at my long red hair. I dig in my purse for a comb. I put on lipstick. I have bright, full lips, and I almost look pretty. Greg doesn't want to get married. He doesn't want any more kids, and he'd rather drop this whole thing. He's fishing in a hole in the ice somewhere in northern Minnesota. The cut on my cheek near my ear is healing up. When I pull my hair back, I can see it's still red along the scar.

We had this accident a few days ago. He hit a deer after we'd been bowling. It totaled the car, not to mention the deer, and now Greg's pissed at everybody. He doesn't mention the fact that maybe he was tanked, and I should have been driving. He never wants me to drive. I don't think it would look cool in front of the guys. They all drove home too, only no doe was trying to cross the road with her fawn. They all just went home and went to bed and sort of remembered it the next morning.

Anyway, there was this deer, and all this blood and broken glass, and I just decided for the first time, I mean,

I remember thinking it as I sat there with my head on the dash and warm blood running onto my hands that maybe I just wanted to die. It would be kind of easy. Not even my fault.

But, this guy took us to the hospital, and all I had was some bumps and bruises and this big gash on my face near my hairline. It doesn't show much.

Greg bashed up his knee, but I guess the baby's fine. Sometimes I feel a little move. Maybe it's the baby, maybe not. I don't know. I need to see a doctor or something.

I have to figure out what to do about Greg too. My sister says it's a different thing. His drinking. I need to make up my mind about him and leave the baby thing out of it. I can't just stay with him because of the baby, and I can't have an abortion on account of I'm too far along, and besides, in South Dakota it ain't going to happen.

I take a little diaper out of the bag. It's tiny, like a plastic bandage or something, and so thin. Where does all the pee go? I can hold the whole thing in the palm of my hand. Newborn. Up to twelve pounds.

I think about the doe. Sometimes I dream about her. Those eyes looking at me. I'm a coward. Downstairs, everyone's drinking and celebrating a new year. I'm pregnant and hooked on a man who drinks too much. He's fishing through a hole in the ice with five of his best friends from high school. The quarterback, two linemen, a defensive end and the star baseball pitcher. They're going to be gone a week.

I'm not his best friend. I know that now. Everything was okay until I tried to help him. Until I tried to help us. Now Greg says I'm acting like another mother, another officer waiting with the Breathalyzer test. He says I should mind my own business. When we first got together, we were like best friends. Now, I'm only baggage.

I'm tired. Maybe I should move out. Take control of my life, but I don't have anywhere to go. My sister says to take it one day at a time. My mother doesn't say anything. I can't call her on the phone anymore. She's gone. The doe never did talk, and Greg just talks back.

I sit and hold the plastic diaper in my hands and think maybe I should buy some cotton ones. Then I could wash them and use them again. I hear a countdown downstairs and then cheers and party horns. It's a new year. I put the diaper back in the brown paper bag, and without thinking much about it, I take the fresh flowers and shake the water from their stems, and then put them in the bag too. They will look good in my bathroom when I get home. Maybe I won't feel so sick all the time if there's something cheerful around to keep me going.

78

AT SEA, REVISITED

At first, I meant to write it down and be done with it. "Therapeutic journal writing." But I got, I don't know, addicted. Everything I said that was true, all that stuff I made up. Christ, it felt like my life, and just maybe it was important.

I wrote the story "At Sea." My name is Cora; my name isn't Cora. Whatever. I was trying my hand at fiction: fiction mixed in with a small town in Iowa where I once spent the summer; mixed in with a beach on the coast of Italy that I remember all too well. I wanted to write it down. I felt compelled to write it down. Like a bulimic who craves food and then throws it up with some sense of disgust, I needed to write.

Then I spent my time worrying that it wasn't good enough, that it wasn't my story, that I had no idea what I was talking about.

So why the whining, you might ask? Because I can. Because this is fiction, and characters can whine now and then, and it is my pen and my paper and my dime. Not a good enough reason granted, but even characters in the story can get testy when given too much power, so I'm wrapping this one up. Like the old man on the reservation said at the pow-wow, "I do not tell you this to make you sad and weak. I tell you so that your strength can come back, so that you can remember who you are."

By the way, I don't know the clean-cut boy at the grocery store or his friend with the new heart. They showed up on their own. There are others who just walked in, had a chair and decided to stay. Very few accepted my offer to be interviewed, but it seems everyone ended up wanting to talk.

I still can't walk through a dark house. I see street lights and think they are something else, something sinister in the distance.

WHEN CAITLYN and I were little, we played this game at night with the bedroom wallpaper. We'd lie on the bed and see shadows on the wall from the light down the hall.

"I see a king wearing a crown," I'd say.

"I see the castle. Over there, up in the corner," she'd answer. "Is he a bad king?"

"Nah," I would say. "He's okay. This is the happy ending wall."

"I see two girls, and they are smiling," Caitlyn would say.

"Yeah," I'd answer. "I see them too."

ABOUT THE AUTHOR

Kathleen Patrick is a poet and fiction writer who grew up on the prairies of the Midwest, riding horses, jumping rope, hula hooping, and writing poetry. Her bestselling book, *Airmail: A Story of War in Poems*, centers on her family's experience with wars, from the Vietnam War to the present. *Mercy*, her first novel, is a coming-of-age story set in 1970 on the plains of South Dakota. *Anxiety in the Wilderness* is her first collection of short stories. *Perfume River,* a novel for adults, is a story about anxiety and hope, about believing in the future and reconciling the past. *The Shoe Box Waltz* is a cautionary tale about two young women in search of adventure. It is her fifth book.

FREE SHORT STORY!

Sign up for my mailing list at the address below and get a free short story! "Anxiety in the Wilderness" is the title story from my recent collection of short stories by the same title.

https://patrickpoetry.com/

ALSO BY KATHLEEN PATRICK

Airmail: A Story of War in Poems

Mercy

Anxiety in the Wilderness

Perfume River

WORDS AND REVIEWS

Airmail: A Story of War in Poems

"I read it in one sitting and thoroughly enjoyed (if that's the right word) every poem." — Tim O'Brien, author of *The Things They Carried*

*"Airmail: A Story of War in Poems…*is a great example of how letters and conversations can be turned into stunning poetry. Patrick shares the words and thoughts of seven uncles who served in the military, five of them in Southeast Asia during the American war in Vietnam. …It's always cool to see letters sent home from war turned into poems. They become letters from America sent back to America. Kathleen Patrick shows us what it can look like when it's done poetically and done right." — Bill McCloud, The VVA Veteran magazine

"Love the voice and reading pace. It's great, and the content is amazing. I am a Vietnam vet and I can relate 100%. Thanks for taking the time to do this project." — J.I.

"Some very strong work here, grounded in correspondence that Kathleen had with her uncles while they served in Vietnam, and also in their correspondence with their parents, subsequent interviews, etc. An amazing piece of work. This is the best war

lit I have read since *The Things they Carried* by Tim O'Brien."
— P.L.

"A story that stays with you. I read a lot of historical fiction surrounding WWI and II, but this collection of poems highlighting the perspectives of a family living through Vietnam was just as beautiful. Reading poetry framed as letters by young men wanting to serve and the loved ones they left behind was powerfully written and even more powerful in the things that were left unsaid. This is a collection that should be read slowly, absorbing the words from each letter. — A. C.

"Wow…Honestly, I don't read a lot of poetry and didn't think I would like it. However, I loved it; it sucked me right in, and I thought it was beautifully done." — L.M.

"This collection distills so much family history into consumable little poems that will leave you wrecked in the best possible way. A beautiful read." — H.C.

Mercy

"*Mercy* is a phenomenal young adult coming of age story that will capture the hearts of readers of all ages!"—K.C.

"*Mercy* is a story of adolescence, but adults would love it as well. It explores the emotional turbulence inherent in dysfunctional families and what it takes to move from dysfunction to love to mercy. Any book that can make me cry and laugh out loud is a winner. *Mercy* is a winner!"—J.C.

"A coming of age, found family, young adult novel. A heartwarming story about a twelve-year-old girl named Sadie who finds the family she always craved in her uncle on a farm. After Sadie's mother struggles with gambling addiction after her father's departure, Sadie has a life of instability and worry. Great short read. The only thing I have to say bad about the story is that it simply isn't long enough!"—K.F.

"Mercy was just a great story and a breath of fresh air!" — L.P.

Anxiety in the Wilderness

"A book of short stories that can only be described as bittersweet. Some parts defiantly pulled at my heartstrings. The author herself said the book was written over a long time period. This comes across in the different scenarios in which the characters are involved in. Each a little exceptional tale of it's own. I especially liked the crossover of characters. I am now patiently waiting for a full novel set in the Iowa wilderness!" —K. F., Goodreads review

"The poetic language of the stories lends a warmth to the storytelling that helps to bring the characters to life. Each story describes a different human worry or anxiety that we all may have experienced at some point in our lives; therefore, each story is relatable in its own way.…Short stories are a disappearing art form, and Patrick demonstrates why we should keep them around. There is no grandiosity of language that detracts from the storyline or from the artful character descriptions. Characters navigate their way through their predicaments one day at a time. The poignant vignettes showcase the rawness of various human emotions, much like a snapshot of an expert photographer. " —B. M., Goodreads Review

"I loved this book! From beginning to end the characters smack of realism and you can see people you know or yourself in them. I wish it were the first book in a series of ten — because I wanted more!"

Perfume River

"It is a beautifully written novel with deep feelings. It is the kind of book that wins prizes." E.S.

"Patrick's prose is smooth, even, and consistent. As with her other work, her use of words is sparse and succinct leaving the reader to indulge in their own imaginings of the space and events. The pauses and silences are evocative." J.S.

"Absolutely loved the main character! Great read!" K. K.

"I enjoy Kathleen Patrick's concise descriptive abilities sprinkled with emotional and intellectual truths." CT

"The characters are well drawn, and the story is both touching and humorous. Worth the read!" E.S.